GRACE

'It was little things one lived for; those shifting leaves, the clematis snowing, each petal white in the light as it fell. The thought of breakfast. The thought of Seabourne. Her precious week at the Empire Hotel . . .'

Grace Stirling, an 85-year-old English lady with a romantic history and a solitary present, decides to take a holiday by the sea, going in search of her own past and a vision of disappearing England. Besides, she wants to get away from the silent phonecalls which threaten her cottage . . . In London, very near the railway line that carries nuclear waste through the heart of the capital, Grace's beloved niece Paula Timms also finds herself the victim of harassment.

Small-time private detective Bruno Janes keeps busy in the house next door, determined to make a success of his new assignment for the security services, getting bolder and more angry as the case seems to fall apart in his hands . . . In the course of the obsessive nightmare that rises to engulf them, Grace faces an apocalpytic revelation about her past and they all face a future which is changed for ever.

Maggie Gee has written a novel of towering stature which has all the stealth and suspense of a thriller. Set in the Britain of today – dirty, violent, disaffected – it is nevertheless a book about courage, and love which in the post-atomic age still has the power to hold together the human world. For *Grace* is also the story of a child, *'tunnelling on towards the world . . . hazarding all, to have life in the light, unprotected but quite unafraid'*.

D1352414

GRACE

Also by Maggie Gee

Dying, in Other Words
The Burning Book
Light Years

GRACE

MAGGIE GEE

HEINEMANN · LONDON

William Heinemann Ltd
Michelin House, 81 Fulham Road, London SW3 6RB
LONDON MELBOURNE AUCKLAND

First published in 1988
Copyright © Maggie Gee 1988

British Library Cataloguing in Publication Data
Gee, Maggie
Grace
I. Title
???? ???? ??? ???

ISBN 0-434-28746-6

Photoset in Linotron Sabon by
Rowland Phototypesetting Ltd
Bury St Edmunds, Suffolk
Printed and bound in Great Britain by
??? ??? ??? ????? ????

This book is dedicated, with love and gratitude,
to my friend Beverly Hayne
who died in 1986; and to my daughter Rosa
who was born in the same year

Acknowledgements

The author wishes to thank Bridget Barrett, Martin Booth, Gary Murray for his technical advice, the London Nuclear Information Unit, Trina Rankin and Daphne Youles.
Who Killed Hilda Murrell? is by Judith Cook and was published in 1985 by the New English Library; *No Immediate Danger: Prognosis for a Radioactive Earth* is by Rosalie Bertell and was published in 1985 by The Women's Press.

1

A man holding a child. In the morning, in a green urban garden. A little girl, with white feathers of hair, hanging upside-down and laughing wildly through her father's legs, shrieking with pleasure, miles from the ground because Arthur is tall, crinkling her pale blue eyes at the sun. She fights him off as he tickles her but her strong short calves cling on for dear life. Then she stops laughing, and dangles, wide-eyed, arching her back to look at the ground, wondering if it's a different world, where flowers hang down from a sky of grass.

Paula, who loves the little girl's father, watches the two of them through glass, and in that instant is pierced with envy. Maybe that was why people had kids. To be part of something else, part of each other. Briefly, the two of them are one . . . but Paula has no children.

Then they split apart, Sally shrieks as she lands, Paula leaves the window, life goes on, Arthur bends to frown at a snail; ordinary life in a dirty city, blowing apple-blossom, scraps of paper.

The following night, the world grew dirtier.

2

AT HOME AND ABROAD

'. . . unconfirmed reports . . . abnormally high . . . over 100 times . . . in Sweden,' the radio said. Grace was at home, sitting in the sun by some bright yellow tulips, listening to Mozart. It seemed such a long way away. Grace was eighty-five, she lived in the country, the tulips were blinding sunshine-yellow. Next day, the reports were confirmed.

There was nowhere, really, to hide. Because air is everywhere and goes everywhere. Air from the inner city, air from the chemical plants, air from Russia, that spring.

She would soon retire after a lifetime of work. Though a lot of life was disappointment, it was worth going on with to the last. There was Paula, her niece. There was her garden. At the heart of all, there were her memories of Ralph. Despite her years, she could still feel young. But they said radiation aged everyone and everything.

Grace had tried to understand. In the wind that was shaking the creeper, in the April rain and sun, through curtains, windows, walls, and her thin hand pressed to the window-pane, through flesh and blood and bone it fell.

Yet part of her didn't believe it. It couldn't be seen or heard or tasted; the ordinary senses let one down. Was it really there then, the radiation, that nervous, whispering spring? Was it in the ordinary green leaves and the ordinary milk at breakfast?

Later there were 'facts' about Chernobyl. The fire was so hot that the plume of radiation was carried up thousands of feet, and blew far and wide over Europe. Radioactive fallout came down again in the rain. In Norway and Sweden, it fell on the fruits of the

forest; small yellow cloudberries, lingonberries, Arctic raspberries.
It fell on moss and lichen.

Lichen eats water, like a sponge. Reindeer eat lichen. Reindeer
meat would for many years be too contaminated for humans to eat.

Human beings are enterprising. They thought they would feed
the meat to mink on mink farms. They were doomed to die, after
all. Gleaming, radioactive mink.

Paula Timms, Grace's niece, is thirty-seven, but today she feels
fifty. She sits on an old pink blanket in her boyfriend's garden in
London, beside a pile of paper. The pen which lies uncapped on
the blanket has been there so long it has dried in the sun.

She is trying to write a novel about a brave old woman. She has
written several plays, but this is her first novel. It raises particular
problems because her central character is based on life. And death;
a real-life murder. Hilda Murrell was murdered two years ago in
Shrewsbury, aged seventy-eight.

Paula knew as much about the real Hilda Murrell as you could
learn from books and newspapers. Hilda was a passionate rose-
grower; unmarried; tall; a conservationist; an 'English lady'; 'full
of life'; a strong protester against nuclear power. Some facts are
neutral, others are not. Paula has stared at photographs, all giving
different messages. A kind face, an austere face, a mischievous
face, a demure face. In the end it's just a face, and the facts are
insufficient. The live woman escapes Paula. She tries to imagine
her, but Grace's image floats up before her and confuses the issue.

Hilda wouldn't talk, or smile. In her place, Grace smiled, confus-
ingly.

Besides that, Paula isn't feeling well. She isn't well, or the world
isn't well. The sunlight tells her not to blame the world, not that she
believes the sunlight. Just below the top of Arthur's kitchen window,
three brilliant camellias bob. She watches them a moment, now crimson, now dull as the leaves slide over and under the flowers. She sees
that they are beautiful, but the pleasure doesn't enter her. They are
right and she is not. Or perhaps they only *look* right.

She has tried to explain it to Arthur, but she can't explain what
she doesn't understand. All she is sure of are the contradictions.
She is hungry all the time; food makes her sick. The taste of things
has changed. She is bloated, although she is eating less. She is tired,
although she does nothing. She goes to bed early and wakes up

3

exhausted. She falls asleep when she tries to write her book, but lies there in the small hours with her mind racing through it . . . She is always drenched in sweat.

She looks down at her naked arms and legs. They are yellowish-white against the pink of the blanket. It isn't a pleasant sight. Since Chernobyl, she's avoided the sun; she is normally brown as a nut by now. It strikes her her flesh has precisely the tinge you saw on the faces of teenage girls throwing up on the cross-channel ferry. And the blanket is pink as the skin on blancmange, an unnatural colour, pink and wrinkled. Suddenly something violent is happening, inside her, outside her, all through her; a very loud silence is ringing in her ears and something is rising, cramping and rising, her whole insides are surging together and on a great wave of relief and panic she bends and is horribly sick on the teapot. She looks up briefly, then retches again.

Little Sally is watching her, paddling down the lawn at just the right moment to catch the action. 'You been 'ick,' the two-year-old crows. 'Dirty Paula, you been 'ick!'

'Go away,' yells Paula, gagging, running out of breath in the middle of the yell. 'Somebody's fucking poisoning me.'

'Someb'y fucking,' Sally nods wisely. 'Someb'y fucking Paula.'

Probable Health Effects Resulting from Exposure to Ionising Radiation

10-50 rem
Short-term effects: Most persons experience little or no immediate reaction. Sensitive individuals may experience radiation sickness. Delayed effects: . . . Premature ageing, genetic effects and some risk of tumours.
0-10 rem
Short-term effects: None.
Delayed effects: Premature ageing, mild mutations in offspring, some risk of excess tumours. Genetic and teratogenic effects.

(The health effects of fallout from Chernobyl in other countries were described by the Soviet Government as 'insignificant'.)

* * *

Grace and Paula are attached to each other. Paul is Grace's only niece, Grace is Paula's only aunt. But Paula lives in London, and Grace lives down in East Sussex. They mean to see each other often, but in fact they end up talking on the phone. *How are you? How are you? How's the garden?* There is nearly half a century between them.

Grace has been a feminist since she was twelve, in 1913, before the First World War. Since 1916 she's been a pacifist. In the 1950s she went round the world with Dora Russell's Peace Caravan. In 1950, Paula was two years old, kicked her mother and made her cry. Paula means something quite different by 'feminist', and doesn't like the term 'pacifist'. But Paula is a train-spotter. She helps watch London's nuclear trains. They carry waste fuel for reprocessing, and reprocessing produces weapons-grade plutonium, and Paula is against the whole lethal business, so some would say she was on the side of peace. And she's written plays on related themes which some people thought untheatrical, and others unpatriotic.

Neither Grace nor Paula breaks the law. But odd things happen to both their phones. Recently, Grace has felt harassed, but mostly they discount it. Empirical evidence isn't enough, and the telephone system has never been efficient.

The 'facts' are hard to establish here. There are facts filed somewhere about the size of the buildings used by the security services, the number of staff, anonymous faces behind well-screened windows. There are facts about the amount they are paid and the number of hours they work, about the colours of curtains and carpets. There are technological facts, about taps, bugs, computers. There are definitions of 'subversive activities': the Home Office tells us that they 'threaten the safety or well-being of the State and . . . are intended to undermine and overthrow Parliamentary democracy by political, industrial or violent means . . .' But you needn't actually do anything illegal, because, as one Home Secretary has noted, it is all too easy to use tactics which are not in themselves illegal for subversive ends.

If you are 'subversive', you may legally be watched. The definition can be stretched to fit. Unless you are an expert in surveillance techniques, there's no way you can tell if your phone is tapped. No way you can establish that it *isn't* tapped, then. This fact is not very comfortable.

5

A lot of the targets of surveillance are domestic.

Grace and Paula go on talking on the phone.

Grace makes phonecalls to Czechoslovakia. She has a friend there, a man, Jan Dvořák. Here the facts are easier to state. No laws prevent the tapping of international phonecalls. A high proportion of all calls entering and leaving Britain are 'trawled' for sensitive information. British and American listening equipment – in Cornwall, in Yorkshire, in London – receives an enormous amount of traffic, most of it in no way sensitive. Phone your faraway uncle to wish him Happy Birthday and the call might be monitored for 'sensitive' words. Traffic to and from the Soviet bloc comes through the 'Minor Routes' Exchange, at Mondial House by the River Thames, just a few minutes' walk from Caroone House, where thousands of phonecalls are monitored. Hot buildings full of wasted time, obscure initials, dandruff, boredom.

'Happy Birthday, Jan,' says Grace.

She's glad she lives in England.

Being English still has a meaning, for Grace. It endures as everything else changes.

That's why she was so angry a few weeks ago when she needed to buy a dustbin. The council specified a special kind compatible with their new automated dustcarts. She went to the new hardware store in her local town, and explained what she wanted. The shopkeeper offered her a German dustbin. 'No thank you, I'd like something made in England.' 'No can do,' he said. 'It doesn't exist, not what you want.' 'You mean we don't make them? Why ever not?'

She would have kept the old one till the bottom fell out. She preferred old things to new. Unfortunately, if you lived long enough the old things started to die on you.

The man stood there with a patient expression. 'It's not a bad dustbin, dear,' he remarked.

Grace had to have one, despite that 'dear'. How on earth, she had wondered as she drove home, the obnoxious black plastic thing rolling around behind her, could a country get by if it didn't make dustbins? In these days, too, when there was so much waste. Every country should have its own dustbins.

*   *   *

Paula and Arthur are arguing as Arthur does the washing up.

'Thing is,' he said as he stared into the sink-basket, a nest of noodles, tea-leaves, half a tomato, 'it's work, isn't it? Britain needs work. We shouldn't be too proud to do it.'

Paula was talking, not helping. She'd never felt at home in Arthur's kitchen. It was like a great gamey animal, bursting with rich undigested food. 'I'm not talking about pride,' she told him. 'I'm talking about toxic waste. Waste disposal is getting to be the most massive industry . . .'

'Well we do *need* some industry . . .'

'You've never seemed very keen on getting into industry. You've never seemed very industrious . . . Never mind, the whole thing is . . . our standards are so low. We're very cheap, but not very safe. So other countries send us their poisonous waste. It's all being dumped on England.'

'Waste has to go somewhere,' Arthur said dreamily, watching the bubbles come up from a cup.

'*Arthur*,' said Paula severely. 'You're not listening. I'm talking about *toxic waste*. Not bottle banks, dear, or recycling.'

'I hear quite a *lot* about nuclear waste,' Arthur half hummed, and smiled at her, despite that 'dear'. He shifted his enormous bulk reflectively from foot to foot. 'It's Saturday night. Don't I get a night off?'

'It's not just nuclear waste,' she said. 'I know you think I'm obsessed. It's every kind of unspeakable chemical. We don't even have a clue what it is . . . lots of it comes in sealed containers . . .'

'I'm not a public meeting, Paula. My old dad would have called you *shrill*.'

She didn't listen; she pressed on. 'What I'm trying to tell you, Arthur, is that Britain's turning into a dustbin.'

'That reminds me.' His washing up was maddeningly slow. 'Grace phoned up. She was going on and on about how she couldn't get one. That's what I mean about industry . . . I tried to talk about it, but she rang off. You know how impatient she is. Like you. I've got mixed up with a family of rat-bags . . . I take that back. I'm fond of Grace.'

'Get on with the *story*, for God's sake! What did she *want*!' She digs him hard in the small of the back. He turns and flicks water at her furious face, then kisses her hard, so she laughs and wriggles.

'Something about a holiday. Grace is going on holiday.'

*   *   *

7

Grace's bookshop is closing after fifteen years. It hasn't failed; it must be a success to keep a bookshop going on for fifteen years; all the same, she doesn't feel happy. There is always something sad about a closing down sale. A book – three or four years of its author's life – marked down to 50p. She'd felt almost wicked, setting the prices. And that dreadful shine in the customers' eyes. 'Look at these, George, lovely big books, 50p.' 'Well these are only 30 . . .' It wasn't the villagers, of course. It was folk from the stream of loud traffic that sliced the village of Oakey in two.

That final Bank Holiday weekend had been sunny. LAST DAYS said an orange notice in her window. She hated orange, but she needed the money. So her shop, which had always felt tranquil, ageless, was suddenly forced into the modern age. That orange sign seemed to say EMERGENCY! RUSH! And they did rush in, fresh from Oakey's new Tea Shoppe, barging into Grace's with cream on their chins, stripping the shop like locusts.

When everything had vanished, the shop looked so small, the shelves so shoddy and makeshift, so grey, like a life after the living person had left it. Was this all there was? Was it all so finite? Must everything finally shrink and fade?

Grace needed a holiday. She'd been on holiday in March, with Paula, but it had been hectic with the child around. Now she found herself longing for whatever was lost, whatever she and her life had been. And so her thoughts turned to Seabourne. Going to Seabourne would be going home. She was born there in 1901, an unimaginable time ago. She has not been there for twenty-odd years, but nothing would have changed in Seabourne. Seabourne, to Grace, was England. And so she arranged a week by the sea.

It offered a return, it offered an escape. No letters to answer (not that many letters came; people didn't bother with letters now). No garden to weed. No shelves to dust.

And the phone – no phonecalls either. She didn't want to think about the phonecalls. Let the phone ring in her empty house. Whoever it was wouldn't have the satisfaction of making her pick it up and hear silence.

The last few times she herself had said nothing. Just waited. To deprive him of the pleasure of her voice. Yet doing it gave her a bad feeling. Not that Grace felt fear; she would not feel fear. The girls of Compton Hall were not raised to feel fear . . . It was disturbing, all the same. As if by staying silent she had joined in the game, admitted the danger, become dangerous herself.

In London, flat on his naked back in the yard of his ground-floor flat, Bruno Janes is ready to play. On his hundredth sit-up, he hardly hurts. The adrenalin pushes, the endorphins flow. The red hairs stick to his fine pale skin. He can do another hundred, easy . . .

As his muscular torso swings up and forward his eyes fire bullets into the sky. Not easy to shoot, as you move at speed. He is doing particularly well today, scoring twenty-six pigeons without cheating. Things are going his way all right, today.

Around 160 sit-ups, it always got tough. That was when character told. Bruno had character, certainly. That's why they're giving him his chance, at last. 170 – sweat breaks out all over his body, but his rhythm doesn't falter. Never any turning back . . . You can't be soft if you want to be hard . . . Bruno's head, swinging up, now forward, now back, is an echo-chamber of tags and phrases. At 180 it's easy again, a downhill sprint to the kill – 200. He hardly pauses, rolls over on his belly. Brief pleasant pressure of the stone on his genitals.

He's into the pattern of his press-ups now. He always does a hundred. The tendons cord on his square freckled hands. It's easy, so easy. He wishes they could see him, *the man of the moment, the man for the job* . . .

For the past five years things haven't been easy. Working for that wanker Harvey in Mitcham, all the dirty work for none of the money, then two dodgy years on his own, pouring out money on crap to impress the punters, embossed stationery, printed cards:

BRUNO JANES, ESQUIRE

Private Inquiry Agent

MATRIMONIAL * SECURITY * INTERNAL FRAUD

Your Every Requirement Discreetly Met

CONFIDENTIALITY GUARANTEED

In the end he had started to make a bit of money, but there hadn't been enough *action*. It was endless waiting with cameras for people who never came. It was break-ins where you weren't allowed to do damage, enemies you couldn't get physical with. What was the point of being hard as nails if you spent your days cramped up in a Cortina parked outside the wrong building?

38, 39. Things were changing at last. They had contacted Bruno; he'd known they would. 41, 42. *A fighting-machine . . . A man's man . . .* They had called on him . . . For Bruno is a patriot. *Queen and Country,* pushing up, coming down, *in the national interest,* 72, 73, *they can count, count, count on me . . .* They had reached him just in time, he thinks. He might not have been able to hang on for ever. London was getting hotter. Things were getting dirtier.

The day before Paula went to meet the journalist, she saw a red-headed man chasing a rat. It was heavy, darkish, going hell-for-leather down the sunny street with the man behind it, running head down in a pink-faced frenzy. But the rat darted in through some gateless gateposts, and the man skidded to a halt. He stood for a moment staring after it, hands on hips, face streaming with sweat. His arms and legs were pink and naked. She didn't like the rat; too fat, too fast. Even more than that though, she didn't like the man. What was he intending to do with the rat when he caught it? Strangle it, kick it against the wall? But he disappeared into a fish and chip shop. Perhaps he had meant to eat it.

There were a lot of rodents in London. Only yesterday she'd seen bits of rubbish moving in the shadows between the tracks at Euston. Things come up from the crumbling sewers.

Underneath the city's shining surface of plate-glass windows, Porsches, computers, essential structures are rotting away. The dark is furry, slipping, sliding. Summer's come early; it's intensely hot. In Regent's Park, Arab women are walking slowly through the rose garden, their black robes humming cones of heat, tired eyes caged in sweaty bird-masks. Behind them, bodyguards pant in suits. This isn't what they meant by England. A trembling desire can be felt in the heat haze through which the sun finally starts to sink; caught in the maze of mirrored towers, trains, rats, telephone lines, everyone wants to escape.

But Paula has to meet the journalist.

The radical journalist is plump and dark, a boyish bespectacled figure. For the first ten minutes she gets to know his back as he plays with his computer. His secretary has showed her into a chair which affords a clear view over his shoulder. The computer has a sky-blue screen edged with emerald-green and he writes on it in white. She reads uncomprehendingly at first, eager to discover his secrets, though they cannot be all that secret if he is offering them to her view. WEDNESDAY 10.00 *Car to service (shop en route)* 11.00 *Running.* He's already got Friday pretty well sorted out: after *Running* there's *Large Pine Nuts etc (Waitrose).* But it's only Monday now, she thinks. And he's already focused on that *Large Pine Nuts.* There are dates, as well, names, addresses, but most of it seems to be rather domestic. His body language says *important, busy,* a busy man with a computer diary.

At last he swings round and shakes her hand, and she tells him what she wants to know . . .

'There's nothing in it,' he said. 'There isn't a shred of evidence.'

'I agree there would have been no point,' she said. 'But a lot of what they do seems to have no point.'

'You know, of course, the security services are no friends of mine,' he said. 'But they're very busy men.' And he flashed a faintly stagey smile, intensely knowing, almost smug (though a radical journalist would not be smug).

She felt herself getting hotter and hotter under the pressure of his disbelief. 'I'm assuming they're paranoid,' she said. 'If they're always plotting themselves, maybe they assume other people are too.'

'They're short of resources,' he said. 'These are grey bureaucrats without enough money. A lot of people think they're being watched, but they aren't.'

'I'm sure you're right,' she murmured. On the instant she decided not to tell him what had happened to her – what she thought had happened to her. The misbehaving telephone, the mail that came late, the envelopes obviously torn open, casually restuck with Sellotape. Most absurd of all, the man in the seven-strong audience at the Poetry Society. She had rather vainly addressed the poets on the virtues of writing against nuclear weapons. He wasn't at all like the other six weirdos; a blockish man in a grey raincoat, he asked unfriendly, unpoetic questions. In the bar afterwards he came and stood close. 'I normally step over people like you,' he said, his grey shoulder too near her face, turned to exclude the other people present. 'I take quite an interest in this sort of thing. I work for the Ministry of Defence.' And perhaps he did, or perhaps he was a fantasist. The story was too far-fetched to tell.

The journalist was leaning back on his chair, examining her like a clever schoolboy, a long way away behind his rimless specs, his computer glinting behind him. That amused expression must be aimed at her. Suddenly irritated, she pressed on. 'It does happen, all the same . . . People I know in the peace movement have had strange break-ins, or their mail messed about with . . . so it doesn't seem that implausible. That it could have happened to Hilda Murrell.'

'But why would they bother with her?'

'OK, I know I can't prove that they did. I'm not sure myself, that's part of the problem.'

'Why would they want to murder her?' He was bored; he wanted to talk about himself.

'No one said they intended to murder her. I would assume it was an accident, or a maniac. There are always mavericks . . . if someone slightly strange was put on to her. A private detective, say . . . it's been suggested.'

He put his hands behind his head, increasing his apparent surface area, then swung his chair back and forwards, splaying plump thighs and stroking them. 'Even I,' he said with great emphasis. 'Even I. I've got files full of stuff which is of interest to them. But I've only had five days of surveillance in my life.'

As an argument, it was unanswerable. Professional men, it seemed to say, would save their attention for professional men. Paula hadn't realised how competitive it was, being a subject for surveillance.

Part of her is happy to believe him, though. Part of her does believe him. Part of her would like to believe everything she's told, by the police, the television, the government; by the famous radical journalist.

That the fallout from Chernobyl is insignificant. That nuclear power is safe. That nuclear weapons protect us. That Hilda Murrell's murder had nothing to do with the security services.

That this is England, for goodness' sake, and nothing ever happens in England.

*   *   *

She would like to believe it, but she doesn't. She thinks a great deal is happening in England. She thinks a lot of it is bad.

She forces herself to know about it.

Every week, ten metric tons of nuclear waste is carried through the heart of London. About 44,000 half-pounds of butter, but it isn't butter they're spreading. The trains carry spent fuel rods from nuclear reactors. 'Spent' is a misnomer, actually. The rods have the highest concentration of radioactivity of any substance on earth. They come by train in huge finned flasks from power stations in the south and east – Sizewell, Bradwell, Dungeness – on their way to reprocessing in Cumbria, where even more waste will be produced. Three or four nuclear waste trains a week, running close to the sleeping backs of houses and the people sleeping behind those walls. All down the line the houses sleep.

Arthur and his two-year-old daughter Sally live 25 metres from the railway line. Arthur has a cheerful temperament, and Sally is too young to think about it, and Paula worries herself sick, though she only stays there a few nights a week.

The day that she went to meet the journalist, though, she had other things to worry about. Racketing back to Kensal Green in a hot train, she thought about what he'd said. If he was right, she should abandon her novel. But was he right? And did it matter? She didn't want to discuss it with Arthur. Half of him didn't like her sticking her neck out, and he would only gloat. What she needed was time on her own; she decided to sleep in her flat in Camden. She rang Arthur at the hotel where he worked.

'You'll have to pick up Sally yourself,' she said.

'I'll miss you,' he said. 'I was going to cook you some spinach. No one was hungry today, there's bags of it left . . . promise you'll eat something decent.'

'I've been feeling sick again,' she said. 'In any case, I've given up spinach.'

'Go to the doctor while you're in Camden.'

'Piss off, Arthur. I'm fine.'

'Take care, in any case.'

'I always do.'

'Hang on,' he said. 'Is anyone on duty this week?'

'I said I might go. But we're not supposed to talk about it.'

'Sod that. Cruise missiles. Gorbachev. Trident. Afternoon boys, are you enjoying yourselves?'

'You're drunk, Arthur,' she hissed, outraged, though she sometimes made the same kind of joke herself. If they were listening. If they were there. What could you do but laugh at them?

'You haven't told me how it went with Machin. Did he think you were on the right lines?'

She wasn't prepared to lose face. 'It was *really* interesting,' she said. 'He completely changed my train of thought. Lots of new things to work on. I'm off to Camden to get on with it. Can't tell you about it on the phone, Arthur.'

As she walked down the road to the station once more, she remembered the rat she'd seen yesterday, how fear made its heavy body seem to fly. Where had it gone, after it dashed between the gateposts. Whose dark kitchen was it hiding in?

She remembered the rat, but she forgot the man, who passed her walking in the opposite direction, returning from work in a light grey suit, his eyes invisible behind mirrored sunglasses.

He turns, briefly, and watches her back.

Greta, her landlady, had gone to Rome. She was the only person in the building that night. Her typewriter echoed. It was quiet and hot. It was 6 a.m. when the thumping began.

They must have thought she would be asleep. Actually she was awake, with the newly familiar feverish wakefulness, lying there staring at a crack in the ceiling.

They battered so hard that the room seemed to shake, and she saw her own hands were shaking too as they clawed at the sheets for comfort. It couldn't be her door they were pounding on. It must be her door they were pounding on. And there were thuggish voices shouting. Drunks? Maniacs? What should she do? Police, she thought fleetingly. Call the police. But they wouldn't come out just for that, surely.

Perhaps she already knew who it was. It seemed like minutes that she lay there listening, praying they would simply go away. In the end, she understood. They would never go away. Everything was planned to happen like this. Part of her life was ending.

So it seemed more frightening to stay in bed and be caught

unprepared, half-naked. She dressed herself clumsily. Her fingers felt numb. As she padded down the hall, they were kicking the door, tremendous blows that made it quiver on its hinges. The anger behind it stopped her in her tracks. Her heart was a hard ball, jumping, hurting. Just as she was going to dart back into the bedroom and phone someone – anyone, someone must help – the letterbox lifted; a draught of cool air; then two mad eyes staring in at her, the violent glitter of something alive. Nothing between them and her. She held herself, frozen with fear.

'Open up. Police,' a rough voice shouted. And she knew that she had no choice. Hypnotised, she opened the door. There were four men, not in uniform, with slab-like chests and contemptuous faces.

Her fear amused them. They stood much too close. They stared at her legs, which were naked. They told her they were CID. They knew her name, they had the right address, but they were looking for someone she had never heard of. They insisted they had 'reason to believe' she was sheltering a wanted man, Raymond someone. 'He's a black fellow. You like black men, don't you? Heh-heh.'

They were already searching the flat – the door of the wardrobe squealing on its hinges, saucepans crashing in a cupboard, the heavy smash of a pot-plant – before she remembered to ask them for a warrant; but she knew it would be useless to ask them for a warrant. She suddenly knew she was going to die, but before she died she was going to be sick, and she rushed past a fleshy, hostile back and threw up her stomach in the bathroom, cramping and retching again and again. She knelt there afterwards utterly drained, too weak to move out of the vomit. Then they were hammering the door behind her.

'Miss Timms? It's no good you hiding in there. We've got some questions to ask you.'

She didn't wash it off. There was a bib of vomit on her T-shirt. When she opened the door their cruel, sniggering faces became uncertain. She'd upset them by not looking pretty. She didn't look *fun*, with sick on her chest . . . watching their unease, her courage crept back.

The biggest man spoke, but he sounded rattled. 'We'd like you to make us a nice up of tea. We don't want to mess up your kitchen too much.'

Her voice, which she called up from far away, astonished her by coming out a shout. 'I'm not going to make you any . . . *fucking*

. . . tea. You bullying sods! You've no right . . .' But even as she shouted, her mouth filled again and with an animal groan she turned back into the bathroom, just managing to slam the bolt across before she was sick in a swooping crescent across the path of the other yellow stain. Blood pounded behind her eyes. She no longer cared what happened. Nothing in the world could matter until her stomach stopped contracting.

She didn't know how long it was before the front door closed. Then the flat was deathly quiet.

In the country, Grace is getting up, watching the nest in the apple tree, the constant flurry of comings and goings. Astonishing, and immensely hopeful, when a bird hatched a second clutch of eggs. She had watched the disasters of the first family – the smashed turquoise eggshell, the bird that jumped too young, hopelessly trying to hide under the hollyhocks – but feels that the second will certainly do better. She needs more blackbirds to sing next spring. As she has aged she's slept less and less, and she loves mornings, so full of promise. The time she is happiest still to be alive. It was little things one lived for; those shifting leaves, the clematis snowing, each petal white in the light as it fell. The thought of breakfast. The thought of Seabourne. Her precious week in the Empire Hotel.

Only one thing is bothering her. She doesn't want company all the time, but she doesn't want to be entirely alone. Maybe Paula will come down for the day. To get away would be good for her, bless her.

Paula will never find out who did it. When she tells the local police that morning, they at first deny that the men were policemen, but a few hours later agree that they were. Perhaps it depends on what kind of policeman. She might have been visited by CID, which is what they had claimed to be. She might have been visited by Special Branch. They might have been put up to it, whoever they were, by MI5's 'A' (Operations) Branch, or perhaps F7, who are interested in, among other people, feminists, pacifists, and trotskyists, or perhaps the AEAC, the very low-profile nuclear police. There's quite a lot of choice in England, you see.

There again, perhaps she imagined it all. She's highly strung and she might have had a nightmare.

One thing's for sure, it wasn't Bruno. He was fast asleep, in the house next door to Arthur's. When he wakes up, he thinks about England. Bruno's ideal of England. A country which is free. A country where people are free to make money. A country which is strong. A country where things are under control. A free country for Englishmen.

All round the coast they stand like a wall of gleaming chalk, shoulder to shoulder, stiff and tall as shining stone, white blondes, powerful redheads . . .

When Bruno thinks of having sex, staring into his steel-framed mirror, safe in that cold and narrow sea, Bruno thinks of England.

A little later, he wants to die; wants to kill, and wants to die.

3

THE EMPIRE

Come to Seabourne, 'the Jewel of England's South Coast', where nothing ever happens except death and holidays. The cliffs are magnificent, everyone agrees, the edge of England plunging sheer to the waves, a 400-foot drop to the red-and-white lighthouse. People stand at the top and peer towards France; couples push, and shriek; a few lonely ones jump, thirty-odd a year, most of them successful.

Westward, the land dips down towards the town. The marine parades look as splendid as ever, seen from the boat that bobs along the coast bringing wild-haired tourists back from the lighthouse.

'Smashing, aren't they, the big hotels?' They wave pink hands at the grand empty balconies. 'You'd need a few bob to stay in *those*.'

They do have their grandeur, these white hotels, set square to the waves, with their flag streaming backwards, flying in splendour from the prevailing winds. Salt eats the paint every winter, and the wood and the plaster underneath; each spring they repaint it, and if the walls have shrunk you would hardly detect it from one year to the next . . . in a few decades, the loss might show.

Coming each year to the white hotels – the Empire, the Sandhurst, the Majestic, the Windsor – the regular guests never notice. Though maybe the Porter looks older, and that *charming* waitress is no longer here, retired, they suppose, to the country cottage she chatted about as she served the soup.

But somebody whispers 'dead', and the waves don't quite carry the sound away. The Porter himself has a nasty cough which gets worse as he bends to pick up their cases. 'I could take that,' says a thoughtful guest, and is shocked when the old man hardly demurs, yields up the handle with a tired smile. Next day, however, he looks chipper again, his 'Yessir' as bright and charming as ever.

There are new staff, too, over the years. The same tiny rooms in the high, hot roof, but the haircuts, the bearing have shifted a little; that waiter looks – well, *foreign*, which does not mean continental; that one has a diamond earstud; another one cheeked your mother at breakfast . . .

The hotel hears, but remains unmoved. Nothing happens, you see, in Seabourne. The flags stream backwards, the balconies gleam, the portico shines at the sea each morning, the Italian woman scrubs the steps, then the Spanish woman, then the Latin American (same uniform, each time a little shabbier, same tiny room right next to the pipes, but immeasurably different dreams and memories hum round the massive English plumbing). Always long before breakfast, the steps are done, so as not to embarrass the guests; a grey light whitening; the dark bodies kneel on the wide-ruled steps above the wider expanse of shivering water.

'I don' mind the wind,' said Marta. 'The people, he ees dirty, but I don' mind the wind. The wind and the rain, I prefer it. Ees cold, but ees clean.'

This year the winds blowing southwest from Europe to Seabourne in spring were cold but unclean. Marta was lucky not to kneel there waiting as the foul grey rain blew across the sea.

The Empire survives, as white as ever, set right in the middle of the long promenade, defying the Russians, defying the rain. Though under threat from Ireland, from Libya, from Syria, from guests who defect to their villas in Spain and guests who die before they honour their bookings, they never lower the Union Jack; the smells of roast beef and treacle pudding still steam out staunchly on Sunday mornings; the piano still tinkles in the early afternoon. They'll be almost full, come midsummer. Each year they look on the bright side.

On the debit side, many of the guests are dying, and there aren't enough younger ones to replace them. One of heart disease; one of liver disease; one of cancer, who might not last out the week (and they won't be sorry. He complains too much).

And one guest, in very good health for her age, is as near to death as any of these.

Grace, who just wants to escape for a bit, reading and dozing on the afternoon train, is sucked towards the force field of absolute violence, in Seabourne, where nothing ever happens, they say, except holidays and death.

* * *

The train was crowded with what Grace would once have called 'trippers', in the days when Seabourne discouraged them. The men were drinking beer from the can and belching, the women were shouting to their children or else stuffing them full of food. Grace watched it disappear with fascination. Crisps, peanuts, chocolate, chewing-gum, popcorn, chocolate, peanuts, crisps. What must it be doing to their brains, she wondered. What must it be doing to their arteries?

When she was a child there had been strict rules. Children ate food so plain it was dull, but every mouthful was good for you. Boiled cod, boiled potatoes, cold boiled chicken, boiled eggs, brown bread, milk pudding. Exotic tastes might make you dream. What terrible dreams these children must have.

Grace had scanned the symbols in the hotel guide. A little black rocking-horse meant Children. The Empire Hotel had no rocking-horse. She was safe from children for a week, perhaps . . .

Little Brian, whose grandparents were dead, stared at the old lady riveted as her jaw dropped open and her head slipped to the side. Her teeth were yellow as a Crunchie Bar.

'Mum,' he shrieked at his mother, who had her headphones on. 'Mum, wake up! I want some more of them crisps. *Mum*. How did that lady get so old? Look, Mum. Is she dying?'

His mother yanked off her headphones. 'Here's a pound. Go and get yourself a bun or something.'

Grace woke up with a start and hauled herself back to the vertical, uneasy – had she been dreaming of dying?

She had a paperback Paula had lent her, and opened it at random, to keep herself awake.

Mrs Randall's dogs almost immediately found Hilda's body. The body was lying face up, and Mrs Randall noted that Hilda's knees were scratched and bloody . . . She was wearig her coat, a pullover and a skirt but no underwear . . . Later the police were to find her hat and a knife, which may have been used to inflict the small stab wounds in her stomach.

Grace closed the book with swift distaste and stared at the title again. *Who Killed Hilda Murrell?* Had Paula forgotten that she couldn't stand thrillers? Grace was too old for invented horror.

She was nearly as old as the century, born before Queen Victoria died. The nearer they staggered to the brink of the next, the surer she was that she belonged to the past. And yet she was in robust health – everyone envied her her health. Strangers assumed she was in her sixties. She still walked three miles without too much effort, as long as the road was flat. Grace herself knew that ten years ago she was able to walk five times as far, but since very few people still considered that walking was a useful skill, she expected no sympathy on that account . . .

On learned to walk as a baby; at the end of life there was a slow unlearning. The brittle legs of an octogenarian, sharp-shinned, cuttlefish white. In Seabourne she had been a chubby toddler. Toes on the sand, a lifetime ago . . .

'Mum,' Brian shouted. He had pocketed the pound. 'Mum! They 'aven't got any buns left. Mum, that old lady's asleep again.'

But she wasn't. She was remembering.

Grace's father, Archibald Stirling, was headmaster of St Sebastian's, which reckoned itself the best of Seabourne's seventeen preparatory schools 'for the sons of gentlemen'. Vanessa, Grace's mother, second daughter of a baronet, might have looked higher than Archie for a husband. She smiled vaguely on the little school, but was utterly bored with details. At Speech Days, though, and the Fathers' Cricket Match, Mother had been a radiant presence, wild-rose cheeks and heavy black hair, perpetually late and always forgiven. She referred to Archie as 'your poor father', which Grace as a child accepted without question; 'poor' must mean 'dear' as well. And he *was* a dear, with his long gentle face and his eyes as blue as the stripes on the St Sebastian's blazer. Much later, as Grace failed to marry and became 'my poor girl' in turn, it was too late to question that 'poor'. And Mother didn't answer questions, in any case. Mother had certainties. (Men were incapable of governing the world; women would do infinitely better; yet women and men were equals. Women must have the Vote, yet suffragettes were a disgrace to their sex . . .)

From her mother Grace inherited impatience, and a careless beauty which dried to handsomeness. From her father she had learned a strict morality, though she was an atheist. Like Archie, Grace strained towards a Higher Good. Like Archie, Grace knew about Duty.

(*In a woman, such things are a little absurd.* Vanessa laughed at her poor dear daughter; and yet she had said the very same thing – 'Be a good girl for your mother . . .' *Luckily I shall be dead, poor darling, before you are quite worn out with goodness.*)

Actually goodness never tired Grace, just the difficulty of achieving it. Badness was what tired Grace. Lesser evil and greater evil. Rudeness, carelessness, wickedness. And sometimes the times seemed so very bad. What would they have thought, her innocent parents, if they could have looked forward from Grace's cradle, from 1900 towards 2000, from the heights of empire to its long decline?

Sitting by the window after his shower Bruno stares down the narrowing perspectives of the paving stones on his patio. ('Patio', he thinks, is better than 'yard'.) Those lines would march to a perfect point if his garden were not so very small. Then he spots something disquieting. He'd dealt with them only two days ago. Now they were back. He would have to take action. The scissors were with Brunnhilde's things.

He finds them in her make-up bag, jogs outside and carefully, stiffly, moves along each line between the paving stones, cutting off the daisies head by head. Then he crushes the last two between his fingers, rolling the petals into dirty grey flaps of skin. Then he flicks them at the cat and feels better. Things are under control again.

Jogging back into the house he is further encouraged by the athlete in the plate-glass window. Whiplash strong but light as a spring. He looks at his body, not his face. His mother always said he was ugly. He supposes his mother must have been right. The snouted face of a premature baby. He grimaces, furious, at that pink face.

Now the face is a fist with teeth in it.

The platforms at Seabourne are endless; no trolleys as far as the eye can see. After 50 yards of struggle Grace gets to the taxi queue. A solitary cab. He's doing the crossword.

A lifetime ago, Grace learned she must never disturb her father when he did the crossword. She waits, politely, for the man to look up. When he finally does, his eyes are impatient.

22

'Can I help you?' he shouts, as if she were deaf. It is like a disease, this horrible new rudeness.

'The Empire Hotel, please. Grand Parade.'

'Empire. Come on then, in you get.'

It *is* a disease. The whole country's infected. Grace gets in briskly, and mentally halves the tip.

Fred Curry had never liked tall women. This old girl was very tall. She got in the back, not the front. Snooty . . . It took her an age getting her baggage out. He's used to that, of course. He makes up for it by overcharging. Squinting up at her white hair as he takes her money, Fred wonders whether to help her carry the case. The steps are steep, at the Empire. But he doesn't move. She's already paid him. That tip was a joke, though her voice said money . . .

Too bad; she'd manage. Or else she'd die. He revs up his engine to indicate disgust.

There are too many of them, that's the trouble. Sharing the cabs so he gets less money. They are turning this town into an Old Folks' Home, sprawled along the front in deckchairs. As if they were waiting for the nurse to come and inject them. Give him a chance and he'd do it himself.

They are like a disease. It's everywhere now. When he went to see his sister last week in London, they were slumped on the streets with bottles of cider. It has all grown old, the whole country.

In Kensal Green, over tea with Arthur, Paula is worrying about her age.

'I'm not sixteen any more,' she says. Arthur stares down at his chocolate flapjack. 'You aren't listening,' she insists. 'You're getting on as well, you know.'

'That's what I was saying the other day,' he says slowly, dipping the flapjack in his cup of tea, watching the chocolate bending, parting. 'You said it was a load of crap.'

'That was different. You were going on about babies. Men always think women aren't fulfilled without babies.'

'I never said you weren't fulfilled.' He isn't eating any more, he is playing, enjoying the total collapse of the flapjack.

'Well, I'm not fulfilled, of course I'm not. Till I do better with my work, how could I be fulfilled?'

'All right, you're *not* fulfilled. And you're not sixteen any more. I hear you.'

'And I feel bloody ill. I feel bloody terrible. I look awful too.'

'You look beautiful to me. You're unpleasant, of course, but you *look* beautiful . . .'

'It isn't funny. I look old. So do you. Let's face it, Arthur, you really do. You never look in the mirror, do you? Ugh. You've got chocolate all over your shirt . . .'

(When she isn't in this atrocious mood, Paula actually rather likes her looks. She thinks she has improved with age, but she wouldn't accept that was true of Arthur.)

Paula is thirty-seven. Arthur, her boyfriend, is thirty-nine. Sally, his child by another woman, is nearly three, and listens to them gravely, sitting on the sofa with her thumb in her mouth. She is sad to think how old they were. She knows being dead comes next: Grandpa is dead, in a hole in the ground. But she herself wishes she were older. Sometimes she pretends to be three, not two.

'You don't look old to me. And I never said you should have a baby. As a matter of fact, I think you'd be mad. You're much too selfish to have a baby.'

Paula is silent, digesting that. Her cheeks are flushed with discontent. 'I'll have a baby if I want to,' she says. 'I'm not too old. I can if I want to.'

'Of course you can,' he agrees. 'It's not what you're used to, that's all. It's hard to imagine you a mother, Paula.'

'I don't have to be what you think I am.'

'Pain in the arse,' says Arthur.

She giggles, suddenly, and gives him a kiss. 'I can change if I want to.'

'You're a child, Paula,' says Arthur.

Arthur is a man who loves children. When Sally's mother left him (for being 'spineless', which meant he didn't hit her when she was unfaithful, and gave too much – 'You're suffocating me') Arthur was desperate not to lose Sally. She was thirteen months old, and adorable, and Arthur's fault, in a manner of speaking, since he'd pressured Gina into getting pregnant, a mistake he would never make again. And he knew he mustn't lose anyone, ever again. No one he loved must leave, or die. He would stick by Paula, through thick and thin. She could do what she wanted; she could be free. Even if she abused him. Even if she was childish.

He has always loved children, since he was a child. Before and after Arthur had Sally he loved other people's children with the effortless ease of a man who belonged to a vast family of children. They had a common language; they shared jokes and toys; they felt the same way about adults who told children not to fidget on trains.

Children like Arthur, too. He is comfortingly large and fat, but his features somehow look small and twinkly, toffee-brown eyes and surprised black eyebrows like dancing hairy caterpillars, cushiony lips, very red, and teeth which show childlike expanses of gum. His features look small because his head is gigantic, with a thick bush of hair like the fur on a bear.

Actually only his nose is small. His mouth is large and it moves all the time. From a distance it looks as though it might be eating, an unfortunate appearance for a very large man. Most of the time he's just smiling, though. No one ever believes this, but Arthur is not a very big eater. He's a man of eccentric passions, for avocado and sardine sandwiches, for buttered brown rice with chopped raw basil, for the perfect hard-boiled egg. He loves to feed other people, copiously, with curious foods. But he always has less on his plate than his guests.

When Paula first considered making love to Arthur she was embarrassed by the thought of his size. She couldn't, surely, have sex with a body that would take up so much of the bed. Could a woman feel desire for a big, soft body? She had always had lean men before (but then, she has not been happy before. Perhaps fat Arthur could make her happy).

And Arthur did make her happy. His body took up a lot of the bed, but his body *became* her bed and her home. It was big, but not soft. It was solid. It had appetite. It indulged them both. Hairy, massive, always warm, the blood pulsing in every part. So big he made Paula feel small.

Why was it so familiar, such a remembering, when they first lay together, her head cushioned on his great furred chest, his heart at her ear, his big hand in her hair. 'At last,' he said. 'Now I can call you darling.' It was fifteen years after the two of them met. Inside her head she said *Arthur, Mother*. Inside her head she was safe, and a child.

Arthur is a man who loves children. Yet sexually, Arthur isn't mother at all. He's a confident, hungry lover who likes sex as much as Paula does. More, in fact, for in recent months Paula has liked sex less. But then, she's liked everything less. She still doesn't know what's the matter with her. Apart from the unwritten book. And the police.

'What's the matter with you?' says Arthur.

'I don't know, I just feel restless. Shall I go to Ralph's show, or not?'

'Why not? Go, for God's sake,' he tells her.

'I've never been to Pandora's before.'

'It's not that long a street. Just go.'

Arriving somewhere new . . . the Empire Hotel was new, to Grace the Windsor, where she'd stayed before, had been turned into a Palace of Amusements). She used to enjoy new places. *I could be anyone . . . let them guess . . .*

But when one is eighty-five, she thought, one is simply an old woman.

Inside the Empire's dark swing doors she met herself head-on in a mirrored wall up which a sweetheart plant was climbing. Heart-shaped leaves, a violent lime, twined up the glass and up her leg (a ladylike leg, long and bony), her camel coat, her pale neck (a ladylike coat, a ladylike neck).

Once she'd had so much energy. She was always too tall and too strong for men. They danced with her as if they were breaking a horse. She is still a tall woman but . . . weightless. As if the sea-wind might blow her away. The figure in the glass is paper-thin behind the bright spikes and hearts of leaf. As she watches, a fly crawls over her face.

She's a negative, now, of the print she had been. Once she had jet-black hair and black brows; now her hair is white. Only the eyes are still dark. In summer she used to tan deep brown, though Mother complained – 'This is just a fad. No lady has a face like a tinker's.' Now the tan has dissolved into freckles and liver-spots, is she a lady again?

How much time they wasted on us girls, Grace thinks as she heaves her case to join her, telling us to be ladylike. Age makes everyone ladylike. You're ladylike, and then you're dead.

The receptionist isn't ladylike. Her smile is vacuous, carmine-red.

'Grace Stirling,' Grace informs her.

26

'Oh yes, Mrs Stirling. Just a minute . . . we're putting you in Room 70.'

'*Miss* Grace Stirling, in fact.' A lifetime of saying those few words. Then faintly but clearly Grace hears the child crying. Inside the hotel. There is a baby here.

'Er – in the hotel guide – I'm almost sure – did it say there were facilities for children?'

The receptionist's face closes down. 'Oh no. You must have misread it. We haven't a Games Room for children here. There isn't much call for it.'

She doesn't understand. Grace persists.

'I thought I heard a child crying.'

'Well babies do cry. It's got its mother, you know. It isn't the fault of the hotel.'

Grace gives up. Never try to explain. Just as long as it isn't in the room next door, sobbing to be fed in the middle of the night. Those cries had such enormous power. How did mothers manage not to hate their babies? Especially now, when one couldn't get staff.

She thinks of the mothers on the train from London, screaming at their children or stifling them with food. Perhaps they did hate their babies. Perhaps that was why the babies cried.

Bruno's always restless on Saturday. He doesn't like being at home on his own. He has all the entertainment he could want – stereo, video, his magazines – but still the flat feels quiet and empty, however loud he turns up the volume. He doesn't like people – they're a waste of time; idle, greedy, self-centred *bastards* – so why should he get a bad feeling when he's been alone all day? As if someone has failed to arrive, or someone left without warning.

He has quiet feet – you need quiet feet in a profession like his – but for some queer reason they sound too loud, selfconsciously loud, today. He watches a fly, rather dizzy from fly-spray, trying to lay eggs on the window. In a second he will squash it with his gun magazine. Then the glass begins to tremble, and Bruno is soothed by the sound of a train.

He has liked the sound since he was a boy and the family lived near the railway station. He was sent to bed much too early, because Mother wanted to dress for the club. His sister could watch and he could not, but he dimly remembers he used to watch, shimmering stockings and pale chemises and then underneath small mosses of darkness. And secretive smells of sweat and perfume. Then he had been shut out for ever. His sister was still in there, in the warm. He would lie in his narrow bed and stare at the strip of cold light coming in through the curtains. He thought they were laughing next door. The curtains moved in the air from the window, a hissing whispering sound, the sound of two women stroking each other. He cried, but he didn't make a noise in case she should hear and punish him.

But the great steam trains were on his side. A slow rumbling growing louder and louder, rhythmical, strong, predictable. If they wanted, they could shake the house down, but they wouldn't, because they would never hurt him. One day the trains would take him away. Somewhat secret, marvellous, where no one would know him, no one would know how wicked he was . . . she told him often how wicked he was. He had seen no reason to disagree.

Now Bruno lives even nearer the line. The North London Link, which joins Richmond to Woolwich, runs along one edge of his garden. The Watford Line isn't far away. Lovely little lines, both of them, above-ground lines through the heart of London. The estate agent was apologetic. 'Shame it's not the underground, but still . . . it means the price is a bargain.'

Bruno didn't think it was a shame. This was a real railway line. These trains weren't those low-slung, tin-can numbers, they were high and solid, with blue and yellow carriages. The passenger trains, that is. The other kind looked even more serious.

He didn't like the graffiti, though. They were ignorant sods, graffiti writers. Bruno tried not to notice them, but of course he knows them by heart, by now. LINE OF DEATH, they say. THIS WAY TO ANOTHER CHERNOBYL. He's pretty sure who painted them. One day soon he's going to sort them out.

He sits by the window now and smiles as a big train passes on its way to Willesden and the cord that operates his white linen blinds quivers and sways, then slowly settles.

Enormous power, very close to him.

Grinding upwards in the mirrored lift, Grace wonders why she's afraid of babies. After all, she was a baby once herself. In Sea-bourne. Eighty-five years ago.

There is a picture of her reaching out tiny hands from a sea of pale frills in sepia shadow. Tucked under some kind of wickerwork hood, stretching out round hands into the sunlight.

She was long and thin even then, but bald, and her eyes stood out of her head with excitement, looking at something amazing off-camera, peering out into the future.

She remembers seagulls, on the front. Not understanding why they flapped away when she only wanted to wave at them. She would watch them till they were right out of sight.

I believed that later I'd fly; first you crawled, then you walked, then surely . . .

Her leg gives slightly as the lift doors open and she makes to walk briskly along the landing. She regains her balance with a gasp. First you crawled, then you walked, then you crawled again.

The picture of Grace as a baby stands in a Moroccan brass frame on a beaded mat on an emerald-green dresser in a messy room full of plants and toys and newspapers in a terraced house in London, a thickness of wall away from Bruno, two or three feet of bricks and mortar, and everything shakes as the trains lurch through, and the baby shivers in the hands of her future.

It takes quite a lot to shake a house. Bombs can do it, effortlessly, but most of London survived the last war. Peace-time trains do it every day. Each peace-time week, three or four trains carry nuclear waste through the heart of London.

They are shorter and lighter than most goods trains, but heavy in proportion to the size of their cargo. Each flask is huge, with walls a foot thick and a lid weighing seven metric tons. One flask plus wagon costs a million pounds. They are spending a lot of time and trouble on this, an awesome quantity of steel and engineering . . .

And nevertheless, there are leaks. The engineers fail to prevent them. Low-level radiation has been found on the flasks, the rolling-stock, the tracks. The unleashed particles fly through the air – city air smelling of grime and summer, a hint of green from London's trees – to find the cells that might be looking for them, waiting to be entered, waiting to be split, waiting to start their extraordinary journey.

A long bright tunnel to the window on the sea, long but rather narrow. Grace should have expected her room to be small – she is old, she is single, no one here knows her.

(No one anywhere knew her any more, did they? What is there to know, after all? In her day she had been a distinctive figure; the tallest undergraduette, the one who wrote; the poet in Belgravia; Ralph's companion, in her thirties . . . the figure in all his paintings. The only woman he ever painted, the only woman he ever loved.

As life went on one grew less important. She would not mind; she did not mind.) In the four o'clock sun the room is clean but a little old-fashioned . . . just right then, for an old woman like her. That radio, a round mesh speaker set into the wooden bedhead, must have been there forever. It had a certain Orwellian charm. Grace fiercely admired Orwell. Big Brother will be speaking to you . . .

The phone startles her, harsh and close, making her jump and drop her wash-bag. Tooth-powder rolls away across the room. Where *was* the phone? By the bed, of course. She is angry to find she is shaking, slightly.

The phone is as old as the radio, dull Bakelite plastic, cold, rather clammy. As her fingers close round it and the horrid sound dies, she thinks with sudden pleasure *It's Paula*.

'Hallo? Hallo? This is Room . . .' (she's forgotten which room) '. . . Room 70.'

Silence. She waits. The silence extends.

She can't believe it. Not here. Blood pounds between the phone and her ear as she presses the receiver close. '*Hallo*,' she calls. '*Ha-LLO!*'

There is a click, then suddenly the receptionist's bland voice.

'Is that Mrs Stirling?'

'*Miss*,' snaps Grace, relief turning to fury.

'Ooh, sorry. *Miss* Stirling. I hope you're comfy in your room, Miss Stirling. I forgot to say, there was a message. From a Mrs Paula Timms. Shall I read it to you?'

'Of course.'

'It came this morning. The other girl took it . . .'

'Please go ahead.'

'Right-o. "Hope to come and see you this week if agreeable. Ring me at Arthur's. Paula." That's it.'

Grace takes a second to digest it. 'Thank you.'

'Everything all right with the room, in any case?'

'Yes. It's quite – suitable.'

'All right then,' says the voice, inappropriately gracious. 'See you later, then.'

Grace puts the phone down firmly. *Why do I have to ring her at Arthur's? Doesn't she ever go home any more?*

Paula, the child of her dead sister Lucy, who Grace loves more than anyone alive. And Arthur Fraenkel, the detested. Arthur, the 'boyfriend', if so youthful a term could be applied to someone so fat and shambling.

She had first encountered him twenty years ago when Paula was going through her hippy phase, living in a commune with mysterious friends. Lucy hadn't been dead very long, and Grace was trying to carry out her wishes, keeping an eye on the difficult daughter.

It was Arthur who answered the door. Grace had stood there speechless, staring at him. A monstrous apparition, red-lipped, red-faced, in a kind of shimmering dressing-gown (or was it a dress? For was it a woman?). The black mat of hair lay over the shoulders, but the jowls were blue and stubbly. He smelled of garlic, and a flowery scent. Enormous bare feet peeped under his hem-line.

'Oh, hi,' he said, and the voice was male. 'You needn't have knocked, we never lock it. You must be Aunt Grace.'

'Grace Stirling,' she had finally managed, extending, then almost dropping her hand (for he smelled of sweat, as well as scent and garlic, and the hall behind him looked very dirty). Something horrible had happened then. The shimmering mountain was in sudden motion, an animal smell as his hair flopped forward and then her hand was being pulled up against something hot and wet and appalling.

He had kissed her hand. How dare he? He leered before her like a pantomime dame. The wetness had clung to her own clean flesh. *Men should be men, as Ralph had been.*

It was true that Arthur had changed since then. The caftan phase had long ago faded to shirt and jeans. He had less hair, front and back. He washed. But he wasn't a man. There was no substance to him. He had no drive. He was nobody.

What did he care about? Food. In the sixties he'd cooked for the commune, now he was a chef, it seemed. A part-time chef, at that. And a part-time hotel manager. The young of today did most things part-time. And a part-time journalist, which meant he'd had a restaurant column in a magazine which had fizzled out after a couple of months. No one had a proper career, these days.

Some two or three years ago, Grace was stunned to realise that Arthur had changed status. He wasn't just one of Paula's peculiar friends, he was a boyfriend. Then *the* boyfriend; and now they were virtually living together. Meanwhile, to Grace's equal astonishment, he'd fathered a daughter on another woman – what could modern woman be thinking of? – and gained custody of her when the relationship ended, so Paula was saddled with the child as well.

Paula's mother would have been so disappointed, thought Grace, as she had thought hundreds of times before, and each time she thought it she knew it was a lie. Lucy's interest in Paula had always been vague. It was Grace who was disappointed. She loved her niece, and she was disappointed.

Grace was a feminist, of course. Men should be manly all the same.

'Sweet! Ooh isn't she sweet! Coochy, coochy, *coochy*!' Brunnhilde is out on the town. In the end, she couldn't resist it. A girl deserved to have fun once a week. She strides down the high street, strikingly tall, turning heads to either side. The six o'clock sun makes a fiery cloud of the curls which break on her shoulders, nylon-shiny, electric red. It's Saturday night, and she's in full fig. Her lips are a pout of crimson lake, her eyelashes bat like spiders' legs as she meets, and spurns, the stares. Ladbroke Grove does not deserve her. Some of the remarks are frankly gross. But she's spotted something which *is* to her taste.

'Sweet! Oh isn't she sweet!' A dear little baby in a pink-striped pram with a rope of matching pink plastic rabbits slung across the front like a necklace.

'Goo,' says the baby, amiably, smiling at the funny lady.

'Sweet little thing! Oh *darling*!' Brunnhilde swoops in over the hood, bending awkwardly down off her three-inch heels, and dangles a hand at the baby. She does not look at the mother's face, automatically polite, automatically anxious.

'What's her name?' Brunnhilde asks, now glittering roguishly across at Mum (how very *old* she looks. How very plain, compared to her baby).

'It's a him,' the mother mumbles. 'A boy.' She's very shy. Her husband doesn't like shrill women. 'My husband wanted a daughter, but I went and had a son.'

Brunnhilde hasn't heard a word of that. 'Don't tell me don't tell me I'll guess!' she protests, and the hand she holds up to hush her new friend is large and pale, a disquieting hand. The baby likes it well enough; to him it's the normal kind of wriggly animal that grows on the end of people's arms. His mother, however, shrinks back a little and tightens her grip on the buggy handle.

'Emily? Louisa? *Miranda* . . .? No? Honestly I'm psychic, I'll have it in a moment. DARLING LITTLE THING!' (She wriggles one long, strong hand under the canopy.)

'We've got to go,' the mother is muttering. 'I'm very sorry, we've got to go.' The wheel of the pram pushes briefly but painfully against Brunnhilde's black nylon shin. 'I've got to meet my husband,' the woman adds, trying the pram at a different angle and jerking the baby, who blows a bubble. 'Bobby, say goodbye to the lady.'

'Ga.'

'*Roberta!* What a *charming* name!' Brunnhilde coos into an absence, for the little pink pram is receding very rapidly, weaving through the bodies with surprising speed. Brunnhilde smiles after it adoringly, then wheels to admire her smile in the window. Sisterhood can be very sweet. She belches behind her hand, and catches a definite smell of beer. A little giggle escapes her. Naughty! Next time she'll stick to gin or vodka, more decorous drinks for the girl about town.

Reflected in the window two men are watching her. The nearer one is rather a dish, thickset, crewcut, the macho type. A little like Bruno, in fact. Brunnhilde's eyelashes beat a tattoo, and she offers a smile both coy and haughty. The wind blows under her copper curls and gives her a bouffant halo. I'm stunning, thinks Brunnhilde. The excitement becomes specific.

It is either that or the evening chill which makes her shiver as she turns towards them and shows, on the hand she brings to her lips, the red hairs bristling at 90 degrees.

'You look my type.' Throaty, seductive. Brunnhilde knows this was meant to be.

The love of her life. A foolish phrase – since life contained a diversity of love – but whenever Grace looked at her photos of Ralph the phrase arrived like a homing dove. How lucky she was to have had him. She'd know of his genius long before the world.

She picks from her suitcase the small silver frame which has followed her everywhere for forty-odd years (though where has she been in the last forty years? Without Ralph, her horizons have shrunk. It had taken all Paula's powers of persuasion to get her to Portugal in spring. And the silver frame had flown with her, so if she had died, it would have been with him).

She props it up now on the bedside table by the paperback Paula had lent her. The frame has two oval insets. The left-hand photograph is brown, with the lights and darks yellowing into each other. The right-hand photograph is grey, but Grace sees it in colour.

A young man is laughing at the camera. The oval is only two inches by three, but he's a big man, muscular, not quite relaxed, though he has had fifty-odd years to relax since the day when the photo was taken. His features are broad, proud, handsome. He is caught in strong sunlight, so the lines which surround his eyes and mouth are black; so are his tensed nostrils; his shirt, which is open at the neck, blindingly white; his skin dark grey, the sky behind him a paler grey, and his hair the palest grey of all, a shining undisciplined crest of it.

Grace still sees the blue of his eyes, the fainter, echoing blue of the sky, the deep red-brown of his face and arms. His auburn hair looked blond in the sun. 'Chancellor Hitler would love you,' she'd said, long before it was simply 'Hitler'. So many things couldn't be unsaid . . .

The left-hand photo shows a baby which refuses to emerge from its sepia fix. How different he is from Grace as a baby (hooded and frilled, little first-born daughter, grasping for sunlight she couldn't quite reach . . .) This child sits still and stares at the camera, plump-lipped, heavy-lidded, recently fed, clutching a rattle like a sceptre. Behind him, symmetrically parted drapes sketch in a cradle which could be a throne.

However much Grace stares – and her eyes have looked at this child too often – she can't make the baby breathe and move. His cheeks are yellow waxworks. It's a photo of Ralph at six months . . .

It might have been Ralph's son.

The thought is no longer a thought but an echo of all the other times she has thought it. She shifts the frame just a little to the left, away from Paula's paperback; both ovals of glass burn blank in the sunlight, Ralph as a baby, Ralph as a man, then both of them have gone.

Francesca, Paula's friend, who did the Visual Arts for *Mean Streets* had passed on the Private View card to Paula. She knew about the family connection with Ralph. 'I shan't bother to go,' she'd said, shovelling a heap of blonde hair back over one eye. 'Dunne's great in his way, but it's all a bit Renoir, isn't it? Those sunny, somnolent women . . .'

'That's my Aunt Grace you're talking about. Well, you've met her, haven't you. There's no one less somnolent.'

'Write us a para, if you feel like it.'

'I don't feel up to a lot, like I told you . . .'

'It isn't essential. He's too mainstream for us. Let's get together later in the week . . . I want to hear what's been happening to you.'

'Too much. You wouldn't believe it.'

'Ooh! Nothing ever happens to me . . . Well, something has, but it doesn't count. You're not leaving Arthur, are you?'

'No such luck –'

'Pig, he's nice –'

'I don't mean it. I'm camping there at the moment. I'll ring you.'

They kissed. The two women loved each other. They'd been friends since they were at college together. Other people were always surprised by this fact, since Francesca looked ten years younger.

Paula muses on this as she walks down Bond Street, looking out for the gallery. The sixties and seventies had left Fran undamaged, the eighties floated her up as calm and shiny as a driftwood figurehead. Time had eroded parts of Paula; links between cells had stretched and burst; her face, she thought, had grown more interesting, but it was elastic from laughing and crying. Francesca, by contrast, had been preserved. The years had bleached and polished her. Perhaps she was getting too thin, all the same.

Pandora's. There it was. Paula glimpses herself in the gallery's window. Nonsense. Fran wasn't thinner at all, it is just that Paula has put on weight.

She feels in her bag for the card. *Ralph Dunne: A Final Darkening* it said. How pretentious, she thinks, and how *un-Ralph*. She reads on. *Pictures of the Second World War ... a cache of hitherto unknown drawings ...* She stands in the street, puzzled, re-reading. There weren't any war pictures, surely. He didn't do a thing after leaving Grace.

She swallows. Evidently he did. Clutching her card, she plunges in.

White walls, steely light, a scrum of people. The voices are sharp as searchlight beams, criss-crossing against the ceiling. A lot of press; she knows the faces. But the atmosphere is somehow different. More heads actually studying the pictures.

They are charcoal drawings, not paintings. Ralph's name is synonymous with vivid colour, scorching Iberian blues and oranges. But here there's only black and white. She looks, as always, for Grace's face. At every show she finds it. He's painted her in a thousand forms, but always vigorous and young. More vigorous than Paula feels. Good old Grace, thinks Paula.

Grace means to go out for a seaside stroll before the air gets chill. It's taken her nearly an hour to unpack; once she would have done it in half that time. Just lately, it seems each bone and muscle has developed a separate voice of its own, reminding her of its limits by a moment of pain or a foolish creak. *We shan't go on forever*, they whisper. *Save yourself. Don't push us too hard.*

But what shall I save myself for? she wonders. What point do I have? Am I wholly useless?

She pulls on a sweater determinedly, a fight she would soon be losing. She will soon have to go into cardigans, what Ethel, the pensioner who helped in the shop, used to call 'cardies' – 'You should get yourself a cardie' – and Grace's heart sank, though perhaps she was right.

But I'm not really old; not like Ethel (yet Ethel was twelve years younger than her). How long that little voice had been protesting, denying the birthdays as they piled. Sixty wasn't really old (and at that age Grace had passed for forty-five). Seventy wasn't really old (and then she'd passed for fifty, still walking eight miles a day after work without more than a little tiredness . . . a growing tiredness). Seventy-five, and she did five miles with occasional pain in her knees and shoulders, five miles *almost* daily, growing slightly slower as the birthdays crept round her and the pain crept with it, growing equally slowly, so then it was four miles, three and a half, leave out the bridge and come back the quick way past the police station and the village shop, no longer climbing the hump-backed bridge to look for the swans that Ralph had painted.

Eighty. But no one believed it, or else they were being kind. 'You can't be. You must be younger than me . . .' What these judgements were worth she sometimes wondered, looking at the wrecks who offered them, hobbled with bandages of extra flesh or bent into strange inhuman shapes. 'I'm not really eighty,' she told herself then, for no one could deny that eighty was ancient. *Oh, but he must be in his eighties* – meaning oh, but he's practically dead.

Now Grace, who has watched for so long from the sidelines as all her contemporaries grew old – Grace herself is over eighty, and walks two miles only every other day, stopping well this side of the river, now, watching sparrows take dust-baths in the churchyard, between the graves as the sun goes down: trying not to remember that somewhere else the sun shines red through the hump-backed bridge and the swans are still vee-ing up into flight from the red and white water, immensely strong, smooth hard necks and violent wings, the world of the young that Ralph had painted.

Suddenly Grace is in pain, staring down the tunnel of her room at the sky. She is old. So much has gone. And perhaps she missed the point.

Grace isn't here. She's gone, vanished. Paula searches, but the face isn't there. So in the end, Grace died for him. Everything died for him, it seems.

Everything wrecked, burnt out; planes falling like broken birds, upturned tanks, battered bodies. She fights to get close to each picture, pressing along the wall. His people are tiny, almost irrele-vant, matchsticks in a torn black landscape. The white seems incidental, dots of paper which escaped the dark. Ralph's pictures had always been of living forms, but these are inanimate, recently slaughtered.

She goes upstairs to the last two rooms. The crush on the stairs is greater still; she fights her way up, panting, sweating. People push and peer like sales-goers. She gets her first glimpse, and understands.

They are all of the same naked figure. The drawing is different, precise and fine, but somehow just as violent. She kneels, she crawls, she sprawls on her face, palms flat on the ground, trying to push upwards. Her back is always to the observer. She is dignified, but with no resource against the eyes which have tracked her down. They are drawings from an anatomist's handbook, painfully clear, brutally truthful. The light is cold and bright.

Paula's heart is beating fast. She no longer notices the mob of people; she is with the woman behind the glass. A phrase keeps running through her head as she stares at the intimate charcoal shading. *In the shadow of death*, she thinks. That body is in the shadow of death. Dead, or dying. Unbearable.

But the last picture shows the woman's face. She looks out proudly from round dark eyes. Her mouth is half-open – sad or tender? The word she is saying might be 'Please'. Sighing with relief, Paula sees it isn't Grace.

She fights her way back to the head of the stairs. The braying voices beat at her temples.

'Extraordinary clarity . . .'

'. . . such courage . . .'

'. . . staggeringly erotic . . .'

'. . . a symbol of fascist oppression, sure, but for me it's much too obvious . . .'

A woman is sitting on the top stair, apparently unmoved by the chaos all around her. From behind, Paula sees broad bare shoulders, golden skin, an amazing head of dark copper hair piled thickly on top, and her face, turned sideways, has a calm, amused, proprietary expression. Paula pauses a second to look. Who is it?

The face is intensely familiar. Full lips, flared nostrils, broad strong features, a look of animal content. 'Excuse me,' says Paula, and the woman looks up, and her eyes aren't brown, as Paula expected, they're a surprising, deep-ocean blue, the unqualified blue of the early paintings. They show no recognition. Must be an actress, Paula thinks. Someone I know from television.

Outside, it's an urban summer evening, the sky just deepening behind the pigeons, grey wings puttering a thousand heartbeats.

Thank God Grace never went to these things. She would read about it, though; she would suffer. At eighty-five, her whole life would be changed.

Here where her life began Grace stands, shivering slightly on the edge of evening. Lapped by the sea and a calm rose light, Seabourne seems wonderfully unchanged.

The three-levelled promenade has survived. On Sunday walks, Father shepherded the family along the top level of the promenade. Grace once complained it was dull – she wanted to run down near the sand. Father told her not to be silly, and muttered something about *hoi polloi*. To Grace the words sounded like dancing.

She had always thought how lucky they were, the *hoi polloi* on the bottom level, since the lower one walked, the better view one must have of the beach and the rocks and the sea – and surely that was the point of the walk? She'd heard them singing, the *hoi polloi*. And the hats which sailed by below her feet, elaborate concoctions of flowers and feathers, were nests for the birds of paradise in her leather encyclopaedia ... immeasurably nicer than her mother's neat boaters. And their parasols were all the colours of the rainbow, where Mother's were always mute and white. Grace reached out one pudgy hand towards them. 'Pretty,' she'd shouted, but could not reach. They had bobbed away on a tide of laughter, and Grace traipsed off to become a lady, a lesson one could not unlearn at will. Mother had taught the lesson well, although she was a feminist.

Grace had been six or seven years old when Mother first thought she could walk to the Lighthouse. Eddy ran ahead on his lucky brown legs whereas she had to walk demurely with Mother, in her Sunday dress and slippery shoes (and the autumn country cried out for trousers, hordes of blackberries ready for picking, hedges bright with crabs and sloes – but Grace already knew the rules. One couldn't pick blackberries in a white lawn dress, though her brother's mouth was black and cheerful).

It was Eddy, of course, who saw it first. He yelled back in triumph from twenty yards ahead, waving wildly against the line of the horizon – 'I've seen it! I've seen the Lighthouse!' – and then disappearing, so she screamed in panic, sure that her brother had gone over the edge, and was running forward after him, she was stronger than they thought, she was going to save him, but as her mother called, 'Grace! Don't run,' and her father intoned, 'Don't excite yourself,' she'd already sprawled painfully to her knees, and she heard the fine lawn of her new white dress give an outraged creak like the hinge on a door, then yield as the skirt ripped away from the waistband.

'It's *his* fault,' she sobbed, enraged. 'I thought he was falling over.' But Eddy had re-emerged, impatient, from the waist upward on the green horizon. 'Come on, slowcoaches! Come and see!' – and her parents left her to pick herself up, hurrying on after Eddy. Grace got to the top on a crest of anger just as Mother's pale hat with its paler ribbon sank down out of view, then rose again. The anger faded as she saw it too, exactly the miracle she had been promised, brilliantly white and incredibly small on the cobalt blue expanse of water.

She sat near the edge as the blood came back to her damaged knee, peering, frowning. How could it be twice as tall as a house, which was what her father had told her? How could there be several grown-ups inside? Was it really very big, or very small?

From above, of course, it could only be small. But you couldn't *see* things from too high up. She had lived her life at a ladylike distance.

Impatient, she strikes straight down the steps to the lowest level of the promenade, near the picking birds and the smell of the sea. She reads the notice on the scruffy wooden building, BOAT TRIPS DAILY. Here's hers: ROUND TRIP – SEABOURNE HEAD AND THE LIGHTHOUSE. Grace's spirits rise. The boats are hove to on the pebbles below, the *Southern Princess* and *Queen of the Sea*. She's glad they're closed for the day. It means she can savour her plan without being distracted by hordes of screaming people.

But she isn't a snob. She will not be a snob. Twenty years ago she missed her chance to sail to the Lighthouse through being a snob.

It was 1965. A group of stout women in miniskirts were waiting to sail, eating candy-floss. Somehow a two-inch gob of pink floss got stuck to the sleeve of Grace's white linen jacket. Suddenly exhausted, she watched her ticket flutter down on to the oil-streaked beach, and her long pale ladylike hand waved feebly towards it, then went limp. No one noticed the candy-floss, or the ticket. She had no will to go after it.

Now she has the will, and the motive. She'll see the Lighthouse or die, this time. From sea-level, like the men who built it.

Saturday night, Saturday night. England enjoys its Saturday nights. Saturday nights, things happen, after nothing has happened all day. Especially if you're young, and bored, and unemployed, and broke, and drunk. Come to Seabourne, where nothing ever happens, except on Saturday nights.

There's trouble in a disco (Seabourne has got two discos, half-hearted affairs where the disc jockeys wear dinner jackets and patent shoes). Half of one group get turned away for failing to 'Dress Respectable'. The half who get inside make trouble on behalf of the ones who didn't. They push and shove on the dance-floor, break a few glasses, shout at some girls. It's Saturday night, after all, and it's summer, so there hasn't been a football match, which means nothing has happened all fucking day, and something's got to happen right here and now or how will they get through another blank week. So the half who got in are thrown out again to meet up with the half who were turned away and got bevvied up at the pub next door, and then there are thirty of them, drunk and angry, starting to panic that the night's nearly over and they haven't had half good enough a time, they haven't done half enough damage yet, and the thirty of them, shouting, shoving, singing, mysteriously swell to fifty, sixty, youths who join in instead of being jumped on, and seventy run through the shopping precinct which is wide and empty and good to run through and by now they're dreaming of kicking in windows, but they're carried on further by their own momentum and the ninety of them end up running down the prom, and by now the phonecalls have been made to the police and a dozen stout policemen come running to meet them and manage to drive them down to the beach, away from the tidy, timid town, and they find that the beach is covered in stones, beautiful slippery-slidey stones, noisy, heavy, imposing stones, sea-cold stones, salt-caked stones, stones which are free and there for the taking, and they start to pick up some nice big stones, each of them picks up his nice big stone, all hundred and ten of them are carrying stones, and then the first boy throws the first big stone, but it's not the police that they're aiming at, it's the sherried glow of the great hotels, the becalmed glass world that they can't get into, and then the first stone breaks the first sheet of glass and a score of wild voices cheer it on, the wind lifts the cheer and throws it inland, and the guests start to stir in their beds and worry, and most of the stones are bouncing off, a clattering shower of summer hail-stones, but three of the largest windows smash with a crack like the South Coast breaking in two and the pieces lie and glitter like the diamonds that summered in Seabourne long ago.

'I blame the police,' says a hotel porter. 'It's those wallies drove 'em on to the beach. Didn't they know there were stones down there? Stupid sods. I blame the police.'

And the youths themselves, as they're rounded up and herded down to the police station, as painful thought starts to squirm back under the edge of their Saturday night bravado – the youths blame all those lucky bastards hiding behind the glass and velvet, the ones with jobs, the ones with status, the ones with money who lock them out.

(Actually of course it's a misperception; the velvet's nylon, the guests are frail, the restaurant takings have shrunk this season, there's nothing inside that the youth would want.)

In London the hospitals are busy, dealing with Saturday's births and deaths, overcrowded and underfunded, trying to staunch the flow of blood.

As the moon slides out of the sea and slips a quivering skin across the Thames, Brunnhilde thinks she is dying. There were two of them, and they brought a friend. They would not consent to be disappointed. Every orifice has been brutally filled. She has screamed, but nobody's heard her except the woman who lives in the flat above.

Mary thinks it's a baby crying. For decades she's wanted to comfort a baby. Childless, she sighs, and turns up the television.

I want to die. I want to die.

Sleep ambushes Graces with her arm half-extended towards Paula's book on the bedside table: *Who Killed Hilda Murrell?* She supposes she ought to give it a chance. But a deep dead sleep sweeps over her.

The phone rings twice and she jerks upright. She waits, rigid, unsure where she is. The light stares down. Her neck aches . . . Seabourne, of course. The phone has stopped. She waits for it to ring again.

It doesn't ring. The silence stretches.

It happens in hotels, she reminds herself. Switchboards make mistakes all the time . . . but the tension doesn't drain away. Grace is left wide awake.

Somewhere down below, a television blares into the night. Sounds of shouting, running, breaking glass. The crash of the glass is unpleasantly real. Why don't they turn the damned thing down. She flicks her book open in exasperation.

'Many of these very dangerous elements would never have existed at all but for man's meddling with the very building-blocks of the universe . . .' She can't be bothered to follow it. The *building-blocks of the universe* . . . Rather high-flown for a thriller.

Idly exploring the recess under the top of the bedside table, Grace's fingers encounter something more solid, a cover that feels like leather. Of course, a Gideon's Bible. Out in the light, the cover is plastic, but Grace is still delighted; she'd stopped believing when her brother died, but at eighty-five she can afford to be tolerant.

Prefacing the bible is a 'Key' which tells the heathen how to find what they need. Some of the key-words ring in her head. 'NEEDING PEACE' . . . 'WANTING REST' . . . 'WORRIED' . . .

Rubbish, she thinks, I'm on holiday. She turns, instead, to 'THE CREATION STORY'. Genesis 1. That seems right for a beginning. The words look certain on the flimsy paper.

'In the beginning, God created the Heaven and the Earth.'

Grace sleeps like a baby.

All through the night the sea does not sleep nor the winds blowing over the edge of England. On the high cliffs, someone walks, bent low, a small person, a stout person, a person who puffs into the wind, bending double as a contraction takes her, pausing and gazing across the black water, afraid to live and afraid to die. The beam of the Lighthouse decides her. Tonight, at least, Faith will not die, since someone has stayed awake with her.

4   .

A GIRL ON HER OWN

One eye opens. Paving stones. Cigarette packet. Shrivelled grass.

Brunnhilde is lying on the pavement. She doesn't know where the hell she is. Why or where. She doesn't know. Blades of grey, disgusting grass.

It must be early morning. The sky is white and hard as cement. A paving stone inside her skull slides heavily from side to side as she tries to sit up, then collapses again. A milk-float squeals against the terrible rawness behind one puckered eyelid.

Wanting something. Wanting to die.

She slips back into unconsciousness.

The next time waking is total. Enormous legs and feet walk past her. Painfully brilliant sunlight. Traffic pile-drives into her brain. She remembers she didn't get home last night. She tries to rise, with dignity, but one of her feet doesn't seem to work. One of her stilettos has broken off.

A sudden rush of memory. The four of them went to the Bar Surprise. She'd never drunk Tequila before; she liked it; she couldn't get enough of it; she liked it more and more. Then there was a jeep being driven through very loud music and brilliantly coloured traffic; she was trying to explain how lovely it was; she had never been so happy; she was laughing, unstoppably, in long chromatic scales.

Then an unfamiliar bedroom. She asked for coffee but didn't get it, and two of them were trying to make love to her, she wanted to know if they loved her, first, and someone was laughing and hitting her, Brunnhilde started to punch him back and then it was there, in the bedhead spotlight, small and shiny and real, a gun; time stopped, the world was six inches long, a stainless steel Ruger Magnum.

Three of them pushing their bodies inside her. Drifting away from the impossible pain, the vile, warmish, salty liquid filling her mouth and choking her . . . She was trying to get under the sheets and sleep but they wouldn't let her, they were dragging her up, shouting, slapping her, the door was slamming and then the world exploded over her, fierce white light, insanely angled corners battering her head and shoulders as she sprawled face-first down a silent staircase, and at the bottom the world went dark.

Now she feels her face, very gingerly. Ugh; something furry under one eye. She brushes it away, but her skin pulls tight. Half-detached false eyelashes. She gropes in her handbag, which lies by her foot. Empty. The bright sun glints on the clasp. No money, no make-up, no hope.

People are utterly evil, she thinks. She heaves herself up by some rusted railings. Passing faces veer towards her. Horror; she feels for her hair. It's gone.

She will have justice. Torture and kill.

For now, though, she's just a girl on her own, and her eyes sting with tears in the sun.

Grace wakes to unusual brightness, ten minutes before the alarm. A child crying, very faintly, in the distance, or else a distant dream of childhood . . . as her eyelids open, the child is gone. Sunday in Seabourne; how lovely. And sunshine. She starts to look forward to breakfast.

Eggs and bacon, perhaps, for once – why not? – mushrooms, a steaming pot of coffee. Then a walk by the sea, a sit in the sun . . . maybe a newspaper, maybe not . . .

It's a morning for the yellow waistcoat that Paula had knitted for her. All her life, since she was a child, she had never bought anything yellow – but Paula said, 'It's for Portugal. Yellow's just the colour for a holiday . . . Do you like it though Aunty? It's not too bright?'

Grace did think it rather bright, at first. But she'd tried it on and it fitted her snugly, showing off her trim waist; it had pockets for all the things she lost – handkerchiefs, keys, small secateurs . . . And no one, not even Ethel in the shop, could say it was a cardigan. She wasn't condemned to *cardies* yet.

She'd worn it in Portugal on windy mornings and Sally loved her in it. 'Gracie all yellow,' she said over and over, laughing as at a brilliant joke, and was eager to sit on Grace's lap.

In the three months since the Portuguese holiday Grace had scarcely worn the waistcoat, though. In the village they knew her in blues and greys, they'd have stared and wondered if she'd gone into yellow and wondered if she was in her second childhood.

I wish I *were* in my second childhood if it meant I could be a child again . . . if I could be bold and untroubled, like Sally . . . the girls of today were so different.

Grace glances through her window; it shows her a brilliant sea. When she was a child, this stretch of beach was entirely lined with bathing-machines. She was desperate to go inside them and be wheeled down the beach like the lucky people who suddenly spilled out into the water. Her brother Eddy could go, of course.

She'd wanted so much to be brave, like him. She was sure she'd be good at swimming, though her only attempt was an icy debâcle, when they went to Wales with their cousins, and Uncle Jack hauled her through the water on a pole, everything too fast and bruising and the swimsuit heavy with freezing water. She'd dreamed of what real swimming would be, shooting through the water like a fish, twisting and turning, so smooth and free . . .

Miss Wigmore's school didn't go swimming, and nor did Compton Hall. By the time she could go on her own account the bathing-machines had turned into beach-huts, and suddenly it was acceptable to walk down the beach from the hut to the sea, then back again with the wet serge costume clinging like death to her shivery thighs and those clumsy collars weighing her down in their futile attempt to hide the bosom.

Never at all like one's dreams. The pebbles, the costume, too many people . . .

Till I swam with Ralph in the river on our way to Portugal, in the blazing sun, in the centre of my life, with those yellow irises, hot yellow tongues, and we were both naked, and quite alone.

That nakedness had its own small courage. For a woman, that is. It was nothing for a man.

All her life she's had this fight to be brave, this struggle against all the layers and buttons and petticoats and rules and fuss . . .It was men who were brave as if by birthright, the soldiers, scientists, explorers, the empire-builders, for all their mistakes.

The lighthouse-keepers; she believes in them.

She walks down to breakfast with the image of the Lighthouse floating before her, intensely white, happy to think this week she'll see it.

– Just to think, when I was tethered in my bassinet, in a nest of bleached frills in the shade of the garden, patrolled by nurse-maids with parasols – at the foot of the cliffs, men were building the Lighthouse.

Paula wakes up with the now familiar metallic taste in her mouth. She's been crying in her sleep. Or is Sally crying in the room next door? She lies there listening. Nothing.

Beside her Arthur snores. Normally she finds it a peaceful sound. He's a soft snorer, a pillowy snorer, and normally she only hears him at night when he falls asleep so much faster than her. Normally when they're together he wakes up before her to see to Sally, and then brings Paula breakfast . . .

Only nothing is normal, now. Every morning she wakes at six. Every morning Arthur is there, still snoring. It's been three weeks since she slept at home . . .

The memory of that terrible morning in Camden floated in a questioning, uneasy silence. None of it seemed quite credible. If she could forget it, would it cease to be true? Arthur was exasperated.

'You didn't imagine any of it. I saw those envelopes. They wanted you to know they were opening them. And I saw you after what happened that morning. If they're leaving you alone – which please God they are – it's because they think they've frightened you off.'

'I stood up to them. I refused to make tea.'

One tiny moment of courage.

There were different kinds of courage, of course. Lying here at Arthur's with his comforting, mountainous bulk unbalancing the double bed, Paula is still afraid, but she isn't afraid of the knock on the door.

She's afraid of her own body. She's hardly worked since moving in with Arthur, but it isn't through fear of the security services. She's waiting to feel better. But she doesn't feel better. She feels sick every day, as if all Chernobyl had blown inside her.

And yet, she's taken precautions. She hasn't drunk milk, because cows eat grass. She's stopped eating green vegetables. She's even sacrificed her favourite salads.

Men with braying voices kept appearing on television, telling people that all food was safe. These assurances convinced her that nothing was safe. There was one particularly disquieting *cinéma verité* visit to a Minister's breakfast table. He sat over his grinning, terrified children, eating their cereal with lots of milk. They waved jugs of milk, they slurped mugs of milk. 'My family is drinking milk as normal.'

They all looked like mutants, to Paula. The brightly lit table was a shoddy stage-set. The 'children' were probably midgets in their fifties, for even a politician, surely, wouldn't poison his own children. (Then she thought about it. That was just what they *had* done.)

In the shops, milk went beyond its sell-by date. Arthur, who was drinking milk as normal – 'You've got to die of something, sometime. And I'd rather die than do without milk' – complained that it was on the verge of turning sour; because it was old, not because of radiation. The lettuces went dark, with unhealthy wet creases, or turned to a greeny-black sludge in the bag. Tomatoes sat waiting, soft and dull. The new season's strawberries would not sell.

For despite the politicians, the public didn't buy. On the other hand, they didn't know what *not* to buy. They didn't buy milk, but they did buy cheese, in the hope that it was made from very old milk, or had simply had a very long shelf-life. In fact, all the usual rules were reversed. The health-conscious looked for processed food, *old* food, or any food without a vestige of contact with the open air, the dangerous oceans, rain-water. Baked beans and doughnuts were suddenly good for you.

They might be good for her, but Paula couldn't eat them. Paula couldn't face it. Paula couldn't eat.

An early train comes throbbing down the line and through her early morning brain. It's everywhere, she thinks, appalled. If only there were some way to escape.

If only Paula were here, thinks Grace, as she pushes open the swing-doors of the dining-room at quarter to eight, and finds it empty. No one to admire the yellow waistcoat . . . all the same she feels a certain pride; the first guest up, and probably the oldest.

A waitress appears with a certain air of tying on her apron in mid-flight. To Grace's joy, she shows her to the table in the middle of the first bay window. Blue velvet curtains, furred with sun: a view over crimson roses, cars, pale-blue railings and the deep-blue sea. She settles herself with the little sigh that's been habitual for the past few years, but stretches it into a sigh of pleasure. Seabourne in June. To be looked after . . .

On her left a tall young waiter appears, Greek or Italian? – wearing very tight black trousers and a very white, very bright smile. He hands her a menu with a flourish. The menu is upside-down. Grace waits a few seconds, out of deference to his feelings, before she turns it right way up again. Yet her eyes skim the card from bottom to top, an impatient habit of old age. She no longer has time to live things in order. She has to know the ending.

(Nor has she time to fuss. There'd been so much fuss about Chernobyl; were the vegetables safe, was it safe to drink milk . . . Grace was much too old to fuss. She minded for the world, but not for herself. She refused to let the boffins interfere with her life.)

White rolls, brown rolls, white toast, brown toast, jam, marmalade, honey . . . Scrambled eggs, mushrooms, tomatoes . . . cereals, porridge (porridge? in *June*?), yogurt, prunes, grapefruit, fruit juices, fresh fruit from the side table . . . coffee, tea, hot milk . . .

Paula, she thinks, would enjoy all this. I'm sure she could do with a break.

Softly Softly wails at Bruno's window. She must have been out all night. Her mewling is horribly like a baby's. Bruno can't stand crying babies. He rolls over heavily in bed – his eyes and his brain come separately, jolting against the bones of his skull – and grunts, 'Fuck off' at the pillow beside him. The pillow is smeared with black and red.

'Disgusting tart,' he growls. 'Fucking obscene disgusting poncing motherfucking tart.'

The cat is crying again. Bruno pulls the sheets up over his head. He will sort her out good and proper later . . . falling into a headachey sleep. Trying but failing to rise to the surface and failing also to fall much deeper, into a dark where the halves could be whole.

Voices pull him back again. Hateful voices, familiar voices. They were out there in their disgusting garden, swearing and shouting and spreading disease. Pollen came swarming over the wall. Seeds of things, spores of things. The hysterical voice of that awful woman. All three of them were subhuman.

*   *   *

49

'Paula!' Arthur is shouting from the garden, overexcited, dancing on the lawn. 'Come and see what Sally's doing.'

A long pause, then Paula throws up the bedroom window. 'What?' she inquires flatly, rubbing her eyes as she stares into the light. 'I was trying to catch up on sleep.'

'Quick, qui-*ick*!' He's beside himself. Groaning and muttering, she puts on a dressing-gown and pads outside. 'Well, *what*?'

Sally is not immediately visible, hidden behind some rampaging giant rhubarb that Arthur won't dig up. As her eyes adjust, Paula spots her. She's wearing, for no apparent reason, her turquoise bikini, wellington boots, and the tea-cosy for a hat, which descends over her white-blonde eyelashes. 'Lo, Paula,' she says. 'Look! Gardnin.'

Paula looks, and sees that Sally has the garden trowel and is sifting patiently through the only spot of naked earth in the garden. Every now and then she trawls at the rhubarb, which almost cheers Paula up. She glances at Arthur's ecstatic face, transported with pride in the Sunday sunlight, utterly sure she will feel the same way, that the whole world wants to admire Sally gardening. It doesn't occur to him I'm feeling like death, she thinks, and briefly, fiercely hates him.

'Well done, Sally,' she says, without enthusiasm. 'I'm glad you've changed your mind about the rhubarb, Arthur.'

'Are you all right?' he inquires, but rather absently. 'Don't you love her outfit. She tells me that they're gardening clothes.'

'I need that tea-cosy. I need some tea.'

'Don't be silly. Wrap a towel round the pot, or something.'

'It's *my* tea-cosy, Arthur, and I want it.'

'You can't be serious.'

'I FUCKING AM!' Suddenly she's screaming, with her fists clenched hard at the senseless, pretty sky, the luxuriant garden, open-mouthed Arthur, rosy-faced in his irritating night-shirt, Sally, who continues to dig, unmoved. 'IS THAT CHILD FUCKING THICK, OR WHAT?'

Sally turns towards her, very slowly, slowly lets the trowel fall from her fingers, and then, speeding up, one anxious hand clutches the turquoise triangle between her legs, and the other hand moves to half-cover her face as it crumples, lopsided, and Sally starts to cry, a wail as loud as Paula's scream, but getting louder, a monstrous wail that sends Paula rushing back into the house with her fingers in her ears, but her second step lands on a metal lorry, lying in wait, intensely sharp, sewing her naked sole like a needle.

'Shit!' she shouts. 'Shit, oh *shit*! I *hate* living here. I hate you both!'

Fascinated, Sally stops crying and stares.

They all stand staring at each other, immobile, frozen in their separate purposes, big, middling, very small, a family of humans on Sunday morning.

Animals, thinks Bruno. They're animals. They've got no shame. They don't care who hears them. They think the world belongs to them. Belching and farting. Laughing and crying. The disgusting things that went on in their bedroom, though recently there hadn't been so much of that. Looking at them, he wasn't surprised. The man was a freak: enormous. And she was squarish, yellowish, with big saggy tits and a lesbian's face and shaggy dark hair hanging down on her shoulders. A weird way of looking at you, too, in the street, out of cow-like eyes with great staring pupils. Today she was wearing a dressing-gown, but all her clothes looked like dressing-gowns. She had no style; she had no shame. They were both so ugly, you'd think they'd feel sick at the very idea of doing *that*.

In fact, she was always going on about sickness. He got quite bored with listening to that, though he naturally hoped she was getting worse. Perhaps she was going to die. That would save everyone a lot of trouble. That would do a favour to the human race. But she mustn't die just yet. He was due to meet Haines again next week. He had to have something more solid by then. He had to have something to inspire respect.

There was something in Haines's attitude to him that made Bruno feel uneasy. Special Branch knew he was a hard man, of course. Of course they knew he was a patriot, after the Smithers business they were sure of that. Of course they knew he had brains, as well. People in his business had to have brains . . .

But in that previous job he never really had to use them. The Smithers affair wasn't what you'd call fulfilling. Bruno hadn't had a chance to show what he was made of. He'd gone over it all a thousand times, but he always ended up dissatisfied.

Smithers was a Labour MP. Fat little commie with a chip on his shoulder, wanted to make a name for himself. Some trumped-up story about faked statistics at a nuclear power station in his constituency. Stuff gone missing, unreported leaks. Smithers was going to ask questions in the House, and although it wasn't true it would have made a stink at a time when the Government wanted to expand. Nuclear power was the future, of course, but lefties like Smithers didn't see that.

He was holier than thou, but he had a habit, although he was a married man with a daughter. Smithers frequented a certain club which Special Branch liked to keep a friendly eye on. It was there that Bruno had first seen Haines, a burly man standing back in the shadows, a man's man who could handle himself. Bruno had wanted to be standing beside him. In the end they got talking. In time they were friends (but Bruno still isn't quite sure that they're friends).

The job itself had been simple enough. They wanted Brunnhilde to perch on Smithers' lap while SB took a few photos. Bruno arranged it, no trouble at all. Brunnhilde had looked especially glamorous. The photos would have been in the *News of the World* if the little wanker hadn't suddenly resigned.

It was neat, but somehow . . . unsatisfying. It didn't prove that Bruno was a man.

This job was different. This job would show them. Initiative, persistence, political judgement . . . Bruno was playing big league now. He'd been certain of it from the morning when the postman absent-mindedly pushed through his letterbox a fat brown envelope for 'Arthur and Paula' at the address next door. After a second he'd ripped it open, for after all, Bruno never got letters except for the boring ones at the office, and Fate had brought this to his own front door . . .

And so he'd found out that disgusting fat wimp and his hard-faced woman were loony lefties, spying on the transport of nuclear waste, trying to sabotage a great national industry. And then Bruno knew he had a mission in life. He believed in Fate, and pattern. Fate had brought him here to live next door to them. Fate had equipped him to watch and listen. And Fate had given him the contacts so he could use what he learned for good.

He had gone to Haines without delay. At last he could talk to him man to man. And Haines was interested, he saw at once, though he played it cool; SB *were* cool. And never too eager to come up with the money. Cash in a mean brown envelope. Haines made him cringe for it, every time. And last time he'd shown that he had a sense of humour, a sense of humour that Bruno admired. As usual he pretended to forget about the money till Bruno reminded him the second time. Haines pulled out the envelope, opened it, took out a twenty-pound note, folded it, rustled it noisily between his fingers, then slipped it into his own wallet, and handed the envelope over to Bruno. 'Expenses. Mine. Buying beers for you.' And he'd smiled a big smile, staring straight at Bruno. Now that was cool. Witty, and cool, though for a moment Bruno wanted to break his fingers, before he saw the joke, and they laughed at it together.

It was what Bruno had wanted all along: to be part of them, to be part of it all, the easy laughter, the brotherhood. It wasn't just selfish, all the same. The thing he was part of now was bigger than Bruno, bigger than both of them. His mind ran over it again and again, the best day of all, the best day of his life, when Haines said the boys in Gower Street were interested. 'Your *friends*,' he said, which was another little joke of his that Bruno didn't enjoy quite so much. 'You say they have an interest in uranium imports. And a prejudice against South Africa. Now *I've* got some friends who'd like to know about that . . .' It was a wonderful moment, except for the joke. So they summoned Bruno to the War Office, not Special Branch but the MoD, and Bruno sat in Room 050, a hot, quiet room in a web of corridors, sweating as he tried to tell them what he knew, tried to impress them with what he had to offer, staring at the glass of the table because he could hardly bear to meet their eyes, the eyes of officers, the voices of gentlemen, officers and gentlemen who'd called on him, and he tried not to listen to the fly trapped somewhere which made his fingers itch at his palms – though perhaps it was only the distant traffic for the world had retreated a long way away, and for half an hour he'd lived more intensely than anything since the terrible day when he was turned down for the Police Force . . . This time they didn't turn him down.

On a bad day, though, and today was bad, Bruno felt that they all despised him. It had started to fade, that certainty that he was part of the gang at last. Luckily, Bruno was strong. Bruno had always had to be strong. Bruno could do it on his own. For Bruno was fighting evil. Fighting evil, fighting for good. For the good of the country, that went without saying, but also for the good of the human race.

If Man could smash the atom, Bruno considered, he was truly master of the universe. You had to have vision. Bruno did. It was what the trouble-makers lacked, of course.

*   *   *

The after-pain in her punctured foot brought Paula to her senses.

'I'm sorry, Sally. Paula's sorry. Paula doesn't feel very well this morning.' She limps across the lawn to the child, and hugs her, patting the tea-cosy placatingly. It isn't so easy to apologise to Arthur.

'I'm sorry, Arthur, but I feel like hell . . .' His forgiving smile drives her back on the offensive. 'And I'm not so sure it's a brilliant idea for Sally to squirm around in the dirt.'

'Why not?'

'Well, cats, for a start. The bloody cat from next door, for one . . . Besides, you know what I'm thinking about.' She's embarrassed; she doesn't want to seem obsessed.

'It's not Chernobyl again, is it? You're not trying to tell me she's going to get cancer? You want to be careful. You're getting obsessed. I don't like you screaming at Sally, Paula.'

Paula's voice has gone sharp again. 'On the contrary. People like you are obsessed, who think cancer's the only risk of radiation. That's why the dangers of low-level radiation are always underestimated. They measure it in terms of fatal cancers. I mean, sure, cancer is one of the risks. But it's not just cancer. It's the whole organism. Low-level radiation ages you . . .'

Arthur looks at Sally, who is sitting on the lawn, filling the tea-cosy with earth. 'Ageing is not Sally's problem,' he says.

'It's everyone's problem. Don't be stupid. It's a problem for the human race . . . *and if Sally doesn't stop that at once, I'm going straight back to Camden.*'

But instead she goes into the house for a bath and broods while Arthur makes her some tea.

How could you ever get it across, if Chernobyl didn't do it? The trouble was, radiation was invisible. It didn't make smoke, or filthy smells. It had no warning system.

The local accidents always seemed small. They were always happening, but always, according to the nuclear industry, 'insignificant', 'no danger to health'. The big Windscale fire, which caused thousands of cancers, was thirty years ago. It was hushed up and lied about until enough time had gone by for people not to panic.

The danger was always at one remove, some time in the future or the past, in another county or another country. People felt glad they were safe for the present, and hoped the present would go on for ever. Surely it would never actually happen, the imagined apocalyptic disaster . . . Ageing by definition took time, like cancer. So what if the processes had speeded up? Even Chernobyl was a long way away, and of course they *would* make mistakes in Russia . . .

No immediate danger, that was the thing. The title of Rosalie Bertell's book. Bertell had a lot to say about ageing.

The gradual natural breakdown of DNA and RNA is probably the cellular phenomenon associated with what we know as 'ageing'. It occurs gradually over the years with exposure to natural background radiation . . . fission products lodged within the body will cause . . . acceleration of ageing . . .

The speeding-up would be gradual though. No immediate danger.

Paula pulls the plug, and waits for the whirlpool. But the pipe must be blocked; the water drains slowly. Its greasy dimples turn her stomach. She hopes that Arthur isn't going to cook.

Grace wades through course after course on her own. Astonishing; no one else is up. The vigilance of the waiter, applied to her alone, is wearing – he is too young to disappoint. Yes, she enjoyed the prunes (*too sweet*), yes, she enjoyed the eggs (*too wet*). She is truly enjoying her honey now but would rather not have to tell him so . . .

But two more guests arrive, at last. A couple with yellow-grey hair who proceed immensely slowly to a corner table where they settle as if they have lived their lives by the spidery palm in its bucket of brass. They are bent and wrinkled as ancient turtles prised out of their shells, forced to totter upright.

Shall I ever look as old as that? Grace wonders. Do I already? Can't I see myself?

Then there were more of them, slowly assembling, a laggard army of the old, returning, perhaps, from some far-away battle, damaged but drifting gamely home. More often alone than in couples; more often silent than hissing to each other; more often shuffling and listing than choosing the rigid erectness which was

Grace's defence against the thinning of so many bones. They couldn't hear the waiter. They would try to lip-read, then finally, in intense irritation, quiz their equally elderly partner: 'What does he say? What's he say, dear? You heard him, *what did he say?*' They had long lists of things they couldn't eat, which they confided to the waiter in a tone of indignation, as if the very offer of such substances offended. 'We can't eat eggs, dear. No. They don't agree with us. Harold never has kippers, do you, Harold? Eh? I said, you don't like kippers, do you?'

The young – for thank God, there *were* some young – came in later, in couples. She supposed they had lain in bed holding each other. They had a reason for staying in bed (and of course, that was why she had risen so early for the second half of her life. Not virtue, but an absence one rose briskly to escape). Do they realise how lucky they are, Grace wondered, seeing how carelessly they strolled in together, how easily a hand touched a shoulder or a hip, how an arm encircled a neck like a garland, how *light* the garlands were . . .

And how much they laughed! It exploded, between the prunes and eggs and toast, spreading outwards from the islands of youth, rippling the stately fronds of the palms and the velvet curves of the curtains (*Ralph, my darling – how I laughed with you*); drowning the tiny sounds of the old, knives scraping and scraping across the plate, a clearing of throats that made ready for silence.

What happens to all our words? she thought. Once we were bursting with words like them. Couples run out, after a lifetime together. And if one's alone . . .

One can't talk to oneself.

'Master of the universe,' mutters Bruno in the unaccustomed silence. Thank God they had gone back into the house. Stupid people. Hateful people. People who deserved whatever they got.

Bruno found most people hateful. All the same, he loves the human race. To be human meant being top of the heap. Humans had brains. Humans had hygiene. Humans had medicine that dealt with germs. Humans had standards of decency; they didn't walk around showing hairy parts. Bruno had gone to the zoo one day. Hairy parts encrusted with dung.

But at least the animals were safely caged. Nature was chaos, mud, darkness, creeping roots, rot, mould. Nature was things which smelled and crawled in next-door's dustbins when Bruno went through them. Going through dustbins was part of his trade; it was always revolting, and he made himself do it, but the animals' dustbin was worst of the lot, it reminded him of things he was too clean to think about. Thrusting, viscous, slimy things, things which might invade his dreams if Bruno had not been too strong to have dreams. Howling spaces, tremendous falls. Under the surface you'd fall for ever . . .

But humans had fought a long battle with nature. In London, victory was almost complete. Acres of bricks and concrete and steel with only the tamest sprouts of green. In London, a man would really feel he was 'master of all creation'.

The phrase had stuck in his head from the days when he went to Sunday School. (His sister never went to Sunday School; his mother never went to church herself; they simply wanted him out of the house.) It was cold in the church, and the pews were hard, but the sun poured in through the stained glass windows. It was Bruno's first brush with beauty since his mother had locked her bedroom door. They stood on a lake of brilliant blue, tall handsome men in flowing dresses, with helmets of golden rays round their heads. They had long curly hair and waving beards and their faces were not at all like his father's, their faces were bright and kind.

There was someone else he had forgotten now. She walked through the world of the windows so calmly and easily, as if you could take her for granted, as if she was there for everyone and yet she smiled especially for you. The woman in blue had what looked like a curtian of long white hair, but her face was young, and a helmet of golden light like the men. The teacher laughed when he asked who it was. 'It's the Blessed Mary, Mother of God.'

Mother of God. So the baby was God. He lay and looked up at her, completely peaceful, her arms surrounding him as certainly as the curve of gold that circled his head. Their faces reflected each other's light. 'Janes! Get up! What are you doing down there? – and two hard hands had yanked him up.

The second time it happened they couldn't wake him. He lay there rigid with open eyes and what the teacher described as a 'cheeky smile'. But the smile wasn't cheeky, the smile was beatific. Bruno had a Mother; he was good; he was God.

Bruno has forgotten Mary now. Bruno has forgotten all the

things he has lost, and many of the things that he never had.

He knows he is nothing now. He knows that Haines is God.

Grace sits for a minute in her window after breakfast, recovering from the stairs. Room 70, her solitary room, is orderly even before the maid, bed-clothes folded tidily back, books placed neatly on the bedside table at right angles to the silver frame with the handsome man and the silent baby.

Leaving the dining-room, she'd looked around for the crying baby of the day before. She couldn't see any babies; there were only half a dozen children all told. They didn't look very happy. A leg was being smacked. A red-cheeked boy was being shushed. A three-year-old was being told not to fidget; her smaller sister fought off a bib. Parents and Others, Grace thought. The world divides into two.

All her life she'd been firmly on the 'Others' side. As a teacher, she called all her pupils 'Ladies' and did best with the girls who were least like children. Babies, to Grace, were frightening anarchists, storms of emotion, bundles of needs, enormous needs she could never have met. How many times had she said it in class – 'Don't be childish,' 'Don't be a baby.' No one wanted to be a baby, however young they were.

'We don't like children, in England.' Paula was always saying it. Grace knew that Paula meant her. When Paula was little, Grace had been hopeless.

I could hardly believe she was related to me. She didn't go well with my sister, poor silly, pretty Lucy . . . Paula was such a graceless child. She copied her accent, alas, from her father. Until she was ten she had his face, Paul Timms's blockish, snub-nosed face and round brown eyes which gaped at the world where Lucy's blue ones fluttered and danced (and faded, in the end. Paula grew up and my sister grew old). Whenever I saw them together, I felt that Paula was a cuckoo. My pale, fragile sister and that swarthy, tough, lower middle class child, tugging at her, demanding attention, screaming with rage when Lucy ignored her . . . I couldn't stand her. She hurt my ears.

(But I love her now, my grown-up Paula. She's so full of life. She'll never be graceful, or . . . gracious. But she's beautiful, in her own queer way, with those vast bright eyes and that sudden laughter. Grace sees her clearly, smiles at the vision, a woman near forty, her head on one side, her hair shading her wide strong face, a mane of thick hair like a glossy sheepdog, staring at life as if she would eat it, eager as a child when her temper was good. How odd that I love the child in her now when I couldn't stand her until she was twenty. I didn't like her. I didn't like children.)

People always said, 'It's too late to change.' But at eighty-five, Grace actually did. She had learned to like a two-year-old. Not *all* two-year-olds; just Sally.

When Paula first said she would be bringing Sally along on the Portuguese holiday, Grace barely concealed her horror. 'How shall we manage to *eat*?' she'd asked, as if food was all she cared about. 'If we want to go out and have supper, what can we do with the child?' 'Take her with us, of course,' Paula told her. 'They make them welcome there. It's only the English who can't stand children.'

If so, Grace grew swiftly less English as that holiday went on. And because the country she'd known with Ralph was so sadly changed – great sprawls of apartments, tourist restaurants with neutral names, the *Beefeater*, the *Golfing Bar*, skyscrapers, motels, marinas – she found herself turning to the child instead for something unspoiled, a hope for the future. By the second week she surprised herself by offering to look after Sally for a night while Paula went off into the mountains.

Sally cried and fretted at bedtime, so Grace stayed awake for most of the night, worrying about the morning. It was six o'clock when Sally woke up. She came over and gently pulled Grace's hair, opened her eyes, said 'Poor Grace' – an expression of pity for her great age, brutally clear in the morning light? – tried to put on Grace's dressing-gown; tripped over it; said, 'Fold them, fold them,' which was a statement of intent, not a command, for Sally started to 'fold' (i.e. crumple, and drop in a heap on the floor) all Grace's clothes, which had been laid out on the table as always, ready for morning – shrieked with laughter as Grace, still flat on her back, told her to stop – then suddenly climbed on Grace's bed, half-wrapped in the long red dressing-gown, tucked her small brown feet under the covers, and fell asleep on the pillow. Astonished, Grace fell asleep as well. And of course, they awoke to chaos.

Grace was surprised to discover just how little she minded that mess. Actually she liked it, it was friendly, a relief from the endless years of days when skirt, blouse, underwear had lain waiting for her like an empty person.

At the end of her life, she could see that shape, a shell of lifeless habits. It was death that dissolved the self, not childbirth. One left a child, or a set of clothes.

She stares again at the silver frame. Two ovals full of emptiness. *I never had Ralph's baby. I always refused to bear his child.*

I was afraid of it – the physical thing. I was narrow, I thought I should tear in two. I couldn't bear to think about breast-feeding. Only cats, and cows, and common women nursed. I wanted to stay myself, complete, I didn't want to be sucked and mauled . . . except by Ralph. I did want him.

I served him in so many things. I put his talent above my own; I bored myself rigid teaching to help us survive until his trust matured; my writing dwindled, and I never complained. But I baulked at letting him make me pregnant. Letting part of him grow inside me and burst its way out and split me open.

I'd had such a struggle to become myself, to be more than my parents' daughter. Serving Ralph, I could keep my pride. Bearing his child, I should have lost my boundaries, lost myself, or so I believed.

She'd been so certain of what she believed. From the end of her life, things looked very different. Certainties dissolved as her body did. In extreme old age, what would they mean, the boundaries that defined the self? In the end, one needed so many props – clothes, drugs, gadgets, artificial hips and limbs and aids – to be a functioning self at all . . . Shoring up the boundaries. But they crumbled away towards non-being. Cliffs, stones, pebbles, sand.

It wasn't quite that simple. One left the things one had said and done. Good and evil; Grace believed in them. What had she got to leave behind?

So many people left wreckage, poison. The tide of plastic in Portugal . . . Humans leave waste where they once left children.

Brunnhilde had made such a mess of the bathroom that Bruno's still cleaning in the afternoon. Cleanliness matters to Bruno. The world he dreams of is glowing, sterile, bright with fearsome hygiene. Nuclear energy is clean, he thinks. The phrase itself has a cheerful ring; *new clear energy*, it sounds like. Immensely powerful but gleaming clean. When more of it came, it would cleanse the country.

On Sundays he especially likes things clean. He's showered two or three times today. Baths are unhygienic, he considers. Horrible to lie in your own fluids, the scaly remnants of your own decay. Surfaces, he knows, are magnets for germs, and germs were waiting in every crevice, wriggling, breeding, mutating.

Morning and evening every weekday, he cleans the surface of the kitchen cupboards with bleach and a nailbrush. The bleach is so strong that the nylon bristles shrivel and meld together. Within a week they are useless. After the bleach, he uses boiling water to scald the bleached corpses of germs away.

The floor of the kitchen, however, is filthy. Bruno makes an effort not to look at the floor. Once it was black and white check plastic, now it is a greasy mottled grey. When Softly Softly crosses the kitchen, she walks disdainfully on pointed paws. Mice will soon come and inhabit the kitchen, licking and scuttling when the cat's away. Bruno will be in Seabourne, padding after something more interesting . . .

His brain hasn't registered anything wrong in his gleaming kitchen, in any case. He keeps his brain at eye-level. But his heart, his stomach are wrenched with horror. Floors, he knows, are women's work. Why does no one look after him?

Where are the women? Who abandoned him?

An insistent knock on the door of Room 70.

'Yes,' calls Grace. She is irritated, unwilling to rejoin the present. A scrabbling of keys, then the door opens. A small person, a stout person, her belly bulging the nylon overall.

'Do you want me to come back later,' asks the black-haired little girl, but even as she puts the uninflected question she is almost inside with her vacuum cleaner, her duster, her clanging brush-and-dustpan.

Young and pushy, thinks Grace. Ill-mannered and in too much of a hurry. 'Can you come back later, yes,' she says firmly. 'I'm going out very shortly.'

'Oh,' says the girl, looking blank. Her features are remarkably unattractive, bulldog jaw, small reddened eyes. She doesn't move backwards. Clearly she has to re-programme her brain before her limbs will do it. 'All right.' She shuffles backwards through the door her fat little bottom has kept ajar. The door slams loudly behind her.

An idiot, Grace decides. She looks as though she hasn't got a thought in her head.

What Father would have called Bog Irish, though perhaps the expression wasn't very kind.

Outside the door, on the landing, Faith is thinking violent thoughts.

It's my last on this floor today and now I'll have to drag the sodding lot back up again. The carrying was getting frightening, now. Sometimes when she heaved the vacuum upstairs her belly wall went hard as a rock, like cramp in your leg, but it went all through her, and she had to stop and rest. She decides to stay put on the landing and wait.

Sighing, she opens her Sunday paper, or rather the paper she'd whipped from the desk. She reads it with distaste. It is meant for people like her, she supposes, but she isn't what they suppose her to be. The headlines are for idiots. 'STAR DUMPS TWO-TIMING LOVER'. 'ROMEO TEACHER GETS THE BOOT'. If foreigners read this paper, what sort of country would they take us for?

Page 6 has a photo of a handsome man, which makes a change from all the rat-faced, simpering girls. Lovely thick hair and a powerful look. Ralph Dunne – she's never heard of him. SEXY SECRETS OF BRITAIN'S PICASSO, she reads. The secrets don't seem all that sexy, in fact; some pictures he'd painted of a mistress, naked, in what the story called 'suggestive poses'. A disappointing story. And disappointing to discover he is dead.

She stares down over her stomach into the nest of grey in her dustpan. She's still exhausted from yesterday, when one conference left and another lot arrived, so dozens of rooms had to be made up. The lot that were going were drinkers, and some of the rooms were sick-making – smelled like a brewery. One man had decorated his mirror with a wreath of toilet paper, a grown man in an expensive suit. There were empty glasses in all the rooms, and contraceptives, knotted, or floating in the toilet like sausage skins, or coming unknotted in her hands.

The old were better than the conferences in some respects at least. They weren't strong enough to make pigs of themselves. They tended not to bath very often, so you didn't have to clean the bath. Most of them were tidy, as long as they were *compos*. But some of them wet the beds. The ones who did it never looked her in the eye, and they often left a large tip. It was a kind of apology for being old.

All the same, she hated it, hated it. She hated her job, and the uniform, and her swelling belly under it. Most of all she hated the Empire itself, the endless conveyor belt of waste and mess. The things she found in the rooms when they left – half-drunk bottles of whisky or gin, half-eaten chocolates they'd bought for a treat, half-eaten trays of food they'd ordered from Room Service, then got too drunk to eat, and stubbed their cigarettes out in it instead.

And then they had the cheek to act superior. She remembers Room 70, just now. From the look on her face you'd think she hadn't got a bum. But Faith cleans up after them. She knows.

Sometimes dirt and mess is all she can see, stretching on into the future. She's bringing a child into a world like this. The dirty country England is.

At tea-time in London it is sunny and blowy, and Arthur's white roses shine like the clouds. The three of them are out in the garden again. Sally has been given an important task. 'You're a conservationist, Sally,' Arthur told her. 'Shnist,' she repeated. 'Shnist. I am.' Sally has been set to look for snails. Snails eat everything they can get to, and Arthur doesn't want them eating his garden.

'What are you going to do with them, Arthur?' Paula asks, imagining slaughter.

'I'd like to slip them over the wall. Get them to slime up Bullet-head's yard. But I shan't. I'll leave them out in the street. There's a bit of grass. Then they're on their own.'

'I've never got a proper look at him.'

'You've missed nothing. I think he's a nutter. I've got antennae for things like that. I had a good look when I pruned the tree. He would jog out of the house and glower. I spoke to him but he didn't reply. It looks like Colditz, over there.'

'As a matter of fact, I did wonder . . . you know the other day, when I saw that madman chasing a rat. I suddenly thought, it might have been him.'

'I told you, he's a nutter.'

'Your vocabulary is so elegant, Arthur.'

Actually, though, they're friends again, sitting on the grass with their feet entwined, her narrow ones taking warmth from his broad ones, her toes exploring his springy hair. They are talking quietly, intensely, now.

'I really want to apologise, Arthur.'

'Go on then. See if you can.'

'I mean, I *am* apologising. I'm really sorry. I've been appalling. I know, I've been like a maniac. I don't know how you've put up with it. And poor little Sally, why should she put up with it?'

'Because she loves you — you're family now. And most of the time you're great with her. Wonderful. I mean it.'

'Recently, though, I've been . . . a shit. But I just can't explain how bad I've been feeling. I would think it was some kind of breakdown, except I'm just not the type to have breakdowns. Do you think it's hypochondria? — I mean, I feel bad in *so many ways* . . .'

'You drive me barmy, Paula. For God's sake go and find out. For God's sake go to the doctor. I've been telling you to for weeks and weeks. You'll get no sympathy from me if you don't. In fact, I'll agree, you *have* been a shit. You owe it to us to sort yourself out. You're going tomorrow, right?'

For Arthur, this is a tremendous speech. Paula recognises that even while she rejects it. The sulky note comes back. 'Don't like doctors. Don't boss me about.' They look at each other, exasperated, then Arthur sits up, roars RIGHT! So I'll just have to put you out of your misery,' rolls on top of her and starts to beat her up, which is a mixture of squashing, tickling and kissing. Suddenly Paula fights to sit up. 'What's Sally doing? She's awfully quiet.'

She's by the ragged hollyhocks. Her head is silver against the dark leaves. She glances across at them with an expression both of them know well, eyes half closed, impervious, secret. 'What have you been doing?' Arthur goes across. 'You've been doing something you shouldn't, I know.'

'I hope she hasn't been eating anything,' Paula shudders, imagining a snail, sliding down the little girl's throat.

'Oh God,' says Arthur. He stands and looks. He tries to sound extremely stern. 'What's this, Madam? You tell me.'

Sally doesn't answer.

'Come on, what is it.'

'Poo,' she sings out clearly, to the sky, the roses, the sunny clouds, to Bruno standing by the wall next door, gritting his teeth and listening. ''s*poo*. Dirty. Nother girl did it.'

'Oh yes,' says Arthur, trying not to laugh. 'What girl was that, I wonder? I can only see a girl called Sally.'

''Nother girl called Sally,' the child explains, looking at her feet, her voice very serious, her expression teetering from comic to tragic.

Paula starts to laugh, then Arthur does something which sounds like a cough but turns into an explosion, and then all three of them are laughing hard, and happiness fills the garden.

It stops abruptly at the garden wall. On the other side, Bruno is beside himself. He goes pale, then red, then pale again. They are vile, vile. They will have to be killed. They will have to be taught a lesson, then killed. There must be a law. There must be a punishment . . .

This was what SB didn't understand. They thought he should start by *talking* to these people. 'Get to know them,' Haines had said. 'That's the best way. Get in their confidence. Couldn't be easier, living next door. We expect good things of you, Bruno.'

How often he'd heard that last sentence again. It was positively warm. And his Christian name. It made up for the coolnesses he'd noticed. The lack of willingness to give him a start. He'd expected to have the benefit of the official tap on the morons' phone, he'd expected them to feed him titbits from the daily trawl of mail. He soon discovered it wasn't like that. He was to tell them everything; they were to tell him virtually nothing.

'Need to know, you see,' Haines said. 'We work on a basis of need to know. And we don't consider you need to know. Officially, remember, you don't exist. Especially if you get yourself into trouble. Got that? We don't know you.'

Except for that day in the War Office, they'd always met in dingy pubs, scruffy cafés miles from anywhere. As if they were ashamed of him, but that was absurd, of course. And in a way, the scruffier the better. It made it obvious how secret it was.

All the same, he imagined that one day after he'd finished this mission to satisfaction, there'd be dinner with Haines somewhere rather expensive. He imagined the two of them smoking cigars. And Haines might want him for something more permanent, something very dangerous but very well paid. (At the moment, there was only the measly retainer, a few hundred pounds every other month, and a strong hint at their last meeting that the money was expected to buy results.)

In fact, quite a lot of the money had gone on Bruno's methods of investigation. He had not made this clear to Haines, but talking to the neighbours was out of the question. The very thought of it makes him feel ill. Talking to people who let their daughter do her business out in the garden! Talking to foulmouths like them!

Technology was cleaner than conversation. And Bruno had got the technology. It was a doddle to fit it with people like them who never locked windows or even doors. Bruno had got the money to do it (well, anyone had the money to do it. The cheapest bug was incredibly cheap, the price of a shirt, say. Or a wig). Bruno, though, isn't using the cheapest. Bruno is using some of the best. Their telephones would look quite normal to them. There was one in the living-room, one in the bedroom. But ever since Bruno paid the house a little visit, stepping with ease through an open window, the telephones hadn't been normal at all. Each receiver contained an infinity transmitter. And even if the animals got suspicious, unscrewed the mouthpiece and looked inside, the transmitter looked exactly like the normal internal mouthpiece. But Bruno just had to pick up his own phone – or his car phone, if he was in the car – to hear anything that was being said on the phone, and anything that was being said in the room. However, these jokers talked all over the house, especially the woman, with a voice like a fretsaw, gabbing away in the kitchen or the study. So in those rooms Bruno had used something else, little gadgets that he particularly liked, adaptors to replace their own dirty adaptors, which sprouted leads like mouldy potatoes. Bruno's were clean, but he knew they wouldn't notice. Clean or dirty, it was all the same to them. Bruno's adaptors had one little difference. They contained low-powered automatic transmitters, low-powered so as not to upset the aeroplanes, though it might be quite fun to upset an aircraft as it zoomed with all those drink-sodden bastards down towards Heathrow . . . (Bruno bites his lips as they start to smile, licks his lips as they start to dribble . . .)

One way or another Bruno had them sewn up. And the cost, for quite a classy job, what some might call almost too thorough a job, was under eight hundred pounds.

He hasn't told Haines what he's doing because he knows Haines would think it flash. Haines would think it was overkill. SB were a bit old-fashioned like that. But Bruno is sure it will be worthwhile.

The one bit of information Haines gave him was something that Bruno had found quite fascinating. That Paula is interested in Hilda Murrell. Acquaintances of Bruno were interested, too. They had taken a close and active interest. Shortly afterwards the woman died.

'Weird, isn't it,' says Arthur to Paula when the paroxysm of laughter's passed. 'We're the only animal whose shit is poisonous. Even that can't be dug back into the earth.'

'True. And think of graveyards. We box our bodies away from the earth. Anyone would think we hated it.'

Arthur is silent. He's suddenly cold, thinking of Paula still and dead. Will she go to the doctor? She will not.

The phone rings. Arthur makes off into the house. Beyond the garden wall, Bruno does likewise.

'Pau-la! It's Grace!'

And Paula feels happy for the rest of the day. She's arranged to meet Grace in Seabourne, on Tuesday.

'It's so like Grace to go there. It's frightfully English. Nothing ever happens.'

5

ROUTINE

When Paula wakes up on Monday at the familiar, unpleasantly early hour, she tells herself to think positive. Don't lie there suffering; use the time. She takes her bag full of papers into the front room and settles on the long table, clearing away with one sleepy hand the rubble of toys, letters, biros, salt and pepper uncleared from last night.

Too many *things*, she thinks. Human beings make too many things. And when they get tired of them, they don't go away. A rising tide of abandoned objects.

With a dead person, you faced the opposite problem. How could you get them back? How could you ever re-create the web of live tensions that comprise the self? The body, of course, would stay behind, inscribed with its sad, banal story. There were many small stab wounds in Hilda's stomach. The neck and face were severely bruised. The facial bruises indicated to the coroner 'a broad blunt impact', probably a kick. Her knees were scratched, possibly from crawling, trying to get help, but here the body was mercifully mute, the painful picture remained uncompleted. There were signs that she 'put up a fight'.

And there, thinks Paula, you went beyond the body. What kind of spirit in a 78-year-old made her put up a fight? 'If they don't get me first,' said Hilda to some friends, shortly before she was found dead in the wood, 'I want the world to know that one old woman has seen through their lies.'

Missing from her home was the final draft of the paper she'd written for the Sizewell inquiry, the public inquiry into the building of a new nuclear reactor in Suffolk. Her spirit was in that paper, sturdy, indignant, scornful of lies, seeing things at their most basic. Hilda had set her mind to the task; so what if she was in her late seventies? She'd taught herself atomic physics, of course. She'd consulted top nuclear scientists, naturally!

Yet Hilda had written from what she called 'the Ordinary Citizen's' point of view, and what she had to say was powerfully simple. Once the atom was split, it could not be mended. The splintered atom split other atoms, in inanimate matter and in animals, in flat fish and in human beings, in flesh, in blood, in bone. It went on doing that for thousands of years. Once the bonds of life had been broken apart, no one could stop the chain reaction. In children and in their children, unpredictably on into the future. No one could know in which generation the damaged genes would surface again.

> Many of these very dangerous elements would never have existed at all, but for man's meddling with the very building blocks of the universe. Nor do they disappear to nothingness, as the word 'decay' might imply. They form decay products ... which are also sometimes radioactive ... Some of these are more danger-ous than the elements from which they started ... Arsenic, mercury etc. existed before man and will exist after him. He is not responsible for their being here ... Man, on the other hand, creates the radioactive pollutants which emerge from nuclear power stations in unprecedented number, concentration and violence. *He need not do it.*

Her spirit was there, in those fierce italics.

But it wasn't enough to base a novel on. More and more Paula felt it wasn't right, making a puppet from a real person. Especially someone brave and admirable; someone dead, who couldn't answer back.

The sun begins to stream through a crack in the curtains and Paula pulls them and peers for a second, then relaxes, stretches in the golden light. She doesn't feel so bad as usual, this morning. Life is immediate, in the spinning dust-motes, in the deep yellow wallflower nodding its head against the dark edge of the window-frame, a vibrant yellow, a high summer yellow ... she imagines the scent outside the window, warm and sweet in the day's first heat. She is glad to be here, however bad the world is, however dirty and threatening the country's becoming. You didn't live in a country. You lived in a moment, a capsule of light. Each moment was a totality. Each moment cancelled the one before.

And that was why it was so hard making characters. Books

couldn't hold all the contradictions. And so you were tempted to neaten, shorten. You left out the zigzags and drew in a norm. Which was all very well with invented characters ... but if you were basing them on real-life people, you risked being wrong again and again. And if people mattered, if writing mattered, it mattered a lot if you got it wrong.

She sits in the sunlight trying to think positive and thinking of all the problems instead. Not just the intransigent spirit. There were cruder problems; the unknown facts.

Yet someone knew them. Someone killed her. Someone, somewhere knew the answers.

The length of two bodies away from Paula as she sits and broods about Hilda Murrell, Bruno is lying awake in bed, waiting for the buzz of his alarm clock. A little adrenalin, just the right dose, circulates through his bloodstream. Monday, not sleepy, boring Sunday. Monday, and he's going debt-collecting, part of the job he always enjoys. Monday, the day before Tuesday, and Tuesday he's off on a jaunt to the sea. The adrenalin starts to pump hard and fast.

The arrangement between the two women on the phone had sounded surprisingly casual, but perhaps they guessed that the phone was tapped. 'Grace' was the elusive Stirling woman, who had a file as long as his arm. He'd seen it; they wouldn't let him take it away. Stirling had contacts with Eastern Europe. She had been a communist for decades, of course, and although she had 'left' the Party in the fifties, nobody ever really left the Party. A feminist. A pacifist. Accused of indoctrinating schoolchildren by parents in the sixties. Distributed subversive literature from her bookshop in East Sussex. Several arrests for breach of the peace, trespass and criminal damage in anti-war demonstrations. Included (like Timms) on the mailing list of the Kilburn 'Peace in Ireland' group, thought to be an IRA front. And the Anti-Apartheid Renta-mob ... It went on for ever; a lifetime of stirring it. The fact she was old made it all the more disgusting – not to have learned anything in life. Perhaps he would be able to teach her a lesson, something pointed, something personal, once he was sure just what they were up to.

In the shower, which he takes cooler than usual to give himself that cutting edge, Bruno broods about what it might be. He has an idea that it's something big. Something big enough to make his name . . .

A terrorist attack on a nuclear train. Much more effective than a bomb in Harrods. A great tract of London would be uninhabitable. If they could cut through the steel containers – and Bruno well knew that an RPG could punch through steel as if it were balsa – the poisonous dust would blow everywhere, contaminating men and women and children.

All the little houses with their fat little children, deaf and dumb to everyone else, smugly following their little routine: then suddenly plunged into a cloud of poison, choking, smothering, running like ants. (Straightening his tie in the mirror, Bruno finds he is smiling hard, Bruno finds that his lips are wet. He frowns severely and tugs at his collar.) It was sick minds that thought like that. People like the vermin who lived next door. People like that should be shot.

Bruno, however, doesn't have a gun. They should be kicked, stabbed, beaten.

Paula drums her pencil down on one particular freckle of sunlight.

Who drove the car with Hilda Murrell struggling inside it to the field where she died? Whose foot kicked her? Whose knife cut her? Were there two of them, or only one? 'I am informed that those involved were men of the British Intelligence service . . .' the MP Tam Dalyell told Parliament, 'persons in Westminster and Whitehall . . . know . . . about the violent death of Miss Hilda Murrell.'

Men of the British Intelligence Service. If he was right, there were lots to choose from. Special Branch, MI5's 'A' (Operations) Branch, F7, or maybe the nuclear police . . . You'd think there were enough of them to stop things going wrong.

However, it seems there are never enough of them. A lot of work gets contracted out, partly because there are operations from which they prefer to keep their distance, things they prefer not to know about. And so they call in the private detectives. Private detectives, for whatever reason, were monitoring the Sizewell objectors. One of them at least had a criminal record for sexual and violent offences. They might have been working for British Intelligence, they might have been working for the nuclear industry, and some would say they were working for both . . .

And yet, Paula knows it is all conjecture. It might just have been a petty crook, a small-time housebreaker who panicked . . .

In the end, conjecture itself seemed obscene. A violent death should shock us to silence. Paula wonders: does it really matter who frog-marched Hilda across the last field? – whose rough voice was the last she heard?

But it would have mattered to Hilda, surely. Her fierce intelligence, wanting to know . . . Something beyond the physical pain.

Paula hears the first chatter from Sally's bedroom. The child would talk and sing to herself for maybe ten minutes. Then Arthur would have to call back to her, and the ordinary, noisy routine would begin. Before that happens, Paula wants to decide.

Some things at least are certain. The State is in love with nuclear power. Those who object to nuclear power are of interest to the security forces. The security forces are out of control. And those three premises spell danger. The sequence of errors will happen again; she needn't write about Hilda Murrell.

A little afraid, she smiles in the sunshine. She thinks she sees what is to be done.

In fact, the novel would never be written. Life was overtaking her, running her down.

Bruno likes to wear a suit for work even when he knows things might get physical. Work is a serious business. Men in suits have a right to respect. Sometimes a suit gets marked or torn, but mostly the marks are on other people. He has to be careful, of course. Once you have a record, you have to be careful, though a record doesn't hold him back in his job. A private detective could have a record. A private detective could be anything at all. There weren't any checks, and there weren't any qualifications, either, which was lucky for Bruno.

He could have got them, of course, if he'd wanted to, but Bruno didn't have much time for school. Or school didn't have much time for Bruno. A teacher had told his mother he was shy. Mr Frewin, who was probably a poofter. 'He's a sullen little monkey,' his mother replied, pinching his arm where he squirmed in her grip. There was no one to talk to at break-times, so Bruno would stay in the library. There weren't many thrillers, but he read them all. And any kind of twentieth-century history, which reinforced him in his view of mankind. Man was a killer, so you got in first. Kill or be killed was the only way.

However, because of the matter of the record, trifling though Bruno's record might be, Bruno was a little bit hampered as a killer. Bruno had a record for GBH; a nasty old bag in a department store had managed to wind him up one day. She had thin grey hair and a thin pale mouth with little puckers where her teeth had gone (people that old should be put down. Especially nasty, spiteful old women). She had answered his questions reluctantly, and her little pink eyes had looked at him aslant. Bruno had started to sweat. When he finally decided on some tasteful items, and came to her to pay, her eyes had jumped in her head like ferrets. 'I know about you,' she'd hissed. 'I know your type, and I think it's disgusting.' She didn't take his things, or the money. She kept her hands under the counter, trembling on the end of her long wrinkled arms, as if they might catch a disease from him. He saw what he was, in her contorted face; less than nothing; worse than nothing. He had to wipe that vision away. They had pulled him off her, and she was bleeding, more blood than you could ever have imagined would have come from someone so shrivelled and pale. Lying there on the shabby brown carpet she'd reminded him more than ever of his mother, who suddenly shrank and withered after she had a stroke in her sixties. She still tried to curl her hair, but it looked pathetic, yellow and thin and frizzy in places, straight in others, and she couldn't speak, she stuttered and drooled, so she'd never be able to say she loved him, as if she would after a lifetime of chances, but he went on visiting, more fool him, and watched her grow weaker and more disgusting. In the end she didn't know him; she never even said his name, though she knew his sister, she talked to her. Good riddance to nasty old rubbish, he thought . . . As for the Grievous Bodily Harm, the woman was walking on her own two feet when she came into court to give evidence against him, so it couldn't have been all that Grievous, could it.

She'd done for him though, stupid old cunt. Because he couldn't have a gun now, could he. Couldn't get a licence for a nice little gun, just because he got aggravated, eight years ago. And Bruno deserves to have guns. Bruno knows more about guns than anyone. Bruno knows all the latest refinements. He can never have it, but he knows what he wants. This month it's a second-generation Coonan with a Browning High Power type barrel lug and cam locking arrangement, a lovely .357 autoloader. He imagines it, heavy in the heat of his hand. Together they could have been so cool . . . A hard bulge underneath his suit. He imagines it, maybe in a high-ride hip holster, maybe tucked into the small of his back.

He wouldn't need to use it, but he'd know it was there, a secret store of superhuman power . . .

As he leaves the house, Bruno hears a train come thundering down towards Kensal Green. The familiar groundswell under their feet, pulling the separate houses together.

There are houses with children, and houses without. The houses with children have a routine so elaborate, so full of fail-safe devices, that the childless observer woud only see chaos.

Into Arthur and Sally's elaborate routine, Paula has been added only recently as a permanent fixture, a new complication. Sally's very keen on playing with Paula. If Paula's there, Sally thinks it's weekend, and Paula has come especially to play with her. She hasn't understood, as yet, that Paula has joined the home team, like Arthur.

That morning when Sally finds Paula at the table with lots of paper, she demands a glider. Paula makes three gliders, then wants some tea, and then declares she has work to do, but tonight she will draw her a fleet of gliders.

'Now,' says Sally. 'Please, Paula.'

'There isn't time. You're going to Aunt Steffie's . . .'

'No. Won't. Stay with Paula.'

'Paula's got to work.' Children are fun, she thinks; but rather *less* fun as a permanent fixture.

Sally stares at her hard, then picks up a sheet of paper and gives it her without a word. Paula refuses it. Sally gets down from her chair with her eyes fixed on Paula, and starts to scream. Arthur rushes in, imagining disaster. Sally stops screaming and smiles at Arthur. But when he tries to put her in her push-chair ready to walk her round to the minder's, Sally arches her back and goes rigid.

He sings to her on the five-minute walk, feeling foolish as her scarlet, accusing, silent face stares up at him. She's saving something up, he thinks . . . and sure enough, when they get to the minder's she screams so hard, with such blind despair, that Arthur cannot leave her, though as soon as the door has closed behind him she stops, and goes and picks up a toy, a little tired but entirely insouciant.

* * *

Bruno walks up the walkway to the Fairfields Estate, trying to look as though he's wearing the Coonan, trying to look as though he doesn't want to use it, but if they force him to, he will. The walkways are long and empty; it's a sunny, windy day, and the wind gets speed up down the slopes of the walkways and pulls annoyingly at his body, disarranges his business clothes, stings disagreeably under his eyelids. He's walking fast, but with the wind against him and the walkway extending ahead of him for miles, he starts to feel smaller, and in slow motion, and his trousers almost seem to flap at his ankles, which can't be right, for the suit isn't old, there certainly isn't any flap in the trousers, it's certainly not, for example, flared, but why are those black kids sniggering and whistling, what will they force him to do to them? He stops and turns, but the sun's in his eyes, and by the time they have adjusted, the kids have gone.

(Bruno's ideas of himself; he is either very small or very large, but he is never large enough. He refers to himself as a 'six-footer', mentally, as if a man could be a measurement. Actually, he was just five-foot-ten when he last lined up with the other boys at school outside the door of the Medical Room. There was a weighing machine with a shaky wooden scaffold. 'Janes! You're standing on your toes. Get down boy!' Giggles from the louts behind. The master reduced him to five-foot-nine, but that was because he hated Bruno.

Sometimes when Bruno falls back through time and becomes the naked germ of himself who howled and howled but no one came, he is small as a spinning fleck of spittle.)

He stops for a moment and checks the address in the notebook in his jacket. These estates seemed to go on forever; the highest numbers were pure science fiction. He'd visited 415 before. He didn't like to visit more than once. This time he would have to make his presence felt. As he walks, his hands turn into fists, and his red-haired wrists shoot out of his jacket, reclaim his fists and return to the dark, but reluctantly, as if they're ready for work.

This time tomorrow he'd be in Seabourne. This time tomorrow would be something else entirely. Today is by way of a warm-up, he decides, which will add a bit of spice to the old routine.

*   *   *

Grace is beginning to relax into the tidal rhythm of a holiday. Seabourne may not be quite what it was, but the sea and the cliffs and the beach remain. She walks and rests in the hazed June sun and feels the tensions ebb away.

The one false note comes in from outside. Grace looks again at the book Paula lent her. Now she sees that it isn't a thriller. Indeed, it isn't made up at all. *What Happened to Hilda Murrell?* is real.

The woman was kicked, stabbed, beaten.

It's hard to believe, in Seabourne. Grace doesn't really take it in; she doesn't want to take it in. After the frantic last days in the shop it's pleasant to sink into a new routine, a routine not of struggle but acceptance, where food is offered at regular times, her covers are straightened, her sheets are smoothed, and beyond the grey levels of the promenade the bands of foam curve up the shore, down the shore and up again, and decades blow away like sand.

Just out of sight round the line of the cliffs the Lighthouse waits for her to come. She's saving it up till she feels quite rested. A final treat, a final test . . . if the boat leaves while the tide is out she'll have to walk down the swaying cat-walks that link the land with the distant boats. They're two planks wide, high above ground, on thin iron legs which rock in the wind; the hand-rail's just a rope.

Once she was good at heights. But in recent years something odd has begun when she's on a high edge or even a ladder, a complaint she feels is someone else's, a sudden shift and lurch in her temples as if the earth were pulling her down. As if she had always been too tall and looked at things from too high up, and now must crumple to make amends.

I'll do my best. I've made a vow.

She's going to see it from below, full-size at last, her beloved Lighthouse. She's going to see the massive weight of the blocks of stone that form the base. She's going to see where the men clung on as the sea came roaring over the rocks and tried to wreck what they'd done that day, and the boat sped in for them just in time.

I'll go with the trippers in the Southern Queen, even if they chew gum and wear Kiss-Me-Quick hats.

Faith is cleaning Room 70. She has to admit, there's not much to clean, no one could accuse the old bat of being dirty. Snobbish, yes. Rude, yes. But Room 70 isn't a secret gutser, and she leaves her things in tidy piles; it needs the merest lick and polish.

Sometimes, Faith has to smile, when she thinks what her mother would say if she saw her. She said I was the muckiest pup in the place, and I end up working as a hotel cleaner. And I've started breeding early, as well . . . so maybe I am my mother's daughter.

I think that this one's a daughter, too (she pats her tummy as she wipes the mirror). I'll just have one, and make her feel special. No, I'll have two, so she has a friend . . .

She doesn't want the child to be lonely, she fears it will be as lonely as her; you were cursed with loneliness if you were unusual, and Faith has always been very unusual, 'fey' they called her when she was a child and some of the teachers thought she was special, but life could not be more dull and normal except for the gnawing loneliness and nowhere to live except the Empire . . . thank God, even now she looks tubby, not pregnant. They'll throw her out, when the baby comes.

Faith's mother had ten and was very forgetful about their names and whereabouts. Even their sexes; Faith was called Paddy or Jack as often as Bridget or Shelagh. When she told her mother she was pregnant, her mother's eyes went narrow and blind, her mother's eyes didn't look at her, her mother went on about a chicken for dinner, killing a chicken, plucking a chicken, Faith and Shelagh would both have to help her, she'd break its neck or strangle it, 'and I don't want to hear any sentiment, mind.'

'It's a mortal sin to have an abortion,' Faith had shouted at her great fat back, and her mother turned round and looked at her finally. 'What do the Holy Fathers know? What do they know about having a baby? I don't want to hear it. I don't want to hear.'

Nobody heard, and nobody listened. She ran away to England so they weren't ashamed. She was hated in Ireland, so what did she lose by going to a country which hated the Irish? She'd talk to the baby, once it was born. For now she'd be silent instead of unheard.

In London, the traffic is hopelessly jammed, an atonal nightmare of angry horns. Thanks to Sally and the scene at the minder's, Arthur is stuck in the worst of it. He gets to the Albion Hotel at ten. So Phyllis, the receptionist-telephonist-housekeeper, raises one overplucked eyebrow ironically above her upswept tinted glasses. She's glad he's late, since she's got a hangover.

'What's this?' asks Arthur, looking at the switchboard where eighty-eight units are showing on the memory. 'Who's just run up eighty-eight units? Banana-face ringing Mecca again?' Since Arthur's late, he's glad about the units, which show on the memory but have not been written down.

Nominally, Arthur is the manager, but he and Phyllis jockey hard for position. It's a game, but serious, and both of them play it although both say that the Albion's a joke, which it is, and an ancient joke at that, all the equipment a decade out of date, shrivelled beige sticks in the window-boxes, curtains hanging down off the curtain-rails.

The Albion belongs to James Pennington, a very old acquaintance of Arthur's, a member of the commune way back in the sixties. He keeps the hotel on as an investment, since the land it's on in the centre of London seems to double in price almost every three years. Besides, he's too lazy to sell it, and it rather tickles him, part-owning Arthur. He looks him up twice a year or so and talks dully about his sons at Marlborough. In his cups he tells Arthur that he's his best mate. This astonishes Arthur, who feels he hardly knows him. The business itself is a tax loss.

Arthur benefits; a nice gentle job which allows him to cook when he feels like it, and also allows him to take time off to be with his daughter and cultivate his garden. Phyllis benefits, though not so much; she wasn't at college with the owner, like Arthur, and she's a woman, so she isn't well paid. But she likes her drink, and the bar's well stocked, and Arthur takes it for granted she nicks it. One way or another, she isn't doing badly.

The people who aren't doing well are the guests. 'Banana-face' is a typically respectful name for one of the Saudis. Arthur doesn't think of himself as a racist, but at the Albion he plays by the rules; the hotel divides into us and them, guests and staff, guests and foreigners, a complex world of invisible walls.

'Good morning, sir,' says Arthur now as Banana-face himself comes down the stairs. He doesn't speak much English, so Arthur sometimes engages him in elaborate speech, elaborate for Arthur, Byzantine for him. 'Ringing the family again, I see. Everything all right at home, sir?'

'No,' says the man, whose face veers to one side, and is long and yellow as the fruit of his nickname. 'No, Mr Arthur, I no ring.'

So Phyllis has been ringing her boyfriend in Holland. Not smart enough to erase the units. 'Will you be leaving your key this morning?'

'Please?' says Banana-face, not understanding. Arthur picks up a key at random from the key-board and jingles it slightly too close to his nose. 'Key, savvy,' he says.

The man shakes his head with dignity. 'No, sir, I keep,' he tells him, with galling politeness, and walks out. As the swing-doors close behind him, Arthur bows at his back. 'Kiss your bum, sir, Mr Banana-face.' He says it partly because he feels ashamed. Phyllis giggles, as always. All the same, he considers, she's getting too confident.

'Has Mr Onassis checked out?' he asks.

'Onassis' is a fat little Egyptian lawyer whose luggage and inter-national phone bill have convinced the staff he's rich. Having one rich guest is essential for morale. And they do still come to the Albion, surprisingly . . . somewhere in the world there must be travel agents who still have copies of long-dead brochures, artists' impressions of window-boxes gay with geraniums, blowing awnings.

'Checked out this morning.' She looks at her finger-nails and purses her precisely-whitened lips.

'Did he leave a nice tip for the girls, Phyllis?'

'Nah. Fiver. Mean little sod.'

So she's probably got twenty tucked away in her handbag. 'Maria will be disappointed,' says Arthur. Maria is one of the chambermaids. She sends money home to South America.

Phyllis is instantly indignant. 'Maria! She doesn't do too badly, one way or another . . .'

Aha, thinks Arthur, so Phyllis is letting Maria telephone her family in Colombia. The Albion's footing the bill, of course.

But he doesn't for a moment begrudge it to Maria. James Pennington could afford to pay. They were all on the fiddle, one way or another, and Pennington was making more money than any of them by sitting on his bottom in the house in Hampshire. He and his cousins owned most of England. Just as long as they didn't decide to sell up.

Springing in his mind like a mountain lion up the bare stone staircase towards the 400s, breathing as steady as a giant cat, Bruno times himself on each flight of stairs and is pleased to see that his fourth-flight time is only half a second slower than his first. He's fit; that's a start; he'll need to be fit; his bodywork is in perfect order.

Perfect man in a crumbling world. Fast as he flashes past the floors, he can't help seeing the tottering towers of graffiti that kids have drawn on the walls, pencilled, inked, smearily sprayed, making their mark as high as they can, standing on tiptoe in the echoing stairwell.

Bruno doesn't notice that the concrete from which the estate had been built in the sixties is slowly falling apart. Tiny cracks, elaborate stresses, unpredicted entropies. From the outside it looks like a pen and ink drawing where all the lines have run in the rain, long grey smudgey stains unravelling from every window or balcony.

What Bruno sees is mess, filth, a dumping-ground for the dregs of the earth, a prison where they deserve to be. It's filthy because the inhabitants are filthy, broken down because they don't look after it, badly designed as a punishment to people who deserve punishing. He comes among them as avenging angel, a fiery blow-torch to blow them away; he would like to raze the estate to the ground with all the inhabitants inside it.

There were rumours that they were going to sell up. That the Fairfields Estate would be privatised. The riffraff inside it would be part of the deal. Pausing on the landing, where one of the strip lights is smashed and the other one flickers sickly, Bruno snorts as he peers at the numbers. You'd have to be barmy to want to buy this. He personally thinks you couldn't *give* it away. Only someone like him can get money out of Fairfields. Someone like him can get blood from a stone. He grins, just a fraction nervously, before pressing the bell of 415. A minute to half-past ten. Perhaps they'll offer him a cup of coffee. He snickers with laughter at the thought. The laugh congeals into a greedy rictus and Sharon Taylor, behind the door, behind the spy-hole which keeps them safe, sees a celluloid monster in the fish-bowl lens, flickering yellow, a jaw full of razors, bone which is shiny, sharp and black.

As carriage clocks ring out the half-hour in dozens of flats in Dorset Square, a gentle walk from Regent's Park, Room 24 comes in to the Albion with a bespectacled Japanese; maybe for coffee, maybe not. She's tall and flashing with a yard of blonde hair, he's slight, polite, about to disappear into his spotless Burberry.

'Morning, Susy,' says Arthur. He smiles in pure appreciation of the way her body creases the leather.

'How are you, Arthur?' Susy Cole asks, in her husky voice, with her sexiest smile, but a smile which also says, Arthur, I like you, it's great that we have a soft spot for each other. It never fails to charm him; though as she disappears with the Japanese trotting behind her like a nervous dachshund, he grins and says 'Tart' just under his breath.

She's lived at this hotel for nearly a year. She's very discreet, though she drinks a little, and her pimp comes in and loses his temper. She's very English, impeccably English, and still very pretty in an English way . . . but she'll have to stop soon, while the going's good. She knows it too. She's approaching thirty.

Around eleven the Japanese leaves, bowing faintly to Phyllis, who leers at Arthur. Half an hour later, Susy rings the switchboard. Phyllis is titivating; Arthur answers.

'Could you send up my usual, Arthur?'

'Course . . .' Arthur's due for his morning cup of cocoa. 'Why not come down and have it in the bar.' Today he doesn't feel like being alone. Alone he will only worry about Paula.

Down in the bar Susy looks a little weary, and asks for her whisky neat. 'Trouble is, there's nothing I can actually *do*,' she tells him, opening her vague blue eyes.

'You've had a good run for your money at this.'

Susy doesn't like people being specific about what she does. She says rather quickly, 'I don't really make a lot of money. There's Gus, you know. And living here's expensive.'

'Get married,' he says. 'Have a baby.'

Her eyes go hard, and swivel towards him. 'What about you, Arthur?' she asks. 'You must be – what, forty? You went to university. What are you doing in a place like this? It's a bit of a dump, isn't it?'

'Me,' he says. 'Oh, I'm just marking time. I'm not really a hotel manager, you see. I'm a restaurant critic.' It sounded very weak. 'And father. That's what I really like.'

A silence extends between them. It seems to pad round the dusty bar, to stare at the two of them over their shoulders, uncertain faces in the tarnished mirror.

Arthur tries to brush the shadows away. 'Some would say you and me were in the vanguard,' he begins. 'We're both in what they like to call the service sector. And that's what Britain is going to be good at. I was reading about it in the paper, yesterday.'

'All Britain's good for, is what you mean. If I wasn't so tired, I would get the hell out. Go to America. Go to Japan.' She finishes her whisky at a single gulp, and he realises she is already drunk. 'If you ask me, this country is fucked. It's not just me, love. It's the whole country.'

Back upstairs, Phyllis is fuming. 'Well is there or isn't there going to be lunch,' she asks when he finally gets back. 'It's just not businesslike. I mean. I'm wasted here. I ought to move on.'

But she doesn't move on, because she's comfortable. She doesn't move on because she's set in her ways. She doesn't move on because she's limited; it hasn't got a future, but it's something she can do.

She doesn't move on because she's English. She knows it's coming to the end of the line. But the knowledge is oddly comforting. It means she needn't take the initiative. She'll sit here fiddling and painting her nails and eavesdropping until she's pushed.

Banana-face comes in with his wife. A strip of bare face with enormous eyes, and underneath a great pregnant belly. Poor woman, thinks Phyllis, and feels more cheerful. They treat their wives like animals. They may have money, but they don't have class. There was the man from Kuwait who performed in the basin . . .

At least the English were *civilised*. She thanks the Lord she's English.

'Open up, Mrs Taylor,' Bruno shouts through the letter-box. 'I'm warning you. Don't waste my time.'

Each shout becomes tremendous, inhuman, as its echoes bounce across the flickering landing. He aims a kick at the base of the door. It rocks the door on its hinges.

'I'm counting up to ten,' he bellows.

Inside, they're having some kind of quarrel, he can hear the woman shrieking at someone.

'One, Two . . . I mean it, Mrs Taylor. You're going to regret it if I have to get cross.'

Suddenly the door opens a crack, and a white little face peers behind the chain. 'My boy isn't well,' she pleads. 'Come back tomorrow and I'll have the money.'

'That's what you told me last week. Just open the door and cut the chat.'

From behind her the voice of an adolescent, could be a boy but high as a girl, screams, 'Don't let him in! You're fucking *insane!*'

'Nasty language,' Bruno hisses. 'Do it. Now. Can't wait any longer.'

She hesitates one dangerous second, Bruno steps back and kicks the door so hard that it suddenly sags inwards with a splintering crack as the chain splits off. He presses straight in against the woman's slight body. She gasps and backs into the wall. He smiles a smile of genuine pleasure, glad to be here, glad to begin.

'All right, Mrs Taylor? May I call you Sharon? We wouldn't want you to go falling over.'

In the front room, the TV is on, and a long thin boy stands beside the sofa, limbs held awkwardly, fight or flight. Black or half-caste, but under the blackness his face is bloodless, yellow.

'This your boyfriend?' Bruno asks her.

'My boy Darryl,' she's whispering. 'He's not very well.'

'Get lost. I want to talk to your mum.'

The boy stares at Bruno, and doesn't move. In the background, the English programme blares. 'Don't look much like her, do you,' Bruno continues, sitting down on the sofa. 'I s'pose your father was African. If she knows who your father was.'

She clutches the boy's thin arm as it rises. 'Don't wind him up,' she pleads. 'Darryl, go and take Shirl for a walk.'

'I'm not going anywhere,' the boy mutters. 'I'm English, just for your information. So's my dad. We ain't Africans.'

From the kitchen, a little girl appears, in a party dress of pale blue satin with a spreading greasy stain on the back. Her skin is as white as her ankle-socks.

'Shirley. You go for a walk with Darryl. He's going to take you down the arcade.'

'Five hundred quid,' says Bruno. 'Five hundred and thirty-three, to be precise. You're eight months behind with your payments, Sharon . . .'

'I've done my best. I got the sack. His dad doesn't pay me. The court said he had to, till Darryl left school. Just give us a chance.'

'You've had your chance. Lots of chances. We don't mess about.' He stares round the room, at the shabby vinyl three-piece suite, the greying cushions, the pink fluffy rug, the row of swans on the mantelpiece. Not much here, but all of it filthy. 'You'll have to give me whatever you've got.'

She goes to her coat and gets her purse. 'Twenty-five pounds. Maybe twenty-three. It's all I've got till Monday.'

'Right,' he says, taking it, putting it away. 'That's five hundred pounds short. Pity. Keen on the video, are you, Darryl? We're going to relieve you of the video –'

'You can't take that. It's a present from me dad.'

'Watch me,' says Bruno as he wrenches out the plug. 'There's nothing else in this dump worth taking.'

The boy comes forward, sharp fists raised, but his mother clutches his arm, a plea, her hand very white against his black one. 'Think of your sister,' she begs. '*Please*, Darryl. Get her out of here.'

Bruno takes hold of that small white wrist, smiling at her, smiling at Darryl, inspecting the cluster of rings on her finger. 'These from Woolworths?' he asks her.

She flushes painfully. 'Course they're not. I know you're thinking I ought to pawn them, but . . .'

'Know what I'm thinking, do you? You don't, you know. We're taking these.' And he's tugging at her thin fingers, tugging the rings against her swollen knuckles, the exciting pressure of metal on bone and her sharp little gasp as the metal cuts her.

Suddenly everything explodes. With an animal snarl the boy leaps on his back, trying to pull Bruno away from his mother, and his hands are clawing at Bruno's face, strong black fingers wrenching at his nostrils, and as pain brings the water to Bruno's eyes he elbows the boy hard in the guts so he shouts with a child's outraged surprise and quick as a flash Bruno flings him off and as the thin body keels to the ground he kicks him as hard as he can on the kneecap, delicious connection of boot and bone and then the expected howls of pain and Bruno kicks him again and again as he lies on the floor, his head, his belly, his hands as they try to protect his face, his hateful, slobbering, ugly face, no longer howling, no longer a face, and the woman's screams are as distant as seagulls, and Bruno could go on doing this for ever.

In Seabourne, Grace has abandoned her book and sits and dreams on a bench in the sun, watching two sea-birds blow in the wind, long and silver as willow-leaves . . . the sudden ease of happiness.

Tomorrow, she thinks. My darling Paula.

6

NOT MEETING

But Paula can't go to Seabourne that Tuesday.

Paula is hijacked by her body. Arthur comes back from the hotel discontented on Monday evening, and comforts himself by cooking an enormous, savorous stew, the tenderest beef, the tiniest mushrooms, the kitchen steaming with tarragon and garlic, Arthur singing as the slow bubbles rise through a thickening liquid towards his spoon, Arthur sniffing and fishing and tasting. 'You're going to love this, Paula. Maybe you're just anaemic . . . this stew is bursting with iron.'

'Great. It smells *delicious*.' Her mouth is watering with hunger.

But when he brings the stew to the table – he's put a cloth on, he's remembered candles, he enters like the Lord of Misrule, red-cheeked and greasy-lipped from cooking, bearing the steaming brown tureen – the water rushes to her mouth again, and she realises, though she wants to please him, she isn't hungry, she's going to be sick.

She isn't sick, but she sits there, grey. It's a moment or two before Arthur notices. He doesn't say much; he eats the stew, the sounds of his mouth unnaturally loud.

Paula stares at the candle-flame. 'I'm really sorry. I'm such a bore.'

'Doesn't matter. I'll heat it up tomorrow.'

'Shan't be there. I'm going to see Grace.'

'Will you be well enough? You look like death.' As soon as he's said it, he wishes he hadn't, a superstitious horror of the word, as if now he's said it, someone will die.

'I know I do. Look, don't let's talk about it. You understand, I don't want to accept it. Every day I expect I'm going to feel better. I do feel better. But it doesn't last.'

Arthur is wiping bread round his plate. She loves him but she has to turn away. He looks very fat, wiping his plate, and the bread drips fat, and the candle's greasy, and Paula stands up abruptly. 'I'm off. Going to look at the novel.'

As she leaves the room, Arthur says over his shoulder in a dull voice that asks her to stay, 'I hate the Albion, you know.'

'I thought you thought it was a bit of a joke.'

'What people do is never really a joke. It's a horrible place. And I'm the manager.'

'You're not really a hotel manager. It's just a kind of part you play.'

'I don't know any more,' he mumbles. 'I don't know why I'm there. I don't know what I really am, or when I'll get a chance to be it. I feel I'll never do anything.' He's on his fourth glass of Beaujolais.

She waits for a second, poised in the doorway, for him to say more, but the pause extends, and she suddenly longs to sit down so badly that she says, 'I'm off. If you want to talk, I'm in the study,' and disappears.

In the silence and the emptiness, Arthur adds a last clause to his lament, staring at the film on the cooling stew. 'I don't know if you really love me.'

Paula knows that she's let him down. He hardly ever talks like that. But her body has a will of its own.

That night she finds it hard to sleep. Though her stomach's empty it feels horribly alive, gurgling and surging under the covers. Nearly full moon. It must be that. She's always felt odd around full moon. Arthur looks happy again in the moonlight, plump and peaceful, snoring gently, but Paula is still gnawed by guilt.

He worries about me so much. I don't take a blind bit of notice. And *I* don't worry enough about *him*. I just assume he'll be all right.

Next morning she wakes and stares at the sun pricking through the fine lacework of moth in the curtains. Outside the window there are summer noises; birdsong, leaves scratching the glass. But her stomach's full of the usual acid.

She sighs. She's going to do as he says. Go to the doctor, get sorted out. Grace won't mind; she'll telephone Grace. She's always treated Grace as family – she's very sure of Grace's love. Maybe she treats Grace rather badly. But Grace would hate me to be ill, she thinks. I don't believe she's ever been ill. *Arthur* never gets ill, either. And Sally only gets things like colds. I'm the sick one. I have to think of myself. And when I'm better, I'll be better to them.

When Grace comes down to breakfast that morning she goes to Reception to buy a paper. '*Guardian*, please.'

'Aren't any left. *Mail, Sun, Star*.'

'Never mind,' Grace says and moves away, but another of the girls remembers her and calls, 'Mrs Stirling? There's a message for you.'

The sharp foreboding proves correct. *So sorry, can't make it today. Will phone this evening. Paula.* It leaves a draining sense of loss.

'I wonder why she didn't speak to me.' Grace doesn't realise that she's thinking aloud, but the girl says, 'We rang your room. We kept on ringing, but we didn't get an answer.'

'Oh dear. I must have been in the shower.' I'm old, stupid, deaf, Grace thinks. No wonder Paula doesn't come and see me.

Today she isn't first at breakfast. A very old man whose spine runs nearly parallel to the table-cloth is eating cornflakes very noisily, his head flipped up at a tortoise angle, two tables away from her own in the window. To her dismay he staggers to his feet as she walks past, and sits down as she does, with a creaking bow.

'Good morning,' he wheezes. 'Saw you yesterday.'

She accords a minimally courteous nod.

'George Kirk,' he tells her. 'Old soldier.'

She's damned if she will tell him her name. But whenever she raises her eyes from the prunes, he's staring at her and smiling. If I weren't so very ancient, she thinks, I'd swear he was giving me the eye. In the end embarrassment forces her to speak.

'Have you been here long?' she asks.

'Have I been here long? I'll say I have!' He shakes with silent laughter.

'When are you leaving?' she asks, coldly.

'In a box,' he tells her. 'I live here.' His voice has to struggle to get past the wheezes.

Sorry for him, she makes a small effort.

'You're very lucky,' she says.

'You think so, do you?' And he's off again, shoulders rising and falling in a paroxysm. Grace feels a fool, and furious. She fastens her eyes on her piece of toast and gets up to go as soon as it's finished.

Faith has discovered she's invisible. That's why the chambermaids are up in the roof, in the dusty attics with mice and damp and tiny windows like arrow-slits.

She passes Room 70 on the stairs, Faith going down, her going up, both of them rather out of breath. Room 70's going up to her room with a yellow waistcoat and a frozen face. As she passes Faith she doesn't even flicker, her eyes look straight through the back of Faith's skull as if she sees something very superior, but Faith and her baby simply aren't there.

It's something to do with hotels, Faith thinks. The dirty work is supposed to be invisible. The dirty workers are invisible too. Not just to the guests, but to the rest of the staff, the smart ones like barmen and receptionists.

The Empire is full of invisible walls. You couldn't get through. You couldn't climb over. Nothing could bring the two sides together. (An earthquake, maybe? A hurricane?)

The trouble with weathermen, thinks Paula, shivering slightly as she comes out of the dark of the tube into sunlit Camden, is that they only tell us a few days at a time. Sun tomorrow, rain today. And so they don't notice the weather's gone mad. We have a heatwave at the end of May, then it flips back to weeks of winter, then June decides to behave like spring.

And the rest of the world has terrible droughts, encroaching deserts, desperate floods. In the far distance the ice-caps are melting. And up above the ozone's fucked. All the old systems are breaking down . . .

And most of it's the fault of human beings.

And despite all that, despite her body, despite the fact she's going to the doctor, the early morning is beautiful, the moment is good, she lives the moment, walking briskly towards Regent's Park. An hour to wait till surgery opens.

In the park, the flower-beds look pristine. The plants for June have just been dug in, straight from the greenhouse, already in flower. The basin of air and cloudless sky in the middle of the city is glorious. Hardly anyone to spoil it yet. She peers into the middle distance and counts one park keeper, two gardeners, three small Japanese children made into navy cubes by British school uniform . . . Leaves on the trees are still yellow and fresh, not quite full-sized, growing, stretching; the horse-chestnut candles came late this year and gleam above her, full and firm; even the pigeons look healthy, washed in the morning sun. The world is alight, and in bloom.

But it suddenly seems like a mockery. On her face, the air feels chill and sweet. Her eyes tell her it's brighter than glass, clearer than water (if water's still clear). It speeds her heartbeat, flushes her cheeks. But she is afraid to breathe in deep. She's afraid of what she can't see or feel. She's afraid of the invisible thing which may have blown across the earth from Russia. Settling slow and quiet as frost on the leaves unfolding, the brightening buds, the new June roses, the three solemn children. Settling, perhaps, in Paula. Making everything old; things which are growing, things unborn, things which are not yet realised; the tender, formless future.

Grace takes a walk into western Seabourne, a long haul rising towards the cliffs. As she nears the place where the house should be, she feels the old mixture of fear and longing, for this time, surely, Carlisle Mount will have gone . . .

But Victoria Parade is weathering well. The vast Gothic piles of brick and creeper look very solid in the modern sunlight. Would they be pleased, those Victorian builders, to find they had outlasted the empire?

Once we all thought it would last for ever.

Grace had been the most patriotic little girl in existence. Only last month, sorting out her papers, she'd found a song-sheet she'd treasured for years, with a beautifully hand-coloured Union Jack and an eight-verse version of the National Anthem. When she was ten, it was stuck to her dressing-table mirror – no one objected, because of the sentiment – swimming above her face each morning, a glorious inspiration. She knows it now for a mis-stressed farrago, rambling down the yellowing page.

> God grant our soldiers strength
> That Peace through breadth and length
> Of land be ours.

Strengthen our Navy too
And make its noble crew
Command the ocean blue
    Excel their powers.
Unite our colonies
O'er distant lands and seas,
    Empire we sing.
Asking in pray'rfulness
Our deeds and actions bless
Receive our thankfulness
    And bless our King.

It had worn spectacularly badly. There wasn't much Peace, these days; we didn't have much of a navy any more; no one was interested in being noble; the colonies were lost, the King was dead, and the Empire was the name of a second-rate hotel . . .

But turning the corner to another steep rise, gasping a little with fatigue and pleasure she sees that Carlisle Mount is still there, a great dark glow behind its hedge of camellia, and just for a second they stand by the door, little Lucy, Eddy, Father and Mother, poised to sail down the gravel and kiss her, welcome after a life away. She raises her hand to the stone gatepost, seeing them through a brief blur of tears, a wrenching mixture of joy and horror. Because she had never given birth, she would only ever have this one family. She'd tried to escape, but she'd come in a circle, and with her death the circle would close. In Seabourne, where the long arc began.

She might have escaped them if she'd had children.

And then she remembers Paula.

Paula's allergic to the Health Centre. Healthy people avoided it. It was full of sneezing, coughing kids; weeping, dribbling babies; screaming toddlers bumping into people's knees; lunatics, who might be any age, rocking, wincing, muttering. You always waited *hours*.

Today the man in front of Paula in the queue speaks too loudly and waves his hands. 'Do you offer Family Planning here? I want to start a family. I want to meet a nice girl. You understand me, a nice woman.' He is red-faced and wild-eyed. One receptionist said to the other, *sotto voce*, 'He's Dr Skinner's patient,' and louder, 'Have you come for your prescription, Mr Dixon? It was waiting for you three days ago. The best thing is probably to take your tablets.'

Paula's lucky; there's a cancellation. Officially, twenty minutes to wait, which means she'll probably be there all morning. The widest empty space on the benches is near a child of Sally's age who has brought her tricycle in with her. It is hard to be sure who is her mother, since none of the nearby women takes particular notice of her, but all look up with a vaguely hopeless mixture of annoyance and conciliation as she runs her trike at their feet, and laughs. She is eating a chocolate bar. It is on her hands, her feet, her dress, her tricycle, her shoes, the floor, and the tiny, yellowed hankerchief with which she sometimes smears at her sneezes.

Paula is a new distraction. 'Lo,' the girl calls, aggressively, staring at her and picking her nose. Paula says 'Hallo' with finality, mostly in deference to public opinion. She wants to read her book. Moreover, her stomach feels queasy again and the melted chocolate and snot aren't helping.

She opens her book. The print looks strange. Her eyes haven't been behaving either. Some days, everything is blurred. Some days, like today, are unnaturally clear, stabs of bright print on the paper, the sickly glaze on the child's red cheeks, and Paula suddenly thinks of the strawberries, rows of punnets at the greengrocers, notices pleading FRESH STRAWS! NEW CROP!!, but nobody had bought them, they sat there glistening, people were wary of buying berries, for where had it come from, the rain that fed them? – darker and wetter as days went by.

'LO,' the child leers, bending into her lap, and the tricycle rams her kneecap.

'*Ouch*,' says Paula very distinctly, raking the row of women with her eyes. Half-an-inch nearer and the chocolatey mess would transfer itself to Paula's skirt. '*Go away!*' says Paula loudly.

A woman speaks from far down the row. She's large and dull-eyed, but her voice carries. 'She's only a child,' she says. 'Come here, love. Never mind. Some women can't stand children,' she informs the waiting-room at large. The little girl pauses, considering. 'Don't wanto,' she shouts at her tricycle.

'Gloria!' The big woman yells. 'COME HERE AT ONCE OR I'LL BELT YOU!'

Gloria peddles towards her, suddenly crying with all the force of her lungs.

'There, there, lovey,' the mother says, pitching her voice for a public address. 'Did the nasty lady make you cry?'

Paula stares at her book and pretends not to notice, but the page she turns to offers no comfort.

The chaotic state induced within a living cell when it is exposed to ionising radiation has been graphically described . . . as a 'madman loose in a library' . . . cell exposure . . . can cause some of the chronic diseases and changes we usually associate with old age . . . If the radiation damage occurs in germ cells, the sperm or ovum, it can cause defective offspring.

Faith gets contractions more frequently. They grip her now as she cleans the bath. As long as it doesn't hurt my baby, she tells herself as she struggles upright, as long as the twinges mean it's healthy, I can bear anything, I'll go on.

Faith has six weeks to wait, according to what the doctor told her. Faith knows exactly when it was conceived, and she suspects that it's almost due, but no one was interested in what she knew, they insisted on working it out with maths, and Faith supposes she has to believe them.

Faith has a jaundiced view of almost everything that's happened to do with being pregnant (including the conception, which was not a lot of fun) – *except* for the baby, which she thinks is a miracle, the one thing nobody, including herself, can spoil, so long as it stays inside her.

A few days ago she'd wanted to die. She couldn't rest, couldn't sleep, tossing and turning against the baby. At last she drove herself out through the darkness, panting along the cliff at midnight, afraid of the bushes, which might be soldiers, afraid of the wind but longing for it to pick her up like a grain of sand and throw her down past the sleeping sea-birds, suddenly weightless, senseless, easy, headlong down to the rocks below. She wouldn't have missed herself at all, she was suddenly tired of being alone, lying there night after night with the baby kicking and dreaming, a world away, or swimming gently in its separate sea . . .

She didn't kill herself, because of the child. What if it didn't die when she did? What if it was left in the dark inside her struggling, abandoned, slowly getting cold, with the cooling echoing sea all round it? For ages the child had kept her alive; that night it touched her and stopped her dying. That and the beam of light from the Lighthouse spreading before her over the water, into the darkness, across to France, lighting the fear of travellers like her.

Someone had stayed awake with her. Somebody cared about other people, strangers, foreigners, not just their friends, sleeping sailors, a swiming child, the single beam held them all together.

Grace peers into the porch and sees that Carlisle Mount is no longer a whole. It has split and split and split again, a labyrinth of separate lives, 109a, 109b, Downstairs Letterbox for 109c ... A crew of strangers who neglect the garden, unpruned roses and shaggy dark grass. The cypresses are nearly as tall as the house, pulling everything back into deep shadow.

Their lawn was once smooth enough for tennis, a grass court perpetually flooded with sunlight. Grace hardly remembers it raining, except when she was at school. She remembers other things clearly; the taste of stolen raspberries – fur, then sweetness which burst on the tongue and had a kind of darkness in; the swarming hum of thousands of bees; the pale freckled pink of a foxglove.

One summer when she was very small she put her finger in the bell of the foxglove and there was a bee inside which stung her. She sobbed, then felt ashamed. And her big brother Eddy, who could be a torment, was suddenly kind and told everyone that the bee was particularly big and ferocious, a *dangerously outsize bee*, in fact; he told them she'd been brave.

It was kind of him, but untrue. I wanted to be *really* brave. But when did I have the chance? 'You're a girl, you can't go swimming.' 'You're a girl, you're not to fight.' 'Little girls don't climb trees.'

But little girls did grow up. One summer the lupins were taller than her, the next summer she was taller than them, and then she understood that one day she would grow out of the garden.

At last she was sent to the big girls' school, Compton Hall, where the skirts looked so long and the waists so small she never thought she'd fit into them. Most of the teachers were mermaid-like, beautiful and impenetrable, but one of them was different: Miss Pitt, who lived with her friend Miss Pelman. One day on a picnic Miss Pitt said something that Grace would never forget. 'The girls of Compton Hall,' she announced, to the birds, the clouds, but especially to Grace, 'will make their way in the world, if they choose to.'

Grace was just thirteen, but she blushed with pleasure, and all through her life she'd heard the echoes of that marvellous phrase, delivered in Miss Pitt's queer adenoidal voice. So a girl might make her way in the world. Girls might even *change* the world . . .

Grace turns away from the big dark house and walks downhill towards the front, thinking about the concentric rings of years which grew around that promise. It held her still; thrilled her still, though as life went on she'd believed it less, and it hadn't come, the chance for courage.

She sits in a deck-chair, immensely aged by thinking back to being young. Can she ever have been *thirteen*? She looks around her; the legs that reach into the sunlight from the adjoining chairs are veined and pocked, or worn to bone. Maybe some of these strangers were once my friends. We shouldn't know each other now.

Impossible to believe. That all of us, once, were children. A scramble of boys doing nature study, shrieking over the rocks like gulls. A crocodile of schoolgirls walking on the front, plait-ends knocking beneath their boaters.

Where have the children gone?

Why is the world so old?

Dr Gross hears Paula's symptoms carefully, then tells her he thinks she's pregnant.

'I can't be!'

'Why not?'

'We use contraception.'

'What kind?'

'The sheath –'

'You *can* be.'

'In any case, I've felt like this for months. I've had *periods* since all this began.'

'You mentioned they were very light . . . it could be what we call breakthrough bleeding. It's very common. They're not true periods. How long exactly have you had these symptoms?'

'*Months*. Since March . . . three . . . nearly four . . . are you saying I might be four months pregnant?'

'We can test, quite easily. You'll have to give a sample. You'll know by Thursday at the latest.'

'It's ridiculous . . .'

'We can probably tell from an internal examination, if you're as far gone as you say.'

'But I stayed on the pill for *seventeen years* . . . I was sure I must be sterile.'

'That's rather a silly assumption,' he says, but his eyes are not unkind. 'I can see you've had a shock. Let me have a look, then we'll talk about it.'

Gone; far gone; as far gone as you think.

Paula emerges from the Health Centre flushed, shaken, terrified. They're mad, she thinks. It can't be.

Her arm stings where the blood was taken, and aches from wrist to shoulder. Her heart is beating uncontrollably. She stares at a paving stone in the bright sun. An ordinary rectangle, flecked with mica; a fringe of grass around the edge; the white and yellow of a bird dropping. *Help*, she thinks. *Save me*. Ordinary things can disprove it all. If they are unchanged, so is she.

But the pavement isn't the same. The feet which tread it are absurd, gigantic. The lemon-yellow opening leaves above her shiver with hysterical laughter.

On the bus, the conductor has to ask three times where she is going. 'I – I haven't decided,' she babbles. 'Victoria, then.'

'That's sixty pence.'

The conductor has learned not to get involved, or else he would have asked her why she is crying. Soon he sees she is smiling, too. *Nutcase*, he thinks, and is glad he didn't ask her. Something wrong with the world, these days. More and more nutcases about.

Paula has chosen Victoria because it is the end of the line. The streets are the usual chaos of tourists, roaring traffic, diesel fumes, stumbling people with enormous cases, rowing couples, red-eyed drunks, a man with dark stains on the front of his trousers, a woman on the kerb, her blouse undone, a can of beer glinting in the sun under what Paula suddenly sees is a nipple, a thing like a crushed enormous strawberry.

London is hell, she thinks, with a detached sense of revelation. She isn't part of this. She isn't really here; she's floating in a cocoon of shock. *England is hell. It really is.* Fluorescent faces; painted faces. A pigeon hops on a rotted foot.

There is something else, as well.

Something she's never noticed before, something she sees but does not believe, like the thing the doctor told her this morning.

Everywhere there are pregnant women, walking with a slightly inward air, protected, perhaps, from the frenzy all round them, holding their stomachs, holding their backs, taking a rest from heavy packages. Some of them are gently rounded, some unbelievably vast, parting the crowd like walking whales, some of them have small children in tow. None of them seems to notice Paula, but Paula follows each one with her eyes. They are there, after all, as a sign to her.

She's gripping the plastic of her British Rail beaker so hard that the orange juice floods her shoe, but she doesn't move; she's listening, trying to make sense of the words in her head.

Arthur's baby. Arthur's and mine. I'm quite far gone. There's a child inside me.

Bruno sits in his office, immensely frustrated, trying to keep himself awake. He needs a computer; he hasn't got one. He needs his typist, but she's off sick, and in any case she's only part time, and besides that she's a woman, and not to be trusted with important things.

But the things in his in-tray are the lowest of the low, a stack of requests for checks on people's credit-worthiness, a handwritten letter from a nutter wanting Bruno to follow his teenage daughter, a man who thinks his YOPS trainees are stealing tools from the workshop, a man who wants Bruno to find his dog, a woman endlessly boring on about her husband's suspected infidelity . . . whingers, wimps, and they want him to help them, as if he had nothing more important to do.

Today should have been quite different. Today he should have been hot on the trail of Timms and Stirling in Seabourne. Today he should have been working for Five, and intead he's back in his dusty little office, getting cramp in his spine from trying to type. Timms had let him down. Perhaps she suspected something. Perhaps Sunday's phonecall had been a front.

The office is yellow, dull and small. The pile of papers sits there, stupid. Three o'clock, a hopeless time. Nothing will happen. No one will come. Bruno will always be alone . . .

He shakes himself, hard. No more of that. He has to see Haines in less than a week. Haines and the rest are counting on him. Right.

Tomorrow he'll go to Seabourne. Whatever the hag next door decides, it's time he got to grips with Stirling.

Lost in the valley of the shadow of the past, Grace misses lunch without noticing and is suddenly starving at tea-time. The restaurant she remembers near the Martello tower has mutated into the Martello Muncher – she hesitates, but she has to eat.

She files automatically along in a row of people peering into plastic cages, fishing out lustreless Fresh Prawn Platters, looking more closely, pushing them back. The salads are determinedly monogamous, unrelieved lettuce and tomato. The radio this morning said salad greens weren't selling since the Chernobyl accident, but rather a lot of them seem to be here – bought up cheap by Seabourne caterers? Then down at the end she spots some surprisingly delectable-looking strawberry tarts, shells of thick cream where the red fruit swim. Her passion for strawberries has outlasted most others. Their melting flesh, their sharp-edged sweetness . . .

Strawberries, for Grace, meant the first school picnic, in 1913 before war broke out. That year the girls of Compton Hall had travelled in brand-new motorised charabancs. The spare seats groaned with hampers of food, tongue and chicken and salted beef, seed-cake, chocolate cake, gooseberry tarts, and a tremendous finale of strawberries and cream. Grace felt utterly happy, flying down the roads through the summer countryside, level with the tops of the hedges, sailing to the future down a river of flowers, saucer-sized dog-roses, pink-striped columbines creamy, wide-open morning-glories . . .

With a most unladylike, specific hunger she was also longing for the contents of the hampers. Growing so fast, she was always hungry. But the school had to traipse around Herstmonceux Castle before they were deemed to have earned their picnic . . . At last they reassembled in a dreamy, chattering cluster round the two mistresses. Grace read the notice on the flower bank; 'Ladies and Gentlemen Will Not – Others Must Not – Pick the Plants and Flowers.'

Grace must have eaten quite half a hamper. There were only half-a-dozen all told, but it seemed that no one else was eating; everyone was on reducing regimes. Grace didn't notice how much she had eaten, she only knew it must be time for the strawberries, and poised herself over a pyramid of fruit. Then suddenly Ginnie St Cloud, who was a prefect, and too beautiful to speak to, said loudly, 'I say, who *is* that second year who's eaten all the sandwiches and most of the tarts? I say, what's your name?'

There was absolute silence, then a swell of laughter. All over Grace's body the sweat broke out. It ran down under the long hot skirt and high-necked blouse so she felt she was bleeding. 'Grace Stirling,' she half whispered. 'I was hungry.' The laughter came again, in a burst, and distracted with shame, completely unconscious, Grace started to eat the strawberries. Laughter broke out once more.

But Miss Pitt, who was sitting two yards away under a yellow parasol that made her look yellower, turned round and stared very hard at Ginnie. 'The food,' she said with unnatural distinctness, 'is there to be eaten. Some of the girls in this school have fallen victim to a foolish fashion for starving themselves. This will not help them make their way in the world,' and surely, now, she was looking at Grace, her grey, slightly bulbous, clever eyes had chosen Grace for a special promise: 'The girls of Compton Hall *will* make their way in the world, if they choose to.' Then her head turned back on its long thin neck with a faintly audible click.

Maybe that look was a trick of the light, but Grace thought to herself, 'My life has been changed,' and less distinctly, 'I love Miss Pitt . . .'

Back in the present, she stares at the sea through the salt-stained windows of the Martello Muncher. Her strawberry tart is inexorably modern. The mountain of cream turned out to conceal a hump of foam-rubber sponge-cake; the strawberries were watery, tasteless. Was anything left that was real?'

On her way out she passes a table with four old people and three modern wheelchairs. Two of the old men are severely damaged – one arm, no legs, a missing eye. They must be veterans, here on a visit.

'Lovely, isn't it, Doris.'

'Alf's doing well with his.'

They've chosen strawberry tarts as well, but they eat theirs with relish . . .

The next school picnic, in 1914, she'd found a dark clotted stain on her skirt and thought she had sat on some strawberries, but then she realised it was blood. Mother explained, explaining nothing. Servants dealt with the bloodied rags, they would disappear and come back clean – what endless scrubbing went on in secret?

Nothing was wasted except their lives . . . A few months later war broke out, and mess and blood were everywhere and Eddy died and the world turned over.

The baby never came to stop the blood. It just dried up, a lifetime later.

Paula sits on in the café at Victoria, prodding at her stomach underneath the table. By now disbelief is in the ascendant. Four months pregnant would be nearly half-way. If she were four months pregnant, she would be *enormous*. She looks again, surreptitiously, at the book she had picked up in the surgery. The title is shameless: *You and Your Baby*. Nobody seems to be laughing at her, but she holds it carefully, only half open, concealing the cover with embarrassed fingers.

At one week old it was a malformed fish, but with startling swiftness it became a baby. Your Baby at 16 weeks – that was her; four months is sixteen weeks. More.

But this was *ridiculous*. YB had tiny hands and feet; an intelligent, enormous head; a childlike way of curling inside her. Good job it *is* curled up, she thinks, since the baby book says it's eight inches long. How on earth could she have an eight-inch animal curled inside her and notice nothing? She stares and stares at the pink and innocent-looking drawing on the page. Then she touches her stomach again. Impossible to put the two things together.

'Your Baby's eyelids aren't open yet.' YB, she thinks, looks so *serene*. Her fingers relax on her belly and start to stroke instead of prodding. Maybe it's true, she thinks. Maybe inside her restless, worried thirty-seven-year-old body, something is sleeping, so quiet and peaceful she hasn't even noticed, safe from the world and safe from her knowledge. Something resting, and smiling . . .

A very definite thought escapes and imprints itself on the plastic table where *You and Your Baby* now lies wide open.

I want it. I do. I hope he's right. It's mine. It's ours. I want this baby.

Grace has been reading, back in her room. The book Paula lent her lies open on the bed; she can't bear to read any more, for the moment.

Waiting for evening, she watches the light on the silvered square of sea in her window. How could one put that calm together with Hilda Murrell's awful death. The more she reads of the Murrell story, the more she is compelled by it. If Hilda Murrell was murdered because she thought, and wrote, and argued, then no one is safe, she thinks. No one is safe any more in England.

Twice already in Grace's lifetime, everyone's lives had been cut off. Whatever meaning they thought they had was made to look ridiculous. The first time Eddy, her brother, died. Two decades later, it was Ralph. Each time she'd felt she should have seen what was coming. Suddenly, now, she has a sense of dread.

She isn't afraid for herself, of course. Her battles are all through. But Paula. She's afraid for her.

Violently scarlet, a speedboat full of screaming people shoots under the pier and bucks across the spread of silver, leaving a chaos of broken water. The furious trail cuts the picture in two.

Straight after supper she telephones Paula.

'Paula, it's Grace.'

'Oh *Grace*, I'm sorry. I was going to ring. I went to the doctor . . .'

'Are you *all right*?'

'Yes. No. Some things have been happening, and Arthur's not here, he's working late . . .

'I've been worried about you.'

'Don't. But I need to see you, Grace. Things I can't discuss on the phone . . .'

'Phones are awful. We have to meet. And I've got the photographs . . .'

'Will I be pleased?'

'Delighted. They're everything we hoped for. You could come tomorrow, Paula . . .'

'I can't, though, dammit. I'm waiting for some news. Something extremely important. I'll know by Thursday . . .'

'Come Friday morning. Same time as before. You're not in any trouble, Paula . . .?'

'No more than usual. I'll be there . . . But Grace, how are you?'

'I'm pretty well. Delving into the Murrell story . . .'

'I've things to tell you about that, too.'

'By the way, Paula, before I forget. I'm afraid that Jan – you remember? – wants someone to do a bit of shopping. Nothing big. I wondered if you . . .'

'Polish, right?'

'Almost. He's Czech. Things one can only get in London.'

'I'm sure I can help. Tell me when you see me. Oh God, that's Sally – I have to go.'

'Go, child. See you on Friday.'

And Bruno, listening, prickles with glee. Secrets, photos, Eastern Europe, a general sense of urgency, a specific sense of things firming up. His penis nudges his wrap apart. *Her* wrap, really; his own is dirty. Brunnhilde's silky, slippery wrap . . .

Bruno's packing to go to Seabourne. He wonders whether to take the shoes. It's work, of course, and middle of the week, but he usually takes them when he goes away. He can pick up the other gear more or less anywhere, but shoes his size aren't easy to find.

He drops them in, and smiles in the mirror. They are white, quite plain, with a three-inch heel.

Early to bed; he needs his sleep . . .

Bruno, who thinks he never dreams, has a recurring dream. Behind his lids his pale eyeballs flicker and twist like the sides of a snake. The dream is a room he enters in sleep and knows that part of him has been here for ever and can never get out again. There's a room inside the room, and a room in the inner room, and so on.

The outside room is blinding white, full of loud noises and enormous people. Compared to them he is utterly weak. They lift him, shake him, turn him upside down. Bruno has nothing to hide himself with. They are laughing at his penis, which is tiny, even for the tiny child he is. He can't control himself, although they all stare in a mixture of terror and enormous relief, he urinates copiously everywhere. At first it is very warm and wet but soon it is icy cold and smells and the huge attendants are going to punish him, they take a knife and stab at his penis . . . the only escape is to crawl back inside, to the dark inner room they had dragged him from, and Bruno can sometimes get back, in the dream, to a tiny space in the windowless darkness where he is entirely safe and warm.

This is the perfect heart of the dream. If he wakes now, without knowing why he'll be happy all day; he'll buy fish for Softly Softly, and send his typist home a few minutes early. But he hardly ever wakes to safety, he hardly ever buys fish for the cat.

Nearly always, the muscles that hold and squeeze grow suddenly rough and turn against him, making him choke and struggle away for now he knows the bitch is murderous, Bruno must wriggle away or die, but the only way out is to press down on the blinding terror of the first white room, violent laughter, the knife coming closer . . .

There is only one way to break the sequence. He has to make himself big, not small. He has to escape from the naked, tiny bundle of terror on the operating table. He has to look down on himself, instead. He has to join the murderous giants . . .

Bruno is not very kind to the cat when he wakes up as one of the torturers.

7

TIME IS EVERYTHING

Grace feels cheerful again today, last night's dread the faintest shadow. She stands in the door of the dining-room and blinks at the brilliant untenanted tables, white light on the squares of linen streaming towards the blue of the sea. In that blaze of morning the tiny old man at the very far end is almost invisible; George Kirk's greeting can barely be heard, and he only rises an inch in his chair before the earth pulls him down again.

Today she is able to ignore him. From the corner of her eye she watches, though, as he tries to summon a waiter. His arm trembles vaguely up from the table, his mouth opens without any sound. To think that yesterday he made her feel threatened! Spotting the waiter he's twitching towards, Grace shocks herself by cutting in and summoning the waiter herself instead with a clear, bold gesture. 'More coffee, please,' she says, and relenting, 'I think that gentleman's trying to call you.'

She finishes her meal at a quarter to nine, but the dining-room's only a quarter full, as if the hotel is emptying, but that's hardly possible, in June, unless everyone knows something she does not – the imminent arrival of a tidal wave? – some frightful impending disaster? – She wouldn't know, she hasn't read a paper.

(Though up in her room there's still an *Observer* she bought on Sunday but didn't read. She means to, though. She doesn't like waste. 'Dunne's Dark Lady', says the headline of the review on page 64, a long review of Ralph's last show. She hasn't seen it. It's waiting for her, a tidal wave, an impending disaster.)

This morning Grace is buoyant at the thought of mass destruction, the azure Channel rising up and washing little Britain away. At least they would all be in it together. And it made her own dying less than nothing. Grace isn't ready, yet, for that. She'd have to deal with it one day . . .

When I'm a hundred, say.
But it could be tomorrow.
Could be today.

Bruno feels cheerful too, although the Cortina is on the blink. A
little bit of an outing. He sits on the train rocking through the
green country, which doesn't seem as unpleasant as usual, it looks
quite smooth, at speed, from a distance, and the trees look just like
the trees in the ads for a classy model housing estate, you couldn't
deny they went into the décor; *trees*, he thinks; *fields*, he thinks,
and *English trees, English fields*. Bruno is a patriot. Put like that,
he definitely likes them.

Grace Stirling, Room 70, the Empire. It's all he needs to know,
for today. Timms's phonecall on Tuesday was put through to
Room 70. Probably not the first floor, which was good, any noise
wouldn't carry down to Reception, though of course he doesn't
mean to make any noise, he doesn't mean to have a confrontation.
Confronting isn't professional. He knows the rules, he knows the
score . . .

But at the same time, he is ready for action. Second post yesterday, like a sign, a parcel had arrived for Bruno, something he'd
wanted for a very long time. It was a replica gun, a Ruger Magnum,
a very good gun but a replica and so not covered by the gun laws,
not illegal for a man with a conviction for Grievous Bodily Harm.

No way of telling, from the outside, that it was a replica. Bruno
knew all there was to know about guns, and he looked the thing
over for nearly an hour, but there wasn't any way you could tell
it wasn't real.

And the evil old biddy who had wound him up and got him the
conviction in the first place couldn't do a thing to prevent him
having this. Anyone could buy a replica gun, a murderer could buy
a replica gun, it was straight-up legal, and now he has his Magnum,
so far as anyone else would know.

All it can't actually do is kill, and no one but Bruno knows it
can't. And if anyone should rumble that it isn't real – if anyone
should fail to be afraid, which is not very likely, Bruno considered,
as he first held the blunt-nosed weight in his hand – there is more
than one way to make people afraid, more than one way of killing
them.

Just after he thought it, he heard the echo, as if someone else was talking through him, and then he heard laughter, somebody laughing, laughter in bursts like a mad machine-gun, and Bruno looked in the mirror, startled, where he was admiring himself with the Magnum, and saw that the gunman in the mirror was laughing, and knew that Bruno had split again.

So today he hasn't brought it along. Perhaps it was all getting too exciting. Perhaps he was in danger of losing his cool, and he must be cool if he's working for Haines.

He travels light wih his overnight case — it may take time to get to grips with Stirling — and now as he's carried through the heart of Sussex, cool as the fields, cool as the trees, he suddenly knows that it's going to be fine, that the old woman will be nice and easy, that Bruno's completely together again (and he arches his back against the seat like a cat, enjoying the regular, sexual vibrations, stroking the leather flank of his bag).

But he has Brunnhilde's wig and shoes.

I'm not one person any more, thinks Paula as she wakes, very late, long after Arthur and Sally have left. There are two people under my skin. But does that make me more, or less?

Yesterday, as the news first sank in, she had felt miraculously enlarged, released from a prison of sameness. She'd felt important, too; bearer of astounding tidings, tidings that would change all their lives, a benign inversion of the sort of importance she sometimes imagined, when very bored: 'Arthur, I have cancer. I'm dying. But it's all right, I'm going to be brave.' Everything would be lived differently now, in the light of this amazing change. Nothing would be trivial any more; they would live in the light of the future . . .

The light hadn't managed to last the day. She rang Arthur at the Albion bursting with news, scared to begin. But he didn't remember to ask how she was, or why she hadn't gone to Seabourne. She waited to see how long it would take him, and listened for what seemed like hours to his monosyllabic complaints about Ian, the young Scottish porter.

'It's not because he drinks. Everyone drinks. But Ian gets drunk.'

'So you've told me. Often. So give him the boot.' But Arthur was too soft to give Ian the boot. When she felt his selfishness was thoroughly proved, Paula rang off in bitter delight. *Right then. He doesn't deserve to be told.*

Ten minutes later he rang back.

'You didn't go to Seabourne, did you?'

'Well done.' (But hearing his voice she begins to relent, ready to love him, ready to tell him, ready to give the amazing gift.)

'Is Grace OK?'

'Nothing to do with Grace,' she snaps.

'Oh that's all right then. I was worried. Look, since you're in London, could you pick up Sally? I want to keep an eye on Ian.'

'Shan't be there, sorry.' (*Right – that's it.*)

'What do you mean, you won't be there?'

'I've got a lot of thinking to do, as it happens. I prefer to do it away from you.'

'Where are you going? *Paula* . . .!'

That was satisfying, in its way, though as she'd sat through the lonely evening in her Camden flat she couldn't help wishing it had all been different, that she had told him, that they were together, and as the regrets became cold and sour she'd felt herself cooling towards the baby; hopeless, hopeless to have a child when she couldn't stand the father; hopeless for a child to have a father as stupid and annoying as Arthur.

The phone rang again and again. She jumped with hope, re-pressed the hope – only Arthur would let it ring twenty times, of course it was Arthur, he had to be punished – said, 'Bastard, bastard', to drown the noise, but when it stopped ringing, she wept.

This morning she feels distant, removed from the quarrel and from the baby. Lying in bed at ten a.m., a disorienting time to lie in bed, she runs her hands over her body. It feels like a body she doesn't quite know. It may have decided to change her life. Do her breasts and nipples really feel larger? They've always been large, but still . . . Her stomach, though, feels perfectly flat, a resolutely unpregnant stomach.

She begins, for the hundredth, the thousandth time since she saw the doctor yesterday morning, doing mental arithmetic. Four months ago was the end of February. Arthur's punctilious about using rubbers, even though she knows he wants a child. She's sure he'd used them every time, she's sure he used them carefully (and as she thinks of him, slow, careful, sensual, tender, entirely reliable, her heart yearns towards him, *Arthur*, and she wishes they were sharing this). So how is it possible that she's pregnant?

It *isn't* possible. Impossible, yes. She's suddenly certain and shoots up in bed, ready for the day, ready for work. Ridiculous, this lounging and brooding. The doctor was mad; she was mad to believe him.

– But is she relieved, or disappointed?

Both, and neither, and both in turn.

Fierce hope and awful despair.

She doesn't feel well. She lies down again.

The hope might be hormones, and the despair. So how can she find what she really feels? How do you escape biology?

Periods. Some nagging memory. Then she remembers, and clutches her stomach. It was spring, must have been quite early spring because it was very cold. Sally was having her afternoon sleep. We got right under the covers, and he rubbed me all over until I was warm. He was very excited, he wanted to do it although it was the end of my period and we had clean sheets just the day before.

He'd used the last condom. Of course, of course. But he wanted me and I wanted him, I needed Arthur to come inside and he did, I asked him, and it was lovely but oh, Arthur, that must have been it . . . and we couldn't keep quiet, I thought we'd wake Sally but before we could worry we fell asleep, he stayed inside and we fell asleep and the sperm, I suppose, swam up inside me and lay in wait until I was ready. My body must have known they were there. I must have ovulated ten days early. Some part of me must have wanted this baby, *if* there's a baby, so very badly . . .

If there's a baby. She has to know. The official result wasn't due till tomorrow. If she waited till then she'd go crazy. There were kits, tests, you could do it yourself, there were things you could get from the chemist . . .

She turns on her side. Now her body feels heavy, as if it lags behind her will. It's not herself but a shadow self, a shadow that has become unstuck, a shadow moving on its own. Not herself, but other. Wherever it goes, she has to go.

Half an hour later, she's standing in Boots, sifting through the wide array of packets. There are tests which turn pink, tests which turn blue, tests which produce a dark ring like an eye . . . The packets have pictures of roses or storks or very young women bulged like camels. None of this seems to apply to Paula. With assumed insouciance, she opens a packet and reads the glossy pamphlet inside.

The pharmacist is watching her. She scrunches open another packet.

'Can I help you?'

'Probably not. I want to see how they work.' She says it in her rudest voice, as if he wouldn't have a clue how they worked.

He smiles at her, disarmingly. 'Take my advice. Buy the cheapest. After all, it'll give you the same result . . .'

It's good advice, so Paula ignores it, buying the fastest and most expensive. She takes it back to her flat to try; a place where she'd never even dreamed of being pregnant, a place where she'd been herself, and free, a place where that lost self might be.

Bruno walks from Seabourne station. He takes the route through the Mariner Centre, a fine new shopping centre, he thinks, acres of sparkling glass and concrete, very new and very clean. Bruno is going to like this town. As he leaves the precinct and comes into one of the wide avenues which lead to the front, he looks judiciously at the hotels, big old buildings, historical, and thinks they too are nice, in their way, nearly as nice as the Mariner Centre, white and hopeful in the sun, and the flowerbeds are beautifully kept, so the heads of the flowers (and he checks this carefully, kneeling on the ground with his head on one side) are almost exactly on a level with each other, tidy as print, geometrically neat.

Not a lot of people about, this morning. He realises with a thrill of pleasure that he hasn't seen a single coloured face since getting on the train at Victoria. Except the ticket collector, but that didn't count. Seabourne's a place for your native English. When he makes a bit of money, he might come here, buy a little flat for weekends and holidays. Maybe it's almost too white, all the same, so he slips his mirrored sunglasses on, but the actual front, as he turns from the shelter of Western Avenue on to the Parade, still makes him pause and shiver a little, and tilt his body towards the land, for half the street simply isn't there and where it isn't, too much stares through, the unlevelled sand, the unbearable ocean, it stretches away to some fearful edge, it shifts and gleams like insanity, and Bruno hurries along the pavement, mouthing the names as he passes them, the safe names, the English names, names that shut out the roar of the sea, the Windsor, the Sandhurst, and now with relief the Empire, at last, he knew it was here, and he stands there a moment and gathers himself, his rigid back to the amazing water.

Grace comes out, and he comes in.

Grace is going out to the Butterfly House, a visit recommended by the Hotel Porter, something unkown and therefore youthful.

Grace is wearing the yellow waistcoat, and as she steps into brilliant sun she smiles a brave unseeing smile, eyes dark cracks in a pale crêpe mask, bracing her face for daylight.

An inch away, in a different story, Bruno passes into the dark, sweating a little in his summer suit, and the swing-doors sweep him safely past her, granting her grace for one more walk.

It's further than she thought. Even as she shrinks, the world extends. The longer Grace stays in Seabourne, the more she realises how much has changed, almost everything, in fact, except the three-levelled promenade in front of the Grand Parade. She doesn't know what she knows, any more. She keeps stopping, now, screwing up her eyes at the little drawing the Porter had given her, trying to see how far she's gone, frightened in case she goes too far.

– And yet I never went far at all. My eighty-five years have been a short round trip. If they'd told me when I was twenty-three, when I made my earth-shattering departure, if they'd said I would end up so near home, I think I should have thrown myself under the train which took me away that very first time.

She'd known what she wanted; not marriage but love. She'd wanted to be able to read Marie Stopes, and talk about her without fear. She wanted to get her hair cut short (she never did; it would have felt too naked). She wanted to use the mysterious, exciting names and addresses Miss Pitt had passed on. She wanted, most of all but least confidently, to write. *To be a writer.*

'One can't be a writer in Seabourne. One can't be a writer without seeing the world . . . Oen has – I have – to *live*, Mother.'

And Mother had stared, petrified. 'What do you mean by that, child?'

Grace couldn't explain about Marie Stopes. 'I mean, one has to see life.'

'Do you think your mother has never seen life?'

'Mother, I didn't mean to upset you.'

(And in retrospect, once Mother was dead and Grace could think about her more clearly, Grace knew that her mother had seen life, had probably lived too much for her father, had probably had lovers as well as admirers to keep her warm in the big dark house. She lived for herself, instinctively, and the only self she'd had a chance to develop was the laughing, imperious beauty who found the family sweet but a bore, who needed her luncheons, her afternoon outings from which she returned flushed and unkind, particularly strict about Grace's behaviour. Both she and Father were clear about that. Grace was to be a good girl; to her brother, her parents, the Missionary Society, God, the war effort, her baby sister.

And I was a good girl. I accepted it. Till it was all too much, and I broke away, but perhaps I never really broke away, perhaps some part of me was always crippled by putting other people before myself. But I tried. I was brave, a little bit brave. It wasn't easy to go to London.

She lived with a friend of Miss Pitt. Edwina turned out to be the daughter of a marquis, thus almost acceptable, though a former suffragette. And so the world began. Edwina was thirty, unmarried, rich: Edwina knew a lot about Art; Grace was overwhelmed by her confidence. Moreover, Edwina had a lover. Not a platonic lover. She would never say so directly to Grace, but Edwina had an affair – and with a foreigner.

One day Grace had managed to broach the subject.

'You must love Vladimir very much,' she said, as they drank cocoa together in a quiet corner of a smoky room where half-a dozen of Edwina's friends were discussing evolution. 'It must have been a terrible tragedy, losing all his possessions. Does he miss Russia horribly much?'

Edwina pealed wih laughter, showing her shiny, oversized teeth. 'Love? La!' she said. 'He's very amusing. He's a darling. But we've only known each other six months. Vladimir left to avoid the fighting, he's really the most frightful coward.'

It was difficult to digest. No one could love a coward, of course. Grace had seen them dancing at parties, their bodies touching from shoulder to hip, and she'd told herself it was love; she hadn't condemned, she had envied them.

'B-but if you don't love him,' she'd stuttered, a skin of cooling milk on her lips. 'If – well – I don't understand.'

'Have I shocked you, darling?' Edwina sighed, finishing her cocoa at a single gulp. 'You are a romantic . . . we aren't all nuns, you know. One has one's needs. One gets on with life . . . Gentlemen!' she called, rushing into the centre of the group of shirt-sleeved men. 'If you've finished your cocoa, have some whisky. It'll make you quarrelsome . . . and who will teach Grace about love?'

Grace had felt the heat then, rising and reddening, making her melt inside her clothes, driving her eyes to the carpet, and she'd risen, knocking her mug from the table, smelling the salt of her own fresh sweat, and told the carpet she was going to bed . . .

She remembers that heat with her whole body, for as she enters the Butterfly House, sixty years later but still on her feet, still sentient, still entirely alive, it comes to engulf her, tropical, heat as solid as the heat of flesh. She wasn't expecting this.

The butterflies swim across her vision, huge and stately, on waves of heat, their silky brightness reflecting the film of moisture on every leaf. Their immediacy is almost frightening; one touches her face, she starts away; the wing feels intimate and firm; then something else brushes against her hair and she shivers, despite the balmy warmth, but turns to find it is only a rising, trembling finger of bougainvillaea.

Touched; being touched. Now no one touched her. It was yet another circular movement; at twenty-three she was almost untouched, at the end of her life she was a virgin again. One took them for granted, the satisfied senses. A peacock butterfly lands on her arm, settles a moment on the blue of her blouse. Its red wings, cream-and-purple-eyed, seem to have the soft weight of velvet, but she knows if she strokes them they will fragment into thousands of severed scales. After a moment, it's off again, veering and hovering behind the verbena.

Red velvet notebooks. She remembers them suddenly, her mother's present when she left home. All this time later Grace still winces. They were much too pretty for a serious writer, but the pen slipped across the heavy cream paper as if she were writing on silk. They looked like sin, to Grace, which could not, of course, have been her mother's intention. Grace didn't actually sin, not yet. But she wondered, guessed, intended – and she wrote it all down, pages of it, in her black and definite copperplate hand.

One night she came back from a day of lusting over naked marble in the British Museum to find Edwina reading her notebook.

'That's private!' she shrieked in awful despair.

'You left it in the bathroom . . . I've read it now, too late to fuss. If you want some advice, *don't waste time*. Some of this guff is a waste of time. You ought to get out and see life . . .'

'I am seeing life . . .'

'Rubbish. You're walking around all day on your own and writing this stuff in the evenings . . .'

'But I want to be a writer . . .'

'Then we'll have to find you a situation. And you'll have to stop

writing about yourself. You ought to be clear and hard, like Pound
... oh darling – do stop crying.'

Grace had bought herself a typing machine, which she thought
would make her clearer and harder and more employable as well.
And she found herself an employer, or rather Edwina did; a Dr
Gruber who wanted a secretary five days a week from nine till
one.

He was a massive man of fifty with yellow-grey hair and striking,
overmarked features, bloodshot eyes under shaggy white eyebrows.
'What are you staring at?' he'd asked. 'Never seen an old German
Jew before?'

Within the month they were lovers. It usually happened in the
early afternoon on the brown leather sofa in his study. He would
ask her to stay to lunch; she always vowed she would not do *that*.
Not till he made it plain that he loved her, as she, of course, loved
him. Why else would she let him lift her dress, why was she letting
him now, again, and his fingers loosened her heavy hair so she felt
its weight fall down her neck and then everything was drawing her
down and she wanted it to go on for ever, the cracked brown
leather would burst in the sun and the power would go on rising
inside her, but Walther always stopped moving too soon, the wave
of feeling didn't quite break though day after day in his dusty study
it rose to the brink of curling over. Perhaps if he'd said that he
loved her ...

She wrote about it, not mentioning love. Never again a word in
those notebooks. Now she used neutral quarto paper and wrote
short poems, which she left for a week and then cut down to half
their length. Out went expressions of emotion, then adjectives,
unless hard and clear, then adjectives, unless negative. Tentatively
she showed them to Edwina. 'A teeny bit lush, but you're coming
along. Send them to whoever pays the most.'

By the time she met Ralph, eighteen months later, Grace was
publishing almost every month; she was almost a Londoner; she
was almost happy, and almost famous, and almost had a real life
of her own – which she threw in the air like a ball of glass, when
she met the arbitrary, amazing stranger.

Bruno looks himself in the hotel mirror, which is overgrown by
some spiteful weed – they must be mad to let it grow there – so
he looks as if he has leaves in his hair and straggling over his

second-best suit. He wants to wrench the thing from its brackets, smash the glass on the marble floor.

Relax, Bruno. Loose and cool. Half closing his eyes to avoid the leaves he checks that he's respectable. He straightens his jacket, unclenches his jaw. Looking good, he's looking good (though his face, as usual, is a disappointment).

It's ten a.m. On a day like this the old bag should be out enjoying herself, but he has to be sure. He approaches Reception, repressing the smile which hovers somewhere for he knows from experience it doesn't please (all through his childhood teachers had said it: 'Janes, don't snigger; Janes, wipe that smile off your face'.)

'Is Miss Grace Stirling in her room, please?'

There are only two girls in Reception. One of them is sorting the mail, and the other is talking on the switchboard. He addresses his question to the latter.

'. . . so I told him, he's got a cheek. I'm sorry, sir, what name did you say?'

'Stirling. Grace. I think it's Room 70.'

'Ringing her for you.'

She turns back to the switchboard, and as she does, swift as a cat Bruno leans forward over the counter and sweeps the key to Room 70 off the keyboard and into his pocket, where it makes a bulge.

Someone touches him on the shoulder. Bruno jerks. Bruno sweats.

'Did you say Miss Stirling?'

A shrivelled little man in a porter's uniform. Old and small. Bruno could crush him. 'Yes,' he snarls, then modifies it. 'Yes, that's right.' And absurdly, before he can stop his tongue flapping in his mouth, 'I'm a relative.'

'Thought I heard you right. Pity is, you just missed her. She must have gone out the door same instant you came in.'

'Oh dear,' says Bruno like an automaton, sitting grimly on the growing smile. From the desk the receptionist calls, 'No answer. She's not in her room.'

'I can tell you where she's gone. She's gone where I recommended her to. She's gone to the Butterfly House, that's where. Matter of fact, I drew her a map.' His nose was a red-veined cauliflower; how ugly human beings were. Bruno swallows his disgust, and tries to look grateful. 'That was very kind of you.'

'Twenty minutes' walk. Say half an hour.'

'I think I'll wait here. If there's somewhere I can get coffee . . .'

'Admiral's Bar. On your right, sir.'

And as soon as no one is looking, Bruno slips into the mirrored lift, *doing fine, doing well,* he tells the faces he find in there, turning to a self on either side, she can't get back for at least an hour, and the key tag bulges his jacket like a gun as he sails up into the roof of the Empire.

Third floor. Very quiet up here. Couldn't be better, from his point of view. He pushes the key into the lock. It turns easily. Bruno comes through.

Test-tube, stand, dropper, alarm clock, instruction sheet, beaker to catch the urine . . . Nothing could be worth all this palaver. Dip-stick. She'd forgotten the dip-stick. It wouldn't all fit on the bathroom shelf. The instruction sheet is very long, and darkly dimpled from falling in the basin. The times it stipulates are very precise. Paula loses any desire to piss. And her brain is playing tricks. However many times she reads through the sheet, she can't remember the steps in order.

Depressing, the narrow, dusty shelf with its load of sterile instruments. Sitting on the loo trying her best, with the seat cutting into the back of her thighs, squashing them out so they look old and fat. And the bathroom still smells very faintly of vomit. The vomit is part of being pregnant too.

The heat, the tenderness. The dance of the flesh. All of it cooled in the end to this.

Arthur thinks about Paula. The Albion gives him time to think. Today the thoughts aren't cheerful. Today the Albion's like a morgue. Phyllis had a visit the night before from a girlfriend who once worked with her. The girlfriend is married now, with two babies. The girlfriend kept saying how happy she was. ('London – I couldn't stand it now. It's a horrible place, is London.') This morning Phyllis is depressed. She's depressed enough to confide in Arthur.

'What do you think?' she presses him. 'I mean you've got Sally, what do you think?'

'Sorry,' says Arthur. 'I missed the question.'

'Whether it's true what Judy said. That children explain the meaning of life.'

'Well,' he says slowly. 'Maybe. Paula would say it was a load of garbage.'

'What do you think though? – Paula hasn't got one.'

'I think kids are great. The best. But hellish. And they're not supposed to give you things. Not meanings or happiness or anything. And life doesn't *mean*, in any case. It *is*.'

Phyllis is gratified by so much speech, but the genuine smile which transforms her face fades as she considers the last two sentences. 'What do you mean, *life doesn't mean*?'

'Well maybe I've missed it, the meaning of life. It's passed me by, unlike your friend Judy.'

'I think you're laughing at Judy.'

'Not at all. I'm just thick.'

'Meaning you think I'm thick.'

'Look, do we have to talk?' he asks, exasperated beyond politeness. 'I'm worried about Paula. She's disappeared.'

This thrilling dispatch is effective in silencing Phyllis for nearly half an hour, but it echoes horribly in Arthur's brain.

She could be anywhere. She could be dead. Or maybe she's got another man. It wouldn't surprise me. I'm no good.

Twenty-eight minutes after Arthur's bombshell, Phyllis forgets and starts talking again.

.'Ian's of the same opinion.'

'What opinion? What do you mean?'

'Same as Judy. Ian hates London. He never wanted to come here in the first place.'

'Why did he then?'

'No work in Scotland.'

'He doesn't do a lot in London, either . . .' That witticism cheers Arthur up enough to feel he's been unkind. 'He's all right, Ian. He's a nice kid.'

'He's a bit of a nutter. You mark my words.'

'We're all nutters, or we wouldn't be here.'

On cue, Ian crashes through the swing-doors.

Arthur smiles at him. 'Phyllis says you're a nutter.'

Phyllis goes scarlet, and plays with her hair. 'You're a rotten liar,' she says. 'I didn't say any such thing.'

Ian's short and wiry, with muscular arms too long for the rest of his body. He has white-grey eyes, startlingly bright, and a charmer's smile with a hint of devil, very white teeth and a pointed tongue, but he cried when a cat got run over in the road outside, and that's good enough for Arthur. Ian gets letters twice a week from his mother, and is usually well away before lunch. Ian's mother once phoned the hotel and asked to speak to the manager. It was plain she was drunk as well. She tried to tell Arthur a lot about her son, she tried to tell Arthur a lot about herself, she told him Ian's father was a lousy bastard, and then she had started to cry; Arthur could handle all that; he cleaned his nails while she cried some more, it was what he was used to at the hotel, most of the staff were either drunk or sad or else they were Latin American and too poor and young to be sad or drunk, working like slaves to send money home, and that in turn makes Arthur sad, that in turn makes Arthur drink, but Arthur is able to handle that, he soon cheers up, and he doesn't get drunk, but then Ian's mother starts to describe her cunt, in savage detail, with desperate hope, and Arthur tells her he has to go, Arthur asks her not to call again, and Arthur is lumbered for good with Ian.

'Bampot McGregor, they call me at home. Real headcase. And they ought to know. In this shitty city I can only get worse.'

Arthur looks at him. At least he's alive. The rest of the hotel is dying on its feet. At least he's young. Unlike Phyllis and me.

'Complaint from Room 32,' he says, but his tone is conversational, gentle. 'She says you fell downstairs with her case.'

'Lost my footing,' Ian smiles. 'A decent hotel should have a lift.'

'And you'd be out of a job, matey.'

'That wouldnae be so awfu'.'

After he's gone, Phyllis makes coffee and brings some to Arthur in the office. He knows that face, both grave and smug.

'Don't tell me. Some frightful fact about Ian.'

'I was going to say. What you said about Paula. I'm really sorry. Has she left you, then?' She can't prevent the lift in her voice. He can't prevent the drop in his spirits. A lump of lead in the middle of his chest. What if she's left me? *Paula*.

Paula is on Stage 2. It's supposed to take ten minutes. The alarm clock is set for the right time. She's trying not to get excited, but it *is* exciting how soon she'll know. After Stage 3, she'll have her answer.

The phone rings. She has three minutes. It might be Arthur. She wants it to be. She misses Arthur, desperately. She shuffles from the bathroom, trousers round her ankles, and makes a flying lunge for the phone.

'Is that Paul?' An American voice.

'Speaking.' Why couldn't it have been Arthur.

'I'm sorry, I want Paul.'

'This is Paula. Who are you?'

'Paul is a man. Is this some kind of joke? Are you some girlfriend? I'm calling from the USA.'

'Well you've got a wrong number, Buster. I hope it wasn't cheap.'

Paula slams the phone down, a victory, and rushes back to the bathroom, but it must be OK, the alarm hasn't rung . . .

Except that she'd failed to set it properly. Damn, damn, damn, damn. She's three minutes late already.

It doesn't matter. It will still work. It will still work because she needs it to. Heart in her mouth, she proceeds to Stage 3.

Time is everything, thinks Bruno, swift, efficient, totally cool. Fortunately the room is small. He'll find what he's looking for in minutes . . .

But there's a sweet, old-womanish smell which disturbs him, makes him want to gag. It's hot, too. The window is closed, the sun streams through the window. It makes him feel unpleasantly visible, though of course there's only the mirror to see him. His suited reflection looks very formal, kneeling on the floor by the bedside cupboard. When he finds the bible, he tries to sneer, but he can't help feeling that it's bad luck, and pushes it back into the tidy dark.

It's hard to be cool when you're very hot. He takes his jacket off, and feels naked. He wishes he'd brought along his gun. He would see it now, in his hip holster, a big dark bulge where he needed one. He wouldn't look naked if he wore a gun.

What if the maid comes back? Of course. The room looks tidy, but she might come back. He takes the DO NOT DISTURB sign, opens the door, shoots a look outside, flips the sign over the doorknob. The silence out there is rather unnerving. It's the middle of the season, isn't it. So where have all the people gone? Maybe they're all in Greece or Majorca. No one was loyal to England now. Or else they were out on the front, in the sun . . . it's as if the world has gone on without him, leaving him locked in this horrible room with the old woman's clothes and the smell and the clutter, leaving him trapped in the past on his own. He wants to get out. He wants this over.

But there's almost nothing here. The only photographs he can find are two musty old things in a silver frame, which can't be what they talked about on the phone. No documents; just some timetables, train timetables and tide-tables, and he looks at his watch; half an hour already since his conversation with the Porter; he daren't stay too long in case she changes her plans . . .

But maybe she expected her room to be searched. Maybe she knew he was on to her. Maybe she carries everything with her.

He sees himself snarling in the mirror, frustration, anger, a growing fear as he feels the plot run away through his fingers. He'd thought that today he'd make contact with something. He'd thought that today it would all become real. But there's nothing here he can report to Haines. There's nothing here except an old woman's clothes, and books, and biscuits, and toilet things . . .

He's in the bathroom, a last resort. A brush full of hair, a very old brush of split yellow plastic (or so he thinks; Bruno is incapable of recognising ivory), the bristles interwoven with disgusting grey hairs. He slams the wall-cabinet open. An empty glass. A round tin of powder. Toothpowder. Must be something for false teeth. He remembers the most revolting detail about the little episode in Barker's. The saleswoman had false teeth, which fell back in her throat when he punched her, cutting her gullet, nearly choking her. In court they said she had nearly died, and it counted against him quite severely. Of course in a rational world they'd be killed *before* their teeth started falling out.

A sudden memory of that sensation, the jolt, the lurch, her rattling breath. He wishes that Stirling was with him now. He wishes he had his hands on her, on her sickening stinking corrupt old body (he remembers his mother; she certainly stank in the last few months she was dying of cancer). Staring at the blank white screen of the bath, he's assailed by the familiar torturing images and leaves the bathroom to push them away.

Back in the bedroom he hides his head in the open door of her wardrobe, buries his face in some soft dark cloth, fleeing the light and the memories of the painful fluorescent on his mother's body, shrunken and naked, glimpsed one day near the end in the Home when his mother was too far gone to care what he saw, wrinkled skin like the skin on blancmange, butcher's-shop bones sticking through underneath, the little pot belly, the angry crimson ridges where the tit should be . . . Most disgusting of all was the swell of pity.

He takes a deep breath to steady himself.

Actually the cupboard doesn't smell bad. There's a perfume Bruno recognises, maybe something Brunnhilde wears, definitely not the smell of old age. Maybe something his mother wore when she was neither old nor shrivelled, something from one of the mysterious fluted bottles which sprayed a rain of fine scent when she pressed the woven gold balls at their necks.

In fact, the cupboard smells – exciting.

Bruno looks at his watch. He's been here now for forty-five minutes. Time's running out, he tells himself. But fear is exciting too. The perfumed garment is a dressing-gown, soft on his face, soft dark wool. Perfume and darkness; Bruno remembers. Time slips away. Time slips past.

I live in the past too much, thinks Grace. This week especially, I've kept looking back.

She doesn't believe in it, harking back. She tries so hard to believe in the future. But it's only natural, she tells herself, now there's nothing more to do in the shop, she doesn't have to play the businesswoman, she doesn't have to talk to customers, and Seabourne is silent except for all the memories. If Paula were here, I shouldn't hark back (for Paula never shows much interest in her past, Paula's more interested in talking than listening, but Paula explains the present to Grace, and that, she thinks, is how it should be).

Grace misses Paula now. The heat in the glasshouse is claustrophobic. She looks in the bag for the Portuguese photographs. Paula laughing, frowning at the sun, her startling eyes momentarily narrowed, Paula with Sally riding on her shoulders, Paula sturdy on a bright blue sea. To Grace, of course, Paula was a child, but she wasn't as young as she used to be . . .

Physically they were so unalike. And yet there was something, a certain look . . .

Perhaps she could come before Friday after all. Perhaps if Grace rang her now, this morning, and encouraged her to come down today . . .

If I walked straight back to the Empire. If I walked fast, I'd be there in twenty minutes. I could ring from my room, in comfort.

Bruno dreams his mother's room, when he was very small. It was full of shadows, and a soft pink light, a lampshade shaped like a pink half-moon with swinging tassels, a darker pink, pretty things he would never get close to later on when he had his own life, his parents told him to live his own life but he couldn't feel it, or furnish it . . .

Her skin would gleam as she dragged off her day clothes and paused, looked at her body in the mirror, it was soft and round with a little dark fur, anointing herself with oils and powders, clouds of powder like smoke in the light, before she dressed herself for the club, in wonderful, silken, lacy things; she had been a dancer or maybe a singer, she was cross and vague when he questioned her, but in any case she performed in the glass, and unless he spoke she forgot he was there and he crouched in the dark at the foot of the bed, sniffing, watching, enjoying her, but he never tried to touch her, because he knew that would make her cross.

Magical things – beads, earrings, boas – would be tried on once then tossed away and lie on the floor, smelling of her, and when she wasn't looking, he'd try them on, stroke the feathers against his face, feel the cold sides of the glittering beads where tiny reflections of the lampshade shone.

When she left she finally remembered him, swooped him up, never very gently (but a magical being couldn't also be gentle) and carried him off upstairs to his bed. Later he learned to creep back down. There was no one in the house; he was quite alone. He found out how to reach up to the dressing-table and press the button so the light came on. Then the dreamy pink world came out of the darkness. The floor would be littered with women's things, wonderful things he could rub against, silent things he could touch and hug, or stand inside them, miraculously changed.

Until one evening he went too fast, reached for the lamp too eagerly and caught the flex with his little finger so the delicate thing came crashing down and fell into ugly jagged pieces he tried to pick off the floor in the dark, cutting his fingers, whimpering, knowing his secret would be discovered and he would be shut out for ever. When she told his father, he picked Bruno up by the tender skin on the back of his neck and swung his body into the wall, slamming his elbow, his knee, his cheek against the hard plaster as if they weren't human, as if they were dead and couldn't be hurt, and perhaps he did wish Bruno was dead for he beat him until he couldn't stand up, 'Dirty little pansy! Little Mummy's boy!' and Bruno knew from his mother's face as she looked at his snivelling, sodden body dragging itself away to a corner that he couldn't ask anyone for pity, never ask anyone for help, and that was a lesson he carried through life; a victim is disgusting.

But he stole, and hid, a soft wool shawl, a pair of lace gloves, a satin petticoat, kept them under his bed, in the shadows, for no one ever cleaned his room, a secret softness to comfort him.

Bruno buries his face in the warmth of the past. He feels behind Grace's dressing-gown. Smooth and slippery. He brings it out. A grey silk blouse, quite classic. A suit, blue jersey, lined, not bad. An overcoat of grey-mauve tweed Brunnhilde wouldn't be seen dead in ... not many clothes for a week away. And the shoes. They were a fright. Great clumpy things with huge rubber soles.

'Darling, I wouldn't be seen dead in those.'

She's talking to Bruno, in the mirror. Bruno isn't snarling any more. Bruno draws the curtains, shuts out the sun. Bruno is pulling off his shoes, Bruno is pulling off his trousers. Bruno stands rigid in his socks and shirt. Bruno's penis sticks out in his underpants. Pull them off, the nasty things.

Soon there is just a nakedness, except for the watch and a down of red hair that shivers, electric with anticipation, an absence waiting to be filled.

For now the nakedness is disappearing. A different person, a missing person appears in the glass, someone tall and slim, a teeny bit awkward in her ladylike clothes. Pity she has no stockings. But the shoes are ready in the bottom of the bag. White will look rather good with grey, and grey is a flattering colour for a redhead. The wig that replaces the one she lost is a softer red, rather more mature, exactly right for the suit and blouse. An austere figure, perhaps a headmistress, someone with class, someone with power.

Skirts, of course, never quite do up. The hips are fine but the waist is not. The gap is hidden by the jacket at the back. From the front she is immaculate, except for whatever distends the skirt. She pats him, teasing. She's no longer alone. She has a secret. She is infinitely strong. She wriggles the skirt round so the unfastened zip now faces the front, and there is her friend, distended with power, rising pink and blunt to her greedy hand.

When she comes, the sperm whips out in a yellow cord that arcs and falls. Glistening patches of dying seed, which will shrivel, by the time Grace stares at it, to a puzzlingly familiar stain.

Walking towards what she takes to be another hall of brilliant colour, Grace is appalled to meet herself, almost touch herself, in a mirrored wall. So thin, so pale, so ladylike, so out of place in this dream jungle. Old, she thinks. How did I get so old. I shan't ring Paula. I shan't interfere. She's young and busy. I've dried to this. It was flat as paper, her mirror image, something which had blown into the Butterfly House, out of place and out of time, for here everything was young.

Ralph would have loved it here, of course. But what would he think of me, grown old. When he saw me first I was twenty-four but he said I looked less than twenty. Twenty-four was old to be unmarried. Extraordinary – *twenty-four was old*! So perhaps he was only being gallant, but we all looked younger, in those days, by the gentle gaslight of evening parties.

'What do you do?' he'd asked. 'You're so beautiful. Where do you come from? What's your name? May I fetch you a glass of whisky? Will you come outside and look at the moon?'

'Why do you ask me so many questions?' She was almost sophisticated, but she still blushed.

'I'm an artist, and I'm falling in love,' he informed her, and she saw he was drunk but also incredibly handsome, with his glossy red hair and fine pink skin.

'Oh Dunne! Come on! Not *again*,' shouted one of his friends, from across the room.

'Do you fall in love a great deal?' she'd asked, willing the heat away from her.

'I used to. But I shan't any more. I shall love you until I die,' he protested, and at that moment a great cheer went up from the people in the next room. 'There you are,' he said, and seized her hand. 'Come out in the square and look at the moon. It's a warm night. I shall pick you some lilac.'

Next morning she sang as she cleared the breakfast table ready for the maid to wash up. She left in the centre a terracotta jug in which the cones of lilac pushed, trembling lightly in the breeze from the window. She was still there staring when Edwina came down. Grace hadn't heard Vladimir on the stairs of late. Edwina was restless, and irritable.

'Can't stand those things,' said Edwina. 'Did you know that lilacs poison the soil? Nothing'll grow near a lilac tree.'

'Can't do much harm in a vase,' Grace said. 'In any case, Ralph Dunne picked them.'

'Be careful, Grace. Stay away from him. He uses women up like paints.'

'He said you'd asked him to paint your portrait.'

Astonishingly, two islands of red, not at all like Grace's solid blush, appeared on Edwina's olive cheeks.

'I was hardly serious,' she said. 'He has talent. But he's conceited. And very young. So very young . . .' she sighed, and stared at the offending flowers. 'He'll stop you writing, Grace . . . Mary!' she suddenly screamed for the maid. 'Throw these hideous things away.'

'No,' said Grace. 'I'll take them. I want them in my bedroom.'

'You should look for another place,' said Edwina. 'I'm too old to live with a circus of people. I've done my best to help you, Grace. It can't go on for ever.'

Ralph changed her life, of course; at the time it seemed entirely for good. Looking back on it, though, a lifetime later, Grace notices what she lost, as well. Edwina; she was a good friend. She had courage, and generosity, and she told me things I had to be told. Grace met her once in Regent Stret when they were both in their fifties, and Grace was at last undergoing her painfully belated menopause. She knew Edwina had done well; she was a keeper in one of the great national museums, the first woman ever to hold such a post. She looked tired out by the battle, but her face was full of intelligent life. She never married, no . . . 'And you?' she asked Grace, more tentative, now, than she ever was twenty years before. 'I know you were in all those wonderful pictures . . . I underestimated Dunne, of course.' 'Yes,' Grace had said, obscurely ashamed. 'You did, a little . . . I'm a headmistress,' and Edwina's face held a little sorrow, perhaps a jot of triumph too, and she didn't have time to stop for tea, the light in her face was already going out, hurrying on to the next encounter.

I suppose she's dead, like everyone else. I lost Edwina, through loving Ralph, and I lost my burning will for fame, and if you don't burn, it never comes. At the end of her life she was quite unknown except as the face that Ralph invented.

Better to be private, though, perhaps. She couldn't have stood people staring at her, poking about, uncovering her secrets, whispering things behind her back. She knew about that side of things, it had happened to Ralph in his late thirties as his fame grew and their love diminished and he grew more bitter and less happy. Some of it he imagined, of course. But some of it was true.

What she never got used to was watching him become a figure in other peoples' lives, people, maybe, he never even knew, people who loved or hated him, people who thought he belonged to them.

Grim and diminished, Bruno strips and dresses himself again, his back to the mirror, his back to the sun, dressing himself with mechanical haste, slipping her clothes away in the darkness. It can't have happened while he was working. It didn't happen, period. Bruno doesn't look at the stain on the floor. Bruno can't bear to see that stain. He stares at the vacancy of the walls, long and narrow, the narrowing future, keep on the straight and narrow, Bruno. It will never happen again.

A dragging, lumbering sound in the distance.

Someone coming along the landing, could be someone very old. The sound comes closer, and sighing breaths. Automatically, he gets behind the door, adrenalin surging, Bruno is ready for anything that he has to do, a man has to do what a man has to do, but he flinches sharply at the knock on the door. After a moment he understands.

The maid, must be. At least it's not *her*. She knocks twice. *Do not disturb*, she mutters; waits; slowly drags away.

Get out fast while his luck still holds.

A last look round. His luck improves. Something underneath the old newspaper, the corner of an envelope. A flimsy envelope, empty. But it has a name, and an address, and the name is extremely foreign-looking, and Czechoslovakia is the address.

Enough to stop Bruno feeling despair. He copies it into his pocket notebook.

In any case, there's no way to give up. The evil (for they are evil, he's sure) has become the thing he is living for . . .

He slips away, by the stairs this time, padding down through the echoing storeys, wondering where all the people have gone, hearing the emptiness circle him, so very little, so little to go on.

(And Bruno needs the whole universe, galaxies must be offered up, since enough of one world has never been given him; Bruno has never had anything to lose. Grace may have lost, but she lost such riches!)

Now she would run away, if she could, but Grace's bones no longer run. Too much at once, too overwhelming. The Ipomea blossoms, brimming with sunlight, wide as saucers, fragile as skin, should never have bloomed so generously in Seabourne's English June. The butterflies should have been spilled across the miles and seasons of distant jungles, not pooled together in a cube of hot glass.

Too much, too dizzy, but – a glory. The yellow swallow-tails dip and soar, a great blue Morpho looms like a piece of satin fallen from the summer sky, and when Grace turns her face away she finds herself staring at the pollen-tipped tongue of a large hibiscus, improbably brilliant, the pistil coated with sun-gold seed. Too much, too soon, too much confusion, objects blurring into sensations, maybe the world's all here and now if she could only dissolve with it . . . Ralph, she thinks. It's Ralph again.

There was almost too much happiness. Six months in Portugal. She told her family she was travelling with her latest employer, a publisher, 'looking for foreign manuscripts'. The story was transparently thin. If they didn't believe her, they gave no sign, so far away on the Sussex coast where the wind blew chill in the evenings and the windows rattled in the empty parlour. They wrote dull letters she only skimmed. Lucy was growing up, they said. They hoped Grace would come and see her sister. Chidhood lasted such a short time . . .

'My childhood seemed to go on for ever,' she mused to Ralph, tearing up the letter as they had torn up so much of the past. He was sitting with her on the rocky terrace outside the whitewashed cottage they were renting, eating a peach, staring down at the sea, his chair tipped back, his feet on the table.

'Well now you've escaped,' he said. 'Now you're with me. We shan't ever go back.'

'The money will run out . . .'

'Then we'll live together in London.'

'I couldn't . . . not in England.'

'Don't say *couldn't*,' he said, swallowing down the last of the peach, swinging his feet off the table. He'd come and kissed her, hot flesh, hot juice, pressing so hard she cried out in pain. 'We can do whatever we want,' he urged her, talking through kisses, undoing her hair. 'There aren't any rules, after that stupid war . . . there's nothing bad but killing. You can *feel* how right we are.'

They'd gone into the house together. The square of window was sapphire blue. She had never known she had so much skin, that every inch of it was smooth and warm and melted into an inch of him, that she wasn't tall and awkward and bony but infinite, fluid, a wave extending through the walls of the house to the sea and the sky; she contained them all, she was not contained, she rose, she swam, she came.

Too much, too fast, too soon. When Ralph got drunk after a bad day's painting and shouted for more in a small hotel, she shrank into herself again. It didn't matter that others were drunk, it didn't matter that the owner laughed. Ralph's face was red and his voice was coarse and he wanted her to be drunk with him, he wanted her to be part of it, but she had gone far away from him. She was Grace Stirling, she was English, she wished she had never left home.

Next morning he'd sleep till ten or eleven and she'd tiptoe into the bedroom to find him covered by a single sheet. The curtains peeled from a blaze of blue; the walls were white in the sunlight; one eye opened above the sheet, opening blue on a hopeful day, falling in love with the world again, pink and naked, and he was her baby.

The country was almost too beautiful, too bright, too rich, too sweet. The western edge of Europe, further south than she'd ever been; walnuts, figs, apricots; miles and miles of shining sand without piers, promenades, breakwaters, just the great Atlantic breakers, surprisingly cold as they curled and fell on the baking beach in a shining line that ran straight as far as the eye could see, going on for ever, it would never end . . .

Yellow mimosa, rose-red wine, wild mauve irises tongued with orange. In the middle months of Portugal, Ralph painted like a man possessed. The colours flared from the canvas, light in living impasto curls. He altered nothing, abandoned nothing; each painting was a perfect birth.

'You make me so creative,' he'd said to Grace one evening.' I could live down here for ever, if I could get hold of some decent paint . . . that's not a problem you run across in your line of business.'

There was a pause. Grace cut a large slice of rough bread. 'I haven't been doing much business.'

Ralph took the slice, bit out a large chunk, and gave it back to her. 'I've seen you scribbling away . . . I've painted you doing it. There's evidence . . .'

'Diaries. Letters. Personal stuff.'

'You'll have to be my muse instead.'

'I can't be a muse for ever, darling . . .'

'You're giving me so much,' he told her, reaching across to stroke her cheek. 'One day you'll see what we've done together. These paintings will hang all over the world . . .'

'I'm glad,' she said, and she was. She had always wanted to give, she had always been praised for giving as a child, she had always wanted to be received. She felt she had given herself completely, so why was she suddenly discontented? Why did she have to complicate things?

Next day the shadow had vanished. She sat in the field against the cool stone wall, her calves two heavy hot loaves in the sun, immersed in Katherine Mansfield. The page was split between sun and shade, everything blindingly clear and simple, she was a woman, she loved a man. Four feet away, Ralph painted her. A butterfly landed on her large bare toe, riffled its wings, then settled. With a twitch of excitement, Ralph touched it in. She knew it would fly in a minute; she closed her eyes and thought *now* and *here, hold this moment, it will always be mine*; she belonged in that inch of baking skin, the featherlight weight of the butterfly's body.

'Damn,' he said, 'it's gone.'

She opened her eyes and saw it weaving up and away across the long grass, vanishing under the orange-trees, but his brush continued to paint it in. 'Never mind, darling, you've caught it,' she whispered.

The money ran out, of course, and so did their supply of contraceptives, and they were in a Catholic country. He couldn't believe she wouldn't sleep with him.

'I'll be very careful. It's a tiny risk. And what would it matter? I want to marry you. I've told you before, you should have six sons.'

Too much, too messy, too much pain. The last five days were hell. She couldn't express it, but she knew what she felt, she couldn't become a mother yet, she hadn't been a person for long enough.

On their very last night, he forced her to talk, by weeping when she turned him down, punching the whitewashed wall and weeping.

The sea was wild outside on the rocks. It was late, and both of them were desperately tired.

'We love each other. I'm part of you. I want you to be part of me. Grace, you're everything to me. I've had so many women, but I've only loved you.' Perhaps he wasn't quite in despair, for she saw his sex was red and erect, though even that looked wounded.

'I can't. Don't ask me.' Her voice sounded cold, but came from levels of frozen pain.

'You don't love me. You never did.'

'You can't say that. It isn't true.' They didn't come, though she summoned them, the burning words she needed.

'You're too selfish to love anyone.' He was still drinking, with savage relish, *see how you make me hurt myself*. His words were slurred and thick by now but the will to hurt her was clear as a knife. 'You've been turning me down for a week. Do you want me to go to someone else? I'm a normal man. I have my needs.'

'You're drunk. You don't know what you're saying.' (For she hadn't been selfish; she had never been selfish.)

'*You* never drink, of course. Oh no. Miss Stirling is too prim to drink.'

'I had a glass. Let's go to sleep, we're going home tomorrow.'

'I can't sleep like *this*,' he roared, lurching to his feet, standing by the bed with his angry penis a foot from her face. 'What are you going to do about it? Do you understand what men want?'

Grace had buried her head in the pillow, then, wishing she'd died before this had happened, the awful shame they would feel tomorrow, and how would she ever love him again . . . He was silent then, as she lay face down, except for his curiously laboured breath, it was almost a sob as she drifted away, wine and fish always made her sleepy and scenes made her sleepy quicker still, the wordless dignity of sleep, but as she escaped she half recognised Ralph's final roar, with its note of loss.

Next day when she woke he was already up, frying some kind of breakfast in the kitchen next door, and she could smell coffee. He was trying to say sorry. She remembered the row, and wished she weren't hungry, but Grace was always hungry. She started to relent. Perhaps it wasn't so bad. He was only drunk, men did get drunk. She opened her eyes and began to sit up. She would help set the tray; he always forgot things, milk or salt or cutlery.

Then she saw the stain on the grey wool blanket, the first night cold enough for them to use it, and knew what it was, and closed her eyes. That stain would always lie between them. Irrelevantly, knowing it was foolish even as the thought formed and would not unform, she wondered, *what would Mother say?* But she knows that Mother would sit there silent, for Grace has entered another world, no longer her daughter, no longer a lady.

It was true, though, everything Mother had said, who had lived her life in ante-rooms, who had come to Speech Day, however late, who had sheltered her secrets behind 'poor Archie'. Once you stepped through here, into this foreign place, there was nothing at all to protect you. Everything dead. Everything dirty. Life, which was sacred, could turn to a stain.

Paula feels a surge of exaltation the moment before she will know the truth, the moment before she checks that it's there, the 'clear blue' that the packet promises, the blue which will prove that her baby's alive, clear blue, the colour of seas, the colour of the place where life began. I'm alive, she thinks, doubly alive. A minute, forty seconds, twenty, ten, and her breath sighs out as she withdraws the dipstick from the test-tube, swallows, plunges it into a stream of cold water.

But nothing happens. Not a shadow of blue. It remains pure white, as white as the water, as white as unending nothingness. She can't believe it. She stares, stupid, turns the tap harder, shakes the dip-stick, and her whole self becomes that pure white ache.

Perhaps it's died ... or it's never lived. She is clutching her stomach as if in pain, crouching on the floor and rocking herself, not knowing what she is doing. If only the baby could speak. If only it could just say it was there. She thinks her body tells her it's there, but at once the conviction ebbs away, how can she know what her body says when all these voices contend in her head.

Instinct won't do. She'll go back to the chemist. The test could be wrong (of course; of course; she left Stage 2 several minutes too long, that would be it, that stupid phonecall).

Heavily, she walks through the familiar streets, which are never entirely familiar, in fact, since nearly every week one shop goes broke and another opens, rashly hopeful. She's been away for less than a month, but there are different beggars, different tramps, and today she doesn't feel like meeting their eyes, today she doesn't feel like giving them anything, but all the same she gives fifty pence to an old woman with a torn frilled blouse and knotted legs half wrapped in sacking, who sits singing outside one of the new estate agents. The woman looks up with shrewd dark eyes. 'That won't buy us much,' she says. 'Babies. Got to feed the babies.' She must be seventy if she's a day.

In the chemist, Paula snatches the first test she sees, refusing to meet the eye of the pharmacist, and walks back home feeling utterly depressed, with nothing to look forward to but messing with urine, alone in her damp unpleasant bathroom, and then a final absence of colour, absence of Arthur, absence of hope.

Which is not to say she could feel no worse, for when she gets home and reads the new packet she finds it only works with the first urine of the day; she can't bear to trudge back to the chemist's again; so now she has to live through another afternoon, another evening of wondering, and she goes to the phone to ring Francesca, if she doesn't talk to someone she's going to go mad, and she only notices just in time, when her finger can still block the final digit, that the number she's ringing, automatically, blindly, is Arthur's number.

Our number.

But pride stops her. *On my own.*

'Was that a single or a double?' asks the man in the foyer of the bed and breakfast.

'Single. I only booked it yesterday.' (*If you haven't booked the room, I'll kick you in the face.*)

'No one of that name here.'

'There'd better be.'

It catches the man's attention. He looks up briefly, then back at his list.

'Oh JANUS,' he says. 'You're Mr JANUS, are you. I thought you said you was James.'

Is he taking the mickey? Bruno wonders. *Janus.* It sounded disgusting. '*Janes*,' he says. 'J-A-N-E-S. I'll pay you now.'

'No need for that.'

'I'll pay you now, I said.'

'Fifteen pounds for a single.'

'Right.'

'Plus VAT. That's sixteen-fifty.'

'Right.'

'Oh, and if you want breakfast . . .'

'Of course I want breakfast. It's bed and breakfast. That's what you call yourselves, a bed and breakfast.'

Once again there is something in his voice that makes the man pause, and decide not to say, as he was just about to, '*if you want breakfast, that's two pounds extra.*'

Going up the narrow stairs which smell unpleasant, a mixture, he thinks, of disinfectant and urine, Bruno thinks about life. A single room. That's what he always asks for. Ever since he had left his family – and you couldn't say he was close to his family – he'd been on his own completely. He supposes he'll always be alone. Good job he's not soft, and doesn't get lonely. The world of the single was what he knew. It was a different world, the world of the double. Briefly he wonders, but he can't imagine it. He and Brunnhilde are fine on their own.

And in any case, if things go right, if this operation goes according to plan, there'll be a lot of people interested in me. There'll be . . . *followers*. There'll be more of us.

Time to go home, thinks Grace. The quality of light has changed. Surprising that here are so few visitors; surely this paradise is worth a visit . . . It seemed a paradise to her. Fragile, but a paradise. And yet, the light is thinner, paler . . .

Were they happy, the butterflies? Did they have any consciousness, or were they just part of the scene she was looking at, attributes like colour or scent?

When she looked back on Portugal (and all her life she's looked back on it) she didn't question their happiness, didn't remember the last five days. She saw two images, paradisal; the open window, a blaze of blue, narrowing, shrinking, but never less bright, and the oranges, groves of orange-trees, dark shiny leaves and burning fruit, oranges as far as the eye could see, so many, so bright, so sweet. She tried not to think of that faint sticky stain.

But now she has remembered it. Thoughtful, she drifts towards the exit.

The big hibiscus is covered in blossoms at different stages in their day of life. The floor underneath has its twisted remnants, still orangey red but going dark, turning back from flowers, it seems, to leaves. A day, they lived, two days at the most, a day of apparently infinite vigour, the pistils, heavy with yellow seed, sticking straight up at the sunlight. In this glass world they could not take root, but the seeds pushed out regardless, prodigal, spilling on the ground and being replaced till winter came and the flowers shrivelled.

It was wasteful, though. It was artificial.

It wasn't paradise at all.

'Are you open all year round?' she asks the woman selling tickets.

'Oh no. Just May to October.'

'What happens after that?'

'We shut.'

'I mean, what happens to the butterflies?'

'They don't live long, butterflies. Some of them lay eggs. So next year we can start fresh. Did you see where they're hatching out?'

Grace walks back in, stiff-limbed. There are rows of bark-brown chrysalides hanging in a glass-fronted case in the corner. They look like last winter's dead leaves, dry and dull and curled in on themselves. Then one of them starts to twitch, and another one further down the row. It's rather horrible, she thinks, to see something quite so intimate, as the twitching increases, becomes a convulsion. Like looking at something buried alive, desperate to get up into the light.

How strange, how frightening birth was. She had never been able to imagine it; a body growing inside your own, getting stronger and larger and more independent, feeding and swelling until the day came when it had to burst out, and you had to let it.

– I never let him make me pregnant. It seemed like a victory, at the time, something snatched from the jaws of defeat. Refusing to be overwhelmed . . . Ten years or more Ralph pleaded with me. I didn't mean it to be final, or perhaps I did, but I fooled myself . . . I was only twenty-nine, only thirty-two, only thirty-four, only thirty-seven, there would soon be more money, I could give up teaching and then I would get my novel written and when it was written there would be more time . . . there would always be more time: until suddenly time was running out, fascism in Spain and Germany, the headlines in the papers going dark, Ralph going off to fight in Spain, but I wouldn't see it, I still kept on – 'One can have a child in one's forties; Mother had Lucy at thirty-nine . . .' On the Pathe News in the cinema there was a bustle of grave-faced men in suits, their gestures more clipped and stern than usual, and in Current Affairs, a girl asked Grace with the innocent keenness of a theatre-goer, 'What was the *last* war like?' – as if the next one were a foregone conclusion, and Ralph said it was, but Grace was suspicious; 'You can't expect me to have a child just because you're frightened of dying!' 'I'm not afraid of anything, bitch!' – it was true, he wasn't, she should never have said it and then perhaps he wouldn't have gone and volunteered the second time: 'I'm only asking you to love me. If you did, you would have our child. Let's go away together, please, tomorrow, somewhere in Europe where we could be happy and paint and have a family . . .' 'It's too late for Europe. You haven't seen the papers. Oh Ralph, you were right, we've left it too late.'

What finished it, then? At what precise point did all the bitter little changes blend together and overturn the structure of things? When did they see it could not be stopped? Why did the train roar off the track?

Very quiet, in Bruno's room. A stick-shaped room, more like a cupboard, not so much a single as a half. 'TV and shower' sounded quite luxurious, but the TV's a snowstorm of black and white and the shower is minute, with a torn green curtain, a corner of the room, not a room in itself, so everything smells damp and faintly unpleasant, and the carpet is stained with other people's dirty water. He'd thought of this trip as a bit of a treat, but he's been cheated, as usual. He lies on the bed, curled on his side, kicking, kicking, scuffing up the yellow bedspread, a frustrating thing to kick at for it catches at his heels, unsatisfying as an empty skin, frustrating as kicking at the body of your mother after she had died and left you alone.

Only violence against a real live victim, while it lasts, is never disappointing.

And the other thing. That's always exciting. To be someone else, to escape, to star.

It's four o'clock. The shops are still open.

Grace has stayed out much longer than she meant. In the Butterfly House one lost track of time, for time and place were fictional. She's suddenly tired as death itself. Coming out into the declining day she sees clouds sprint across the expanse of sky as if life has slipped into one of those films she used to show at school in the sixties, where buds opened in a couple of minutes and shrivelled again before one's eyes.

Perhaps someone's eager to get her life over. Perhaps they have grown bored with her, and the sun will start to sprint round the globe until the whole sequence is finally through. God knows it's been long enough already, and after all this standing, walking, staring, her bones are aching with weariness.

It's your blood sugar, she tells herself sharply. She goes to a kiosk where a bored young man goes on listening to the radio and smoking for nearly a minute while she stands and waits, and life is back in the familiar slow motion. She's disappearing, losing impact, in the end she'll be soundless, without dimension, only habit will keep her here, alive, and only she will notice it.

But she wants to be here. She will raise her blood sugar. 'One ice-cream cornet, a large one, please,' she says very firmly, and he looks surprised.

It's worth going on, just to surprise them. In any case, she is still not bored. She still wants to know what's just round the corner.

Afraid. That night, Paula's afraid. Francesca can't make it till Thursday night. Paula goes to bed very early, at nine, intending to wake up early, too, and do the test at the earliest moment. The flat's very quiet; the flat's very large. As she passes the doorways to empty rooms on her way to bed with a cup of hot milk, the flat seems very dark indeed, and not entirely quiet after all, full of small clicks and rustling noises she hadn't noticed earlier that evening, sliding clicks and rustles and falls. She closes her door with a sense of relief, but then she feels shut in.

Buildings, she thinks, never have this power unless you are alone in them. They never get listened to unless you're alone. At Arthur's, the house is inaudible; Arthur's house has been overrun. The three of us made so much noise . . . in Arthur's case, it was not so much talking as singing, walking, making things, cooking, shifting about on the furniture, which groaned under his massiveness. Arthur bumping into things; he was much too big not to bump into things. Very big and surprisingly strong. He could pick her up as if she were a baby, whisk her in the air like a pastry brush, and she weighed nearly ten stone: but then, Arthur must weigh seventeen . . .

Arthur. He was her security. Arthur was ballast for her heart, for her bed. Arthur kept off the rustles, the shadows. Arthur wouldn't let them break down the door, Arthur would die before he let her be frightened, Arthur had *told* her he'd die for her, soberly and quietly, not asking for comment, one day out of the blue when she thought he was asleep, lying on the floor with sleeping Sally. His tone was so dull that she didn't hear him, she thought he'd said something everyday like, 'Give me the paper' or 'Close the door'. After a moment she realised she hadn't heard him. 'What? she said, without much interest. 'You know I'd die for you or Sally.'

But now she lies in the dark on her own and the rhythm of the train begins again, in Camden the sound is a little further off, but the same line with the same trains and the same sense, when you can't see them, that any of them might be carrying poison, and now the poison's for someone new . . .

If it is there, under my skin. Tiny and bare as a sleeping mouse. Arthur has gone so far away, and no one is here to help me protect you.

(Impossibly hard to protect a baby. One has to see so far in the future. In 1957 Paula was nine, and the 'peaceful atom' was fairly new, *Sunshine Atom*, bringer of warmth, but all new things have teething troubles and that October at the Windscale power plant a massive uranium fire broke out and the plumes of radiation blew far over Europe, though the government said, once it managed to say anything, that there was nothing to worry about; cows from an area two hundred miles square had their milk tipped into the Irish Sea, waves and waves of dirty milk, but still there was nothing to worry about . . .

Twenty-five years later, somebody noticed that too many women who had lived near Windscale were giving birth to Down's Syndrome babies. Some of those mothers who had 'lived near' Windscale were not, as conventionally understood, 'alive' in October 1957, some of them were only waiting to live, they were babies themselves, unborn babies, foetuses curled in their own mothers' wombs, protected as well as flesh could protect them but not well enough to protect their egg-cells, not well enough to protect them from their futures . . .

Although their mothers had dreamed of grandchildren, how could they protect what was only dreamed?)

*   *   *

When Grace gets back to the Empire she finds that things are breaking down.

That cross little girl had not bothered to clean. Her bed is exactly as she had left it, pulled up neatly but not properly made, the pillow unplumped, the corners unmitred. Anger renews her energy. She rings Reception and makes her complaint.

'Room 70 is it? That'd be Faith . . . hang on, she's just come down the stairs.'

Faith is put on the line.

'Grace Stirling. Room 70. My room hasn't been cleaned.'

'Well it's tea-time now. I'm going off duty.'

Grace is speechless with fury for a second. 'Then put me through to the manager.'

Faith is afraid. Till the baby is born, she has to be invisible. 'I'm going to get some air,' she breathes. 'I'll have a look in when I get back.'

'It's not good enough, is it,' Grace says, using her cold, headmistress's voice. 'Not cleaning a room till past four o'clock.'

'But I tried,' squeaks Faith, utterly indignant. 'I knocked and knocked. You had your DO NOT DISTURB sign up. It was about eleven. You must've been asleep.'

'Nonsense. I never sleep till eleven . . .' but Grace is tired. It doesn't matter. 'You'd better come up and do it now.'

When Faith appears, Grace is glacially cool, and Faith's demeanour is hardly appeasing, indeed she expresses the essence of huff with her bustling tummy and sharp black eyes.

'I'll go out and let you get on with it.' Grace's voice intimates what a nuisance this is, but nothing seems to get though to the girl, who actually mutters, 'Good idea.'

Glancing back, however, as she lets herself out, Grace is disconcerted to discover that the door-handle bears a DO NOT DISTURB sign, just as the maid had said. She must have been too tired to notice, earlier. Some mistake. Forget about it. Too old to fuss, not enough time left.

Faith knows she is doing too much, too much for herself and for the baby. She'd been longing for a gentle walk in clean sea air, a sit in a café. She'd have talked to the baby in her head, telling it to rest while Mum rested, gathering strength for what was to come.

She'd have said she was sorry for flinging it about, an eight-month baby couldn't enjoy being bent and squashed as its mother cleaned . . . Now the evil old bag had to haul her back and make her work some more. They were evil, some of them, no other word for it, Room 70's face was thin and mean when she made her point about having to go out, she only thinks about herself, she wouldn't give a thought to me and my baby. People like us don't exist, for her. If her room was clean, she'd rather die than let the two of us through that door.

Faith spots a stain on the carpet that she hadn't noticed yesterday. She doesn't want to get down on her knees, but life means doing things you don't want to do, and she's lurching towards a kneeling position when suddenly the phone rings. She steadies herself, then picks it up. *I expect its Fräulein Hitler, asking if I've finished, I'll tell her to go and stuff herself . . .*

'Hello,' she says, submissively.

There's someone there, breathing quietly. 'Who is it?' Someone, but he doesn't speak, or else there is a fault on the line. After ten seconds, she puts it down, and forgets about the stain on the carpet as the baby kicks high under her rib-cage, look, I'm here, I'm getting impatient.

Bruno telephones twice more that evening, touching base, getting close to Stirling, he's hated that voice for quite a long time, a shiver of excitement as he waits for it. The first time he rings, she isn't there, but the voice that answers, sounding nervous, or cautious, is a woman's voice, young, and very Irish, which is interesting given the Irish connection the files suggested from the start, and Bruno replaces the phone well pleased. The second two times he gets the old bag herself.

It's a bit like using binoculars, creeping up on them when they can't see you, so close you could almost touch an arm, a bitten lip, a patch of bare neck . . . Now he's so close he can hear the faint arthritic catch as the old bitch answers, 'Hallo? *Ha-llo?*' – he leaves her hanging.

Right where he wants her, waiting for him. Tomorrow he'll come and see her again.

The phonecalls leave him overexcited. He's restless in any case, tight with adrenalin, much too big for this damp little cage with its sad blurred television. He pulls back the curtains, claustrophobic, battle is coming, battle very soon, and sees it staring at him, white and clean, the perfect circle of a full moon.

Half a mile away along the front Grace Stirling stands before her open curtains, looking at it too, asking it questions, glad that the winds have cleared the cloud. Is it the same moon she's seen all her life? – the face a little sadder and older perhaps but also more mysterious, wearing away like an unspent coin . . . Then she looks again, and it's actually smiling. The third time she looks the face has gone but the beautiful silver landscape remains, out of our reach, still there, still serene, and she longs to draw on that circle of calm.

For things are a little unsettling. Silly things, they may all be nonsense, she isn't unsettled, she won't make a fuss.

All the same, there was a stain. A stain on the carpet. It's still there. After the stupid little girl had gone. Not that Grace minds about dirt that much At first she thought it was any old stain and was only surprised she hadn't seen it before, but then she was suddenly perfectly sure that it wasn't there till this afternoon, so perhaps it had happened while she was out . . . But a stain, just any stain, wouldn't have mattered . . . till she went to her wardrobe to change for dinner and found it was on her skirt as well, the same familiar sticky shadow.

It was nonsense, of course. It couldn't be. Thinking back had done it, in the Butterfly House, dwelling on things that were best forgotten . . . Of course she has better things to think about, the future, she tells herself, sternly, now, looking out at the predictable, glorious path of silver leading across the sea. Around the corner of the cliffs, just out of her sight but in her mind's eye, there would be another path of light, narrower, yellower, man-made light, sweeping out from the Lighthouse across that dangerous stretch of sea. Tomorrow or Friday she's going to visit. The brave little boat, think about that. Don't dwell on the past. Don't sit here brooding . . . and Grace decides that she has to go out, at once, this minute, in the wind and the night.

For the room has felt a little like a prison since the phone rang last, half an hour ago, and she answered gladly, assuming it was Paula who had tried to call her earlier that evening, Paula ringing to confirm Friday's train – but there it was again, when she lifted the receiver, a breathing silence, hanging there, stretching.

An error, of course. Like all the others.

But she wouldn't wait for it to happen again.

Which is why, as the round moon fills the sky with a brightness that dims the lights on the front and bleaches everything flat and white, two tall thin women pass each other, one of them old, her white face carved with coal-black eye-sockets and cavernous cheeks, almost a skull, and the body that carries it is almost a skeleton, but eager life still pulls the strings and she still walks briskly; the other one young, as tall as the first, walking awkwardly, a tethered gallop, looking taller than she is in high-heeled shoes which clop like horses on the stone promenade, the hectic colour of her cheeks and lips turned a weird bruise-grey by the leeching light.

A prostitute, thinks Grace, as she passes, it must have been less than three feet away, and she feels a mixture of small thrill (for at eighty-five she's still seeing life, still seeing things that would have shocked her mother) and large pity for the woman's sadness, the awkward mincing gait of those shoes; the moonlit face is so strained and queer, and a gaggle of youths are following her, shrieking and hooting ten yards behind her.

(Were those the ones she would go with, then? Some of them looked no more than fifteen, but the faces that pass Grace are bestial, brutal, the savage animal face of the male.)

Brunnhilde has the advantage, of course. She had seen her quarry emerge, quite by chance, as she waited, debating whether to try the Empire's bar for a little drinkie, a little risk, a little game. They meet by chance, but she knows who it is, though the photographed face has grown very old. Very much older than she had imagined. Too old for anyone to bother about. I'd be doing the world a favour, she thinks, and then brushes the thought aside.

Next day he will wonder in some irritation what held him back, when he had her so close.

But the moonlight stood like a skin between them. Until it is broken, Grace will be safe.

What force restrains things from happening? What gravity pulls us back, on the brink, before the fountain of blood and tears, before the fire that can't be put out?

A Chernobyl every seven years, they say, in the current world of nuclear power. What miracle keeps things stable for six, as the little links break, as entropy gathers, as everything moves to the snapping point, and we all start to feel, that nothing will happen, we'll always be safe?

8

BEFORE THE STORM

Next morning as Grace drinks her first cup of tea Major Kirk is
supported into the dining-room, breathing stertorously, rolling so
far on the arm of the tight-trousered waiter that she can't tell
whether he's nodding to her. Charitable, she says a cool 'Good
morning', then drops her eyes to the table-cloth.

What can be keeping him alive? she wonders. 'What still makes
him a living being, when all over his body things are breaking
down, slipping away from him? She can't identify at all. She is old,
she creaks, but she still . . . coheres. I'd kill myself, if I were like
that. I'd be doing the world a favour.

He orders with terrible dragging breaths, drowning in-breaths,
hawking out-breaths, enough to put anyone off their grapefruit,
enough to give old age a bad name.

And yet, she supposes it will happen to her. What will she be
like at ninety, say? Falling apart, almost certainly.

Would she really rather die?

I suppose I'd fight, like him.

If only one's death could be glorious, a testing ground like giving
birth, not blurred and protracted, full of small defeats (but Grace
knows nothing about giving birth). An opportunity to show one's
mettle.

Bruno's breakfast, as in 'bed and breakfast', is hardly worth the
title. They knocked and left it outside the door, three bits of dry
toast in cellophane, which only got good marks for hygiene.

He needed eggs and bacon. He needed sausage and chips. He
needed *healthy* food this morning, food for a warrior going into
battle, but they give him this feeble women's food. He tosses it

down; it scratches his throat. For all these small humiliations they'll pay, when Bruno finally has some power.

(Last night, for example, he'd had to get changed in a smelly toilet down on the beach, climbing over the door and barking his knees, trailing his skirt in the pan in the dark, and then back again after his outing, once the boys had tired of following him. Bruno can still feel the bruise.)

He will pass it on, every bit of pain.

Paula has fretted through the night, not really asleep, not really awake, a night of bad dreams and adrenalin. Around five o'clock she sinks finally into a deep and dreamless sleep, and does not wake till nine, with a sense that she has missed something.

The baby. She'll know, today.

She drags herself up, eyes smeared with sleep, and pads flat-footed to the phone in the hall where the Health Centre number is pinned up. She rings, a heart-beat for every digit, but finds the line engaged.

Grace goes to the desk for a local paper. The girls are deep in conversation.

'. . . *frightful* this morning.'

'Awful.'

'Nurse Stephen said we didn't really ought to keep him.'

They're mumbling rather. Grace tries not to listen.

'Old Bamber hates it when they snuff it on the premises.'

'Well turning them out doesn't look very nice.'

'Rows of OAPs don't look very nice.'

'Excuse me,' says Grace, peremptorily.

The girl who spoke last blushes furiously, and Grace realises, with that familiar surprise, that to them she is just another OAP, and she longs for the moment when she'll show them different, for she *is* different, isn't she?

It hadn't come by close of day.

That day was a day when they all waited, as the impetus of

frustration gathered, as the drive to action worked to break the airlock under the muffling surface.

Arthur waited for Paula to ring; Paula didn't ring him.

Paula rang the Health Centre, again and again until she got through and was told to hang on, and felt hopeful; put through to Ante-natal, more hopeful still; left hanging for ten minutes, a little less hopeful, cut off without warning, despairing and cross, so it was nearly midday when she finally got a human voice out of Ante-natal, and the human voice said Sorry, no: there'd been a delay, her results weren't through.

And Arthur, grim-faced in the Albion, waited for her but also for Ian, mysteriously absent all morning, so Arthur had to carry up the cases himself. They were light as a gnat to a man like Arthur, but still it didn't do. Ian finally rolled in at two with a spike-haired girl, both reeking of whisky, and gentle Arthur was furious, though most of the fury was aimed at Paula: '. . . irresponsible . . . left us in the lurch . . . could have been dead, for all we knew . . . just a big kid, aren't you? . . .' By the time he had finished Ian's face was white and his lips both curled and (faintly) trembled.

'Now piss off and get sobered up. I want you back on duty at six.'

Then it was Ian's turn to wait, once the world stopped spinning and turned to an ache and short-term memory prevented sleep, waiting till six in his echoing room in the hateful hotel in the hated city, but most of all he hates himself, staring at his hands, the familiar tremor, peasant hands not city hands, and the stubby wrists with faint white scars.

In a scruffier part of the same grey city a typist in her first situation waited in the office for Mr Janes. At around eleven Bruno rang in and mentioned coolly he was 'tailing' someone, 'in Prince's Park. In Seabourne.' Elsa squawked like a mynah bird. 'You had an appointment at ten. They showed up here and they wasn't very pleased. And you got another one at two-thirty . . .'

The girl's familiarly horrid voice was even more horrid on the telephone, somewhere between a buzz and a whine, the sound of a clapped-out vacuum cleaner, a voice which sucked away the pleasing faces in the mirror of Bruno's phone-box – the face of a spy, the face of a hero, Brunnhilde, beautiful and bold, the face of a man on to something big – and left him with the face of a small-time detective, a man who'd forgotten today's appointments, a man who was starting to lose control, and Bruno knew that he had to go home.

Too bad. He'd been having the time of his life, with his heavy binoculars hooding his eyes, watching Grace Stirling watching football. American football, to be precise, his favourite programme on the television, and she looked as if she was swallowing a lemon, she looked as if she was choking on the ball, her mouth was a stupid great hole of surprise when she first saw the giant shoulders of the team and the cheerleaders waggling their parts on the sidelines as everyone waited for play to begin, and he'd found it inexpressibly exciting, moving in so close to the evil old face, watching it twitch and sneer and gasp, watching the thin mouth worrying and the bony grey neck craning up, up, so thin he could see it was only waiting for a breath of wind, or a blow, to snap . . .

That day there was no wind. That day Grace did not snap.

She realised, simply, there was little time left, not for herself but for England, for England and perhaps for the world, for why should she find in Prince's Park (where once there was only an oval lake, but that was enough, it was once so lovely, a lozenge of sky-blue light in the green) – these monstrous, cartoon muscle men, playing some monstrous warlike game? Endless abortive ritual fights, then the whistle blew and it began again. They were padded and visored like motorbike riders and like no sportsmen she had ever seen, and there were women humiliatingly tricked out as little girls who wiggled down the edges in unison, chanting songs, waving giant pom-poms, and this, she was told when she asked a perfectly respectable looking middle-aged man, was something called American Football, and no one but her was at all surprised.

– But why do we have it in England? Why has it come to *Seabourne*?

– Why was the park not enough in itself, why did everyone crowd round the foolish pitch so the oval lake lay alone and blank with its little green boats still chained to the jetty, waiting in vain for the children to come?

Walking back through eastern Seabourne towards the Empire

where she hoped to get tea, Grace suddenly perceived that the urgency – the jostling, nervous combativeness, that sense of only ten seconds to go before the whistle stopped one dead – had spread from the football field to the streets. All the shop windows were shouting, as if they had to buttonhole their customers on the very last day before they died; their offers were raucous, desperate, handwritten cries on fluorescent pink or green, EVERYTHING MUST GO: 100% REDUCTIONS!!, DON'T MISS THESE AMAZING PRICES, WE SELL HOT FRESH SOUP, SPECIAL OAP FISH'NCHIPS, WALK IN AND LOOK AT OUR FABULOUS JEWLLRY, GENUINE GOLD AND SILVER PIECES NOW AT KNOCK-DOWN PRICES!! – but why, she wondered, this urgency, why were so many shops closing down, why was everything being reduced, why did everything have to go? What terrible thing were we waiting for? What had foreshortened life so much?

It was in the streets, it was in the papers, it was why she no longer listened to the news. Why was the *country* being knocked down? Why did it not seem to matter any more if it simply got rid of everything it had, its gas, its oil, its water, and left all its other possessions to rot, its hospitals, its schools and libraries, even its books, for Paula had told her the British Museum – the *British Museum*! – was begging people to 'Adopt-A-Book', as if books were so many unwanted children . . .

What did these people know about the future that told them none of these things had a use, that all we needed was spending money, and that should be spent today?

Distressed, she tried to cut through to the front, but she found the beaches of eastern Seabourne were strewn with a scum of plastic containers, coils of cable coming uncoiled, broken toys, glittering tins, metal drums which had lost their lids, and what horrible substances had they contained? It seemed that whoever cleaned the beach had got discouraged by the flood of waste, or perhaps the people who sunbathed here (and they must have rather peculiar taste to come this far east, or else they were poor) simply no longer noticed the mess; or maybe the service had been – what was the word, when they skimped on something to make a bit of money? – maybe the service had been 'privatised', and the rubbish would lie on the beach forever until the whole view was a dense mosaic of jagged metal and glaucous plastic.

What did it mean? she asked herself. What loss of hope underlay all this? What final, wordless failure of nerve? What unacknowledged common vision of a sea that would one day come sweeping in over miles and miles of poisoned sand and find no naked human child?

How had this happened behind her back?

– Perhaps I simply don't understand. I'm a different generation, of course. Because if I'm right, why aren't people frightened?

Tomorrow, tomorrow Paula would come and explain it all. Grace would wait till then.

That evening Paula was waiting again, this time for her friend Francesca, in an East End winebar she once knew well when she worked, like Fran, for *Mean Streets*; but now the décor is unrecognisable.

Two years ago it was vaguely ecological, with wholefood recipes chalked on a board, swags of dried flowers, candles, beams. Now it glittered; now it burned. Masses of chrome and theatrical mirrors, the staff wore white jackets and black bow-ties and Paula counted at least five champagne buckets, no, six, I don't believe it – standing in thickets of pin-striped suits. It was pretty, after her shabby flat, and rather cheerful till she spotted herself, sitting alone in a brilliant mirror, with ratty hair and dated clothes and all the lines of her face dragged downwards, so very unlike the bright young women who hung upon the pin-striped suits, women with sculpted, boyish hair and fancifully girlish clothes.

And everyone looked so rich. How could they be so rich, so young? (Why didn't *we* think of trying to be rich?) How could they spend so fast? (as table after table ordered more champagne . . .) They wouldn't stay rich for very long if they poured their money away on the ground (that foolish way of shaking up the bottle before opening it, like football players, so it whooshed and frothed all over the carpet, *wasteful*, and daylight would show the stain). Some of them couldn't be much more than twenty. *I don't believe all this can last* . . .

Francesca came and seemed abstracted, thinner, drier, more distant than usual. But when Paula told her she might be pregnant her face appeared to shiver apart, small pale fragments of changing emotion, and as they settled she stubbed out her cigarette and her long white arm reached across the table and clutched Paula's wrist in a torturing grip, 'Oh darling. Good. Oh good. It's the future.'

In the rush of feeling that held them together Paula asked if Francesca had changed her mind. As a twenty-year-old she hadn't wanted kinds, then a year ago she wasn't so sure . . . But a kind of cuticle passed across Francesca's beautiful, intelligent eyes. 'I shan't have a child,' Francesca said, and the conversation slipped on to other things.

After several hours and a litre of wine, Paula asked, 'How are you really, Francesca? You've hardly said a thing about yourself,' and Francesca, turning away from the light, revealing a profile which was startlingly hollow, said, 'Actually, there's something wrong,' and Paula suddenly knew she was dying, before the difficult words came out.

She'd been coughing for eighteen months; she'd got to think it was normal; she waited too long before going to find out . . . and now they were advocating a heavy programme of surgery, radiation therapy, chemotherapy. 'They're outraged I'm still walking around, but I've told them I haven't made up my mind. I bullied the most honest doctor, actually I think he fancied me, into admitting my chances were thirty-seventy, even if I do all this ghastly stuff . . . I think I'll just accept it.'

'Of course you won't die,' said Paula, stupidly, thinking *You'll die, and I can't bear it.*

But how was it possible, she wondered, heading back to Camden on the garish tube, how can someone my age possibly die? How can *Francesca* have cancer? And suddenly she was longing for Arthur, what if Arthur died, oh please . . .

She jumped off the tube and made for Kensal Green, half ran up the shabby road in the moonlight, remembered the baby, *don't hurt the baby*, slowed to a panting, racing walk. No lights, and he didn't answer the bell, she used her key and burst into the bedroom but the bed was empty, it wasn't even made – not there, and nor was Sally.

So then another kind of waiting began, full of regrets and razoring worry.

What if he's finally got tired of me? He'd have every right, I don't behave well . . . What if someone has taken him in, him and Sally, some motherly woman? Another woman's hands in Arthur's wild curls, another woman cuddling Sally . . .?

And she thinks of Francesca, her face a skull, the mouth, un-believably, no longer talking. Impossible; Francesca gone . . .

The images grew so real in the dark that Paula put the light back on and looked for the book Francesca had given her just as they parted, she hadn't even looked at it, but anything would do, anything would help . . .

The book was far from being *anything*, though. On top, a review slip; not yet published. A memoir of Ralph, yet another memoir, but Paula gasped as she turned it in her hands, for this one, the book jacket brutally told her, was written by 'Dunne's last mistress', as if Aunt Grace had been one of a chain . . . It must be the woman in those pictures, that exhibition I saw last week. And I've hardly thought about Grace since then. I've thought about nothing but myself ever since the doctor said I was pregnant. And while I wasn't looking it's all gone wrong, Grace is going to go mad with pain, Francesca has cancer, Arthur's run off, and I still don't know if I'm pregnant or not . . .

Grace. Paula suddenly remembers. She expects me tomorrow. I can't possibly go, I'll get my results from the Health Centre, I'll have to sort things out with Arthur . . . At eleven-forty-five, feeling nervous as a schoolgirl, she rang the Empire and spoke to her aunt.

The brief phonecall left her sweating with guilt, hitting her forehead, talking to herself. 'You're stupid, stupid; you hurt people's feelings; you forget everybody; you're no good.'

For Grace had sounded gravely surprised. 'I'd hoped to take you to see the Lighthouse.' Grace had sounded very, very old. They'd made a new date for Saturday evening, but Grace would have gone home by then, they'd meet at her house in Oakey now, and Paula suspected there was something more than a silly old lighthouse Grace wanted to show her, something Paula was meant to learn, but now it was gone, she would be too late, and what, she thought (as the window banged, something fell and broke, stupid, pointless, and yet all day there had been no wind), *what if Grace should die* . . . she's eighty-five, and I take her for granted.

Please don't die. Please wait, Aunt Grace. I've so much to tell you, but that's nothing new. So much to ask you, though, as well. If I have a daughter I'll want to tell her everything about your life. But I don't know enough. I don't ask questions. I don't listen when you tell me things. And if you died it would all be lost . . . I'm going to change. Please wait. Don't die.

Grace Stirling had lived eighty-five years. More than thirty thousand days. So how could a day's delay upset her?

And yet it did. She was badly hurt. Lying in bed she remembered all the times that Paula had let her down. Always when it most mattered, a birthday say, when she was on her own, or when Grace was ill last summer, and always Grace had forgiven her and thought that she would change, in time, but now she knew it wasn't so. She'd gone on living partly because she wanted to see how Paula turned out, but now she saw she was already fixed, Paula would age but stay a child, a selfish child who punished the world because she'd had a selfish mother; now she knew there was nothing to wait for, and the silent dark was too much to bear, Grace was suddenly bolt upright, anchoring herself with a column of light, groping for anything to read, not the Murrell book, please nothing grim, and she saw what she thought was the local paper among the shadows on the dressing-table, good, just right, there would be births and weddings, flower-shows, royal telegrams . . .

But it was the *Observer* from a week ago. Ah well. It looked pristine, docile. She opened it and began to read fast, then very fast, with a sense of fear, skipping from story to story in the middle – stories of pollution, stories of corruption, stories of irradiated Russian firemen, stories of radiation hot-spots in England, stories of sheep being painted blue to show their flesh could never be eaten, stories of thousands of reindeer buried under signs saying RADIOACTIVE WASTE . . . then duller and less comprehensible stories, one or another politician 'reiterating our unchanged commitment to renewable sources of energy' and all that meant was nuclear power, they hadn't learned anything from Chernobyl, they were going ahead as they were before, and the night bore down from every side upon this sprawling nightmare world which must have been here for years, decades, but up till now she had somehow ignored it . . .

She turned to the 'Review' in desperation. Art must offer her some escape. The pages were smooth. They sighed as they opened. 'Dunne's Dark Lady', she read, it was Ralph, and her heart began to flail in her chest like a child in a cage as it takes its beating, and everything else recedes to a blind grey fog compared to this, this the disaster she's waited for, this is her world's apocalypse.

Only Faith, in her attic, trying to sleep, and Arthur, far away in London, both of them doggedly trying to be good, were waiting for something physical . . .

*   *   *

Arthur, bereft of Paula, having washed her clothes, dried her clothes, patted her clothes as he folded them, was left with itchy fingers, hitting his great barrel chest in pain since he couldn't admit that he also wanted to kick her clothes around the garden. He found her appointments diary, instead. A few dates, a few addresses, and he read them hungrily, hoping to get closer. Nothing at all to help the pain. But against today she'd written ? TRAIN WATCH ? A sneaking grin; he knew her so well. The double query meant she didn't think she'd go, but felt the possibility improved her diary.

Which gave him a way of pleasing her (it gave him a way of getting back at her, but he wouldn't admit he wanted to do that. She thought he was a slob; he would prove her wrong; he would show the world he was better than her). He tucked a quarter of whisky in his pocket, tricked Sally into thinking it was *her* idea to go and stay with Amelia again, wooed Amelia's mother into thinking she was saving the life of a poor wifeless man, and sent himself off into the summer dark, a hand of bananas in the other pocket, ready to wait for the train till morning, ready to wait all his life for love.

They'd been here before, on this hump-backed bridge, in winter, for once they had done this often, when Paula first learned about the nuclear trains, before the keenness ebbed away. He remembered the powder of ice on the wall. He'd made her come inside his big coat, he'd wrapped his scarf around her Paula-smelling hair, he'd held her small strong hands in his pockets, and although it's summer it's tonight he feels cold, sitting alone on the blackened brick with his feet hanging over the long drop down to the silent rails and the oily sleepers.

Things have gone wrong with the world, he thought, watching the railway lines, steely in the moonlight, sheering away into the distance, an impossibly complicated tracery of metal, and he quite liked the sound of his thoughts in the darkness (for Paula said he didn't think at all, Paula said he was a vegetable, 'Come out of the garden or else you'll *sprout!*'). Somewhere in the dark those lines would meet. But no one understood the whole picture any more, he worried, side-saddle on the high wall, nobody saw what it actually meant, the unseen point where the lines converged.

Nobody sees where we're going any more (he unscrewed the top of the bottle, one-handed). We all have a sense we're not going far but it's as if there was nobody left to care. (But Arthur cared, even if he was useless.) The world had been split into littly tiny bits, and the clever people were all specialists, so nobody felt responsible for anything big or vague, like the future.

The future; that's what I worry about. I worry about Sal, and the other kids. And there are kids all over the world. But I'm naïve, people would say (the whisky was brave and warm in his throat). I'm a sixties person. I'm a dreamer. Even Paula thinks I'm a stupid old sod. And I don't do anything to make things better . . . (he kicked with one foot, but only met air).

He was here tonight, though, wasn't he?

Even if the train isn't going to come. And if it does, I'll note it down, and that's one more sighting to add to the network of information that's being built up. Maybe lots of us care, in the shadows . . . lots of us hate what's happening to England. Lots of us trying to understand, lots of us doing what little we can. In the end (and it's Paula he's pleading with, but she has dismissed him as a sentimental fool) surely things have to change?

And I'll be ready. *Arthur is ready.* He raises his bottle to that . . .

– Oh yes, and here's the train. That curious welcome for the most unwelcome.

The sound of the engine is light, almost cheerful, only one flask, as usual, and an empty wagon on either side, so the engine doesn't have to work very hard to pull the spent fuel rods through sleeping London. The moonlight glints on the side of the engine.

(How would you know there was a man in the cab? How would you know what the man was feeling? Probably nothing; it's just routine. It's him who makes the train alive, but buried in that great nose of metal he's very small, he doesn't feel responsible. And yet, there he is, one particular man.

He was young or old; perhaps he had children; perhaps he was afraid of the endless small leaks they found on the flasks and the wagons . . . But he rode his cab towards Willesden Junction, and anything else was too big to think about.)

The flask was wearing its smooth metal cap, which shone for a moment as it caught the moonlight, leaving the parallel fins of the sides in striped shadow as the moon slipped past. It was always smaller than you remembered, fixed in the middle of the long flat wagon, small and squat and powerful, and Arthur shivers as it dips beneath the bridge and rattles slowly underneath him, resisting an impulse to leap to one side, for the highest readings of radioactivity were always over the top of the flasks; it was minuscule, statistically, and he stays where he is, he doesn't want to look silly, perhaps the world is watching him . . . *Arthur would never be a coward.*

(The train has passed through Kensal Rise, where houses actually straddle a bridge, their windows overlooking the rails. He'd always liked them; they were almost medieval . . . but now he just wonders who lives in them, whether they're pregnant or have children, whether they know about the nuclear trains, whether they lie there and wait for the thing that rocks so lightly down the line.)

And Faith? She waits for the child to come, a week, she thinks, two weeks at the most, but all that night the child is working, bearing hard down to the pull of the moon, burrowing through the soft bones of her pelvis, tunnelling on towards the world with its tender, planetary skull; unaware the world contains anything bad; hazarding all, to have life in the light, unprotected but quite unafraid.

9

A LITTLE DREAD

Morning falls on the minor ruins; a little wind has blown in the night, an odd little cool capricious wind, a wind for winter, not for June. The bodies lie ruffled in their beds, sleeping, yes, but discontented, tossed into awkward frowning angles, grey or yellow in the morning light, lips pulled tight with a little dread, as if the little wind was just a warning.

At the Empire, the chambermaid has a shock when she pulls the curtains in a ground-floor room, for Major Kirk has changed in the night, the old man is dried and shrunken, he lies across the bed in a frozen lurch, as if he had made a last gallant struggle, but the smell in the room is death, she knows.

Grace does the impossible: she sleeps till after half-past eight, and the sharp little wind blows in through the window (she never sleeps without an open window) and lifts a white hair across her forehead, as if it were worried she would not wake, but Grace has been given no dispensation, Grace has to wake and suffer at last, Grace has to lie there as her heavy lids lift and try once more to absorb the pain.

She can't. She crumbles back to sleep. And dreams of Ralph. He looks the same as ever, but has moved a little further off, she is looking at him as if through glass, as if she were a woman at an exhibition and she daren't press close, there are too many of them, and the sorrow wakes her up again.

But it isn't true. He was mine, mine.

Luckily Arthur has left for work, banging around more clumsily than usual, Arthur not singing or whistling this morning, Arthur cutting himself as he shaves – Arthur has gone, without saying goodbye; lucky for some of Arthur's dreams, for even Arthur couldn't look at Paula lying in bed with her head on one side, the flesh puffed up with misery, fallen across towards her ear, the forehead ridged with angry lines, and think her beautiful. It's a thwarted, childish, needy face, unchanged from the face that hid in the darkness when Arthur stumbled in at four, cheerfully drunk, smelling of whisky, and tripped on the rug and fell on Paula, which he thought was a joy and a miracle for the split second before she screamed. And went on screaming, wild with rage even after she'd realised it was him.

Now she sighs as she drifts back to life and a gnawing sense of damage done. 'You clumsy fool. Where the hell have you been?' she'd spat at him, beside herself, and she could almost hear his brain creak in the dark, he was silent for a good half-minute, and when he did speak he was trying to adjust to something gigantically, globally unfair. '*Me?* Where have *I* been? What about *you?*'

'You stink of whisky!' (She'd meant something else; *I was worried; I was frightened; hold me, Arthur.*)

'I'm allowed to have a drink.'

'Who were you with? Where's Sally – poor little girl, as soon as I turn my back you farm her out somewhere so you can get pissed!'

'I don't believe I'm hearing this.'

'Well *tell me*, pig! You've been seeing some woman!'

'If you know so much I don't have to tell you. And *stop shrieking*. You sound barmy. I'd almost forgotten what you were like . . .'

Last night everything was passionate muddle. This morning the facts are uncomfortably clear.

– I suppose I forget what I'm like, as well. I am a bit barmy. I always was. Grace told me I used to have awful tantrums to make my mother take notice of me; not that it worked. And I do it still. Because I feel safe to do it with Arthur. He's a better mother than my mother ever was. So I do it if ever I feel abandoned, if ever I feel hurt . . .

And usually Arthur could deal with her. He held her somehow. He enclosed her. Absorbed whatever it was she felt. He was usually ready to be stronger than her at the moment she needed to be weaker than him . . .

But last night it was all too much. She'd gone too far, at the wrong moment, and he didn't rise to the occasion. He didn't play the game she knew, the game that always made things right.

(So maybe the game didn't always work. Maybe things had to go another way.)

– But we didn't make up. He wasn't *nice* to me. He didn't let me fall asleep in his arms. He just stopped talking and slept himself.

The last thing he said had salted her guilt. 'I've been *train-watching*. Got that? And I didn't have a clue if you were ever coming back. I couldn't get in touch with you. Now I'm going to sleep. I have to leave at six-thirty.'

She'd listened as his breathing steadied, and then, afraid he had gone beyond her, she'd said in a voice that was small and rueful and hardly hers at all, 'I didn't go anywhere. I went to my flat. I was mad at you. I didn't answer the phone,' and she would have gone on and said about the baby, but he didn't answer, Arthur was asleep, and Paula was stuck with it, she was alone.

Now there was a hard awakening. Time for Paula to think about change. Time for her to feel her way towards being a parent, as well as a child, whether or not there's a baby inside her, for Arthur must be getting tired of always playing mother.

But Arthur has other things on his mind. Arthur has hardly given Paula a thought since he pushed through the doors of the Albion, where the minor damage of this chilly morning has gone much further, where wreck has run wild.

The lobby is strewn with glass and blood. He blinks, frowns, rubs his head, looks again and the vision holds. Apart from the mayhem, everything's quiet. Blood and glass and silence.

God. There's been a murder here.

Then he sees the body, or rather a leg and a foot poking out of the top of the stairs going down to the dining-room, and he runs to see where the rest of the man sprawls down the staircase, blood on the shirt, blood on the hands, much more of it on the chalk-white face, an upside-down face daubed over with red. There's a smashed bottle at the foot of the staircase, lying in a pool of dark on the carpet. The lights have blazed on these stairs all night.

Arthur's on his knees wih his head against the sodden shirt-front, listening for a heartbeat, before he sees that it's Ian. And then he hears the heart's dull beat and the breath which comes in reluctant roars and smells like a fire in a whisky still, and fear begins to give way to anger, for he starts to divine that this wasn't a murder, it wasn't an attack, Ian must have gone on a drunken bender . . . yet the smeared face looks entirely innocent when he has wiped away the blood, losing itself in a drugged sleep, stripped of its nervous watchfulness.

Arthur sighs as he gets to his feet and starts to assess the damage. Why is he surrounded by psychotic children? Why is he always clearing up their mess?

The worst things are probably the till and the mirror. The till was the last non-computerised till in London, a lumbering grey metal monster with keys which had always looked indestructible, and had therefore never been replaced. Only now it is destroyed. It is full of great dents, the drawer hangs open, limp and disjointed, its back broken, and the keys stick out at bizarre angles; others have snapped like twigs. And the mirror, which had for decades reflected vanity, panic, lust, despair as the guests passed by and inspected themselves, the rather elegant thirties' mirror inscribed with the legend *The Albion*, the mirror which had sealed its fate by staring across at Reception last night so unforgivingly – and Ian, desperate, must have stared back – most of the mirror now lies on the carpet in great dramatic pieces of ice, a giant jigsaw for the very young, a heart with a crack in it, a simplified swan. Beside it the axe from the store-room. Ian had run amok with the axe.

Why didn't I see this coming, he asks himself, gingerly picking up the biggest piece of glass, then realising he has nowhere to put it, replacing it clumsily, cutting his hand, just a little cut but it stings like spite; why didn't I see how wild he was getting. He told me often enough. He said he was a nutter. He asked me not to leave him in charge at night. But I didn't take him seriously. I wanted to think he would be all right. I'm an optimist. And where does it get me?

At six-thirty-five one chambermaid, then another, then the third, comes in, is appalled, and raises her hands in Hispanic lament, but they soon set to with their normal energy, clearing up the mess other people have made.

Arthur is pierced by a pang of regret as the massive, lethal pieces of glass are muffled in newspaper and carried away. Perhaps they made up a message, a semaphore from below the surface, telling him something he needed to know, something that pierced to a heart of things that he had lost touch with along the way, a rhythm he no longer heard (for he knows why Paula treats him like this ... a sudden paroxysm of pain; she no longer loves him; she's bored. How could she be happy with a man like him? She guessed at the blood behind the door, she saw the flash from the edge of the future).

'Too beeg,' Anna squeaks from the head of the stairs. Arthur sighs, and goes to lift the ordinary body. That was his function in life: to *bear*.

Grace gets up in a rush, fails to imprison all her hair in grips, hurries stiffly in to breakfast aware she's impersonating a dotty old woman but what does she care what she looks like? What does she care what she eats? She is only afraid of missing breakfast because it would be a sign of despair.

And Grace does not despair. She is reeling, but she will not despair; she has given herself instructions, seeing a hint of droop in her bedroom mirror.

Why is she hurrying, all the same? There's a quarter of an hour before breakfast ends, what is she escaping from? (and her clumsy foot catches a table-leg on the way to her table in the window . . .). Sitting down, she holds the arms of her chair and clings to them until she's steady. That and the sea, the sea, the kindness of its purblind gaze, the light grey clouds scudding over it, everything carrying on the same, as if her life had not been changed, except for that little shift in the weather, nothing much, a small sharp breeze.

And she tries. A slow deep breath. She tries.

She has to learn it was not important, the little track that her life had made, the small dark corners she had not seen. It was all nearly fifty years ago. If Ralph had lived, after all. If he came in now in the flesh and passed me, I'd look straight through him, he'd be an old man, I'd be an old woman, there'd be nothing left.

And yet she keeps feeling that someone has died, and Kirk, she sees, is not in breakfast, a middle-aged couple are sitting there, perhaps she is looking at the wrong table, the woman is fat with an orange, irrelevant, greasy face that she stuffs with toast, Grace looks again carefully, no, he's gone, but Major Kirk is a resident, it's an absolute outrage, their taking his table . . . she's going mad; she closes her eyes, and sees his body lying there, of course he had died, he was right to go, anyone could see he was tired of life, but somehow Grace had failed to notice, somehow Grace had not been told, and so she had failed to make the effort, and now he has gone, her love, her Ralph.

 — But he wasn't your Ralph at all. He died loving someone else. Don't lie to yourself. The truth is what matters, you always fought about that with Ralph, he didn't see why you were so 'pedantic', he didn't see why you were so 'stiff-backed' . . .

What was the truth, in any case? Perhaps she wasn't so honest. The last time she saw him was a solid lie, every move, every breath she took was an act. (Grace realises she hasn't touched her coffee, and sips it, weak and black.)

He left in the spring of '39. One final row as they lay in bed seemed no more final than all the others. She'd left for school that morning with the familiar feeling of dry despair. Coming back she found canvases stacked on the stairs. Inside the flat it was chaos; Ralph and Bunny, his closest friend, were sorting his books away from hers.

Then pride took over. She didn't ask questions. She hadn't even asked where he was going. She went and sat in the kitchen, trying to stop her legs from trembling. In a minute, she'd made some tea, and forced herself to sit and drink it, staring at the columns of stupid print.

Sometimes they passed the kitchen door; from the corner of her eye she watched Ralph's profile; it never seemed to turn towards her. She'd scanned the pages, *act to the end*, tinkled the teaspoon in the cup, checked her hair in the kitchen mirror – in the last two years she had worn it up, though Ralph had begged her to keep it loose; she'd tucked the last tendrils back into place, driven the hairgrips firmly home.

'Are you all right, Madam?' She realises that she's sitting there with her eyes squeezed shut, clenching her fists, clenching her jaw.

'Perfectly,' she answers, crisp and cross, forces a smile, then tells the young waiter, 'The coffee is a little cold.'

'I'm sorry. I'll bring you another pot.'

And that was an act, as well. It salved her pride, like all the rest.

But in the end she had not been proud. She had next seen Bunny in '45. All she knew was that Ralph was dead. They passed each other one night in a little road near Trafalgar Square; it was blackout, and almost dark; but she spotted him just in time, as he lit a cigarette on the edge of the pavement; she stood there trying to get her breath, then ran across the road to catch his arm (five years before she had refused to so much as lift her head from her cup of tea).

'Bunny,' she'd said. 'It *is* Bunny. Bunny, it's Grace. Please talk to me. Please, you have to. I'm desperate.'

They'd ended up in a dirty café with shadeless bulbs behind the blinds.

'It's hard for me to believe you,' he told her, grimacing vilely at the barley coffee. 'You didn't seem to turn a hair. Ralph couldn't stop talking about it, how you sat there reading your paper and drinking your cup of tea.'

'Acting,' said Grace. She had nothing to lose. 'It was the only way I could stop myself screaming.'

'You should have screamed. He didn't want to go . . . he didn't really want to volunteer, either . . . the Spanish war put him off all that. But I do think he wanted to die.'

'Don't say that,' she'd begged him. 'Please.'

'I can still hardly bear to talk about him. He had so much talent . . . such a bloody waste . . . and talking to you, of all people. I've felt ever since – if you want to know the truth – all of us felt you had blood on your hands.'

'But that's absurd,' she'd cried. 'I'm a pacifist. I always was. I didn't even know he was going . . . I tried to dissuade him in '36 . . . I won't accept the blame for his death . . . he *wanted* to be a hero . . .'

'He did die a hero. You can't change that. The citation said "conspicuous gallantry".'

In the long years that followed, their talk fragmented, re-formed into a nagging chorus. *You didn't turn a hair . . . Ralph couldn't stop talking about that . . . I do think he wanted to die . . . all of us felt you had blood on your hands . . . accept the blame for his death . . . accept the blame for his death.*

Grace finds she is walking along the front, pulling a strand of hair from her lips that the freshening wind has fretted across, walking faster than she has for years, and running above her, outstripping her, the clouds have started to sprint again, the film of her life is on fast forwards . . .

Suddenly she stops. It's enough, she thinks. Of course it is. Of course it was always far too much. She turns her face to the wind from the sea, narrows her eyes at the fitful sunlight, and when she's used to it, she stares; at the stony beach, how it shines, then darkens, at the lines of waves, white-tipped and fast, strong-backed, taller, fiercer waves than those which lulled her through the week, and the hundreds of thousands of separate stones, their size, their roughness, their comforting reality, and knows that a lie is the thing that's died, knows that she has been set free.

For if Ralph slept with someone else. If there was an Italian, after me. If he loved her, even. And painted her. Before he went to Monte Cassino to die. It was awful, and yet it absolved her. She hadn't sent him off to die. Her failure of love had not been final.

At last she can reject that guilt, and the gulls fly over very fast in a casual arrow that breaks apart and they fall to the sea as windblown snow, the white sun brilliant on every feather.

Arthur is talking to his old friend James, the ever-genial Pennington, but today he is sounding cagey, on the phone. Arthur is ringing about Ian's rampage. He needs authorisation to buy a new till. He tries to tell the story as a bit of a joke, but James doesn't seem to find it very funny.

'We needed a new till, in any case,' Arthur insists. 'It was out of the ark.'

'Hmm . . . Arthur, we should have a drink. Tomorrow morning. Meet me then.'

'Saturday?' says Arthur. 'I'm off on Saturday.'

'I really would like to see you, old man . . .' (and Arthur realises, uncomfortably, that it isn't an invitation, it's an order). '. . . things we ought to talk about,' James continues, a tiny edge to his long-familiar voice that mixes drawl and strangulation, '. . . other options we ought to consider . . . how full have we been, this summer?'

'Eighty per cent,' says Arthur. 'Well, seventy-five, maybe. Libyan bombing, you know. Yanks stayed away in droves.'

'Winter?'

'What?'

'How full in winter?'

'You never used to be interested . . . sixty, seventy per cent, maybe.'

'We could be a hundred per cent all the time. Ever thought about screwing the DHSS?'

'Screwing the DHSS?' Arthur repeats, mystified.

'Homeless. You know. You must have read about it. It's an excellent wheeze, I believe. They put these homeless families in. You can drop all the frills like the bar and so on, and charge ad lib. You can't go wrong. The councils have to cough up, old boy.'

Arthur is speechless, breathless. 'That's not a *hotel*,' he gasps. 'That's not a *hotel* you're talking about. I couldn't do my lunches. I've read about them in the papers, yes . . .' but James over-rides him as Arthur mutters '. . . they sound like hell. You're not serious'

160

— 'We'll discuss it in detail tomorrow. Think about it in the meantime. I've got a few other ideas up my sleeve.' And then his voice smoothly changes gear, dozy, drawly James again. 'I'm seeing my boy this evening.'

'Rupert?'

'No, Alexander.'

'How did he like the first year at Christ Church?'

'Didn't I tell you? He turned it down. Said the dons were earning less money than a dentist. Decided to join a firm in the City. Clever little bugger, he's doing rather well. Doesn't miss a trick, my Alex. He's started telling *me* what to do.'

Arthur wonders if it was Genius Junior who put up the DHSS idea. He hopes Sally doesn't turn out like that. If she does, she won't think much of her father.

Phyllis, back from her night at her mother's, takes a call on another line, staring sadly at the long white scar that Ian's axe has left on the plastic.

'Albion Hotel?'

'Arthur, please. Give me Arthur.'

So that bitch Paula has turned up again. She didn't sound sour, as she often did. She sounded – *lively*. Even happy. (No wonder; Paula had been dancing round the room.) Phyllis pretends not to recognise her voice.

'It's *Paula*, Phyllis. Just hand me to Arthur.'

Phyllis at her most prim. 'I can't at the moment. He's on the other line.'

'I don't care. Interrupt him.'

'I don't think I could do that, Miss Timms. You see, he's talking to Mr Pennington.'

'Oh *James*,' says Paula with an easy contempt that is deeply galling to Phyllis.

'I'm sorry, Miss Timms. I'll ask Arthur to phone you. As soon as he's finished with Mr Pennington.'

Phyllis puts the phone down.

Paula laughs and struts down the hall, trying to do Phyllis with her bottom sticking out, then the jubilant notes in the reggae music that thunder round her living room make her start dancing again, but carefully, since the Health Centre says she *is* having a baby, 'Timms, Paula? The result is positive,' Paula is pregnant, no further doubt, dance with me gently, little baby, and the window rattles in sympathy, but then she realises it's the wind, a rustling, marvellous wind is blowing, rocking the creamy, showy blooms of the

Indian Balsam tree in the road, and everything is so alive, the rocking trees, the blowing birds, the clouds that pass like flying lace, white lace over darker lace, the blood that swells and falls in Paula, the child she's carrying, Arthur's child, that Paula stands and cries again, cradling herself and *yes, my baby, yes, my love, I knew you were there, dance, my sweet, we'll tell your father.*

'Tomorrow, then. Be there at eleven.' It's James who puts the phone down on Arthur, and after he's gone Arthur sits and broods for a good ten minutes before leaving the office. Things are getting colder, he realises. Not just at home, but here as well. Perhaps he won't be wanted any more. Suddenly he longs to talk to Sally. *Sally* loves him. She's at the minder's.

Phyllis gets him the number. 'By the way,' she says as she begins to dial. 'Your *friend* called' (that special note of irony). 'She wanted you to call her back.'

Yes, he thinks sourly, she would. She wants me to make the running, as usual. Wherever he looks, today, there are problems, and Paula is the least tractable. She could wait. 'I'll speak to my daughter first.'

'Of course, Arthur.' Phyllis approves.

Sally's minder, Stephanie, sounded slightly fussed. 'She's quite all right, Mr Fraenkel. Well maybe a little bit tired today.'

Guilt pierces Arthur with a red-hot pin (*she missed her Daddy, she could not sleep*). 'I'd like to have a word with her, please.'

'Daddy,' says Sally. She sounds overjoyed. The next moment, she sounds depressed. 'Can I come home tonight?' (As if he never let her come home. The pin wiggles between his ribs.)

'Course you can. I'm coming to collect you.'

'Now? Daddy come now?' Sally's ecstatic again.

'No,' Arthur sighs. 'The usual time. Daddy'll come when it's time for tea.'

'Sally's frightened,' she wails, and in the background he can hear Steffie's voice, trying to placate her.

'What's the matter, darling. Tell Daddy.'

'Gonna be a nurrican,' she's crying, then Arthur hears wails as the phone is removed and Stephanie's talking again, too much, with Sally's unhappy voice underneath.

'It's nothing to worry about, Arthur, I'm afraid I had the radio on, I didn't even know she was listening, and there was this special weather report, I'm sure it was nonsense, it was local radio, but someone was talking about hurricanes, Sally asked me what 'hurricane' meant and I foolishly tod her, didn't I, and now she seems to be in some kind of state, she'll be quite all right when she's had a sleep . . .'

Arthur holds the stream of sound away from his ear and tries to think. Of course there wouldn't be a hurricane, nothing like that ever happened in England, but he couldn't bear Sally to be afraid. He wishes he didn't have to work, he wishes he didn't have to earn money, he wishes he could just be a decent father, he isn't even a decent father . . . He wants to get out of the Albion, with the ghost of the mirror darkening the wall and the guests glancing nervously at the battered till and the bloodstains they couldn't remove from the carpet . . .

'I'll come and collect her now,' Arthur says, but just as he says it the doors push open and two policemen come in, 'Mr Fraenkel?' – and he knows they want a statement from him about Ian, who's sleeping it off at the station, 'I'm sorry, something's come up,' he sighs, 'I shan't be able to come till tea-time,' *I'll never escape, or do what I want to, my life will be wasted in this sodding hotel . . . at least Ian managed to break out. I know why people smash things up.*

Bruno's back on the treadmill today, back in the office doing paper-work, shipshape in his suit and tie, and he narrows his pale lashless eyes at the light, tries to make them fierce and keen, squares his shoulders against the chairback and then swings round to face the mirror, preparing himself for Judgement Day, for Haines had called when he was in Seabourne, Haines is waiting and Bruno must come . . . but Bruno hasn't returned the call. Bruno is repressing a sense of panic.

He remembers now what he's tried to forget, that when he last met Haines a month or two ago he'd felt on the verge of being misjudged, Haines's large brown eyes behind clever glasses seemed to look through Bruno's fragile shell and see some boneless thing inside (but Bruno flexes his well tuned muscle), a novice who might not know anything at all (but Bruno is on the verge of such knowledge!), a dreamer, even, all words, no action (but very soon Bruno will do such deeds . . .). He will do far more than they ask of him, he will do such things as will surprise them all.

In the first place, he's going to visit Stirling's home. 'Visiting' vacant premises is easy. And the premises are vacant till tomorrow evening when the old bag is scheduled to return from Seabourne and reconnoitre at last with Timms.

And surely there – surely then – he runs his fingers through his pale red hair in something more than anticipation, something which shakes him to the bone, he drags the nails across his scalp, pulls at some strands, he wants them out, lifts them clean from the bloodied roots – surely at last in Stirling's home he will find the wealth of clinching evidence, the photographs, letters, documents which will win astonished respect from Haines?

For Bruno deserves it. Bruno is hard. Bruno shows all his teeth in the mirror. He holds the uprooted hair in his hands. When it comes to the crunch, Bruno won't play games.

But he sees a movement behind him in the mirror and swings around in unconsidered relief, for Elsa has recovered from her sudden flu, Elsa has come in after all – but it isn't Elsa, nor anything human, it's just the big tree outside the window waving its branches furiously, and he sneers at it in extreme dislike, and turns his back, it's beneath contempt, but something jerks him round again; the glass in the window has a very faint hum as if a great shaking is growing in the distance.

Something strange. The hairs prickle. It's growing dark as it used to once in the winter afternoons when his father came home and tracked down Bruno in the empty house and the voice came first, 'Bruno! Bru-no! It's your father! Come here and take what's coming to you!', and wherever he hid the voice would find him, his father pulled him out from his hiding-place and shook him till he could no longer hear, no longer see, no longer breathe, could only crawl, but not far enough.

He snaps the light on in a frenzy. Why do they leave him alone like this? Why have they always left him alone? There must be a way (and he's holding his hands, clenching his fingers to feel his hands), there must be a way . . . he can't finish the sentence, he forces his eyes to the pile in his in-tray, there's work to do, lots of credit card checks, thousands of people applying for credit, and *that* (he's laughing) is good for business, since hundreds of them will get into debt, and debt-collecting is what he's good at . . .

There must be a way, for he's nearly thirty, he's lived alone since he was sixteen, and no one has touched him voluntarily, they've touched Brunnhilde but never him (and he drives his nails through the palms of his hand) – *there must be a way of getting close.* And the words flash up in front of his eyes, *kill, maim, suppress.*

As Bruno used to beat his toys until they no longer stood up to

him, and when they were limp, when they lay there passive, he
dared to creep up for his kiss.

Grace peers through the window of the Martello Muncher – no
one in sight, what can it mean? – and sees a couple kissing, a
waitress's uniform and a customer, two young bodies pressed
together, yellow hair against a dark shoulder, and smiles a little,
for a kiss is a kiss, a kiss is a sweetness she hardly ever sees – but
they go on kissing, and her smile dies, for don't they care if anyone
spots them? Grace walks round and opens the door, grateful to
slip in out of the wind, and at once the yellow head breaks away
and she sees it isn't a girl at all, it's a middle-aged woman with
chemical hair.

'We're closed,' she says, not very agreeably. 'There's a notice.'

'I didn't see it.'

The man, who's not much younger than the woman, is more
loquacious. 'Closed for repairs.'

'That's rather odd, in the middle of the season.' But Grace spots
that one of the half-dozen giant panes of glass in the window is
smashed, cobbled over with cardboard, and the tables aren't laid.
'Oh dear,' she says. 'Has there been an accident?'

'Accident!' he snorted. 'That was no accident. The Muncher
got done last night,' he continues. 'Police don't say much but we
think it was boys. There's a gang of boys go breaking in everywhere.'

'No respect,' the blonde woman says, and Grace finds herself
nodding her head in agreement, grateful to join the gloomy
accord.

'I mean this was a *Martello tower*,' the man says. 'You know
what those were. Stone Age forts. Well Medieval. Got the
Seabourne War Museum in the basement. They protected
England, the Martello towers. Now they get done by a load of
boys.'

The woman feels he's stealing her story. 'I came in at eight,
as usual, and the mess, you wouldn't believe your eyes. Glass all
over the floor, of course. And they took whatever was in the
till.'

'Dreadful,' says Grace, and 'disgraceful,' but inside she's feeling
something very strange, a desire to laugh, a desire to dance.

'It wasn't just that though, was it,' the man cuts in, warming to

165

the tale, for something has happened to them at last, something that would get into the local papers, both of them have become more real. 'It was the mess they made. It was pointless. The little buggers took out all the eggs, she must have had five dozen eggs in that fridge, and they smashed 'em on the counter.'

'Of course,' says Grace and then realises she has said the wrong thing, she has felt the wrong thing, for this is an outrage. 'Of course that's the sort of thing they do, alas,' she added hastily. 'The young.'

'I'm not old,' the woman says sulkily. '*I* never wanted to go and smash things. They're going abnormal, these days. You can't imagine how slippy it was, I was skating about all covered in eggshell.'

'Terrible,' says Grace, as sternly as she can, but she's fighting a desire to become hysterical, there's something phoney in their solemn tone, the Muncher, after all, was ugly and hateful, no wonder the boys threw eggs around it. Why had she never, in a very long life, thrown eggs at anything or anyone? Pamphlets were much less satisfying . . . Why had she never broken out? Why was she always so English?

And why are the English such hypocrites, always simulating what we ought to feel? They didn't feel gloomy really, those two. They'd got a day off work, after all, and they were kissing, forgetful of everything else, until she arrived to be an audience (and why did I object to their going on kissing? I kissed enough in my day).
'I was going to visit the War Museum,' she says, after a little pause.

'You won't get in there today,' the man tells her, with melancholy satisfaction. 'They smashed the door down there, an' all.'

'The War Museum! I ask you,' the woman repeated, theatrically disgusted, and once again Grace hears it as comedy, she'd bet a hundred pounds that woman had never set foot in the War Museum. Or any other museum . . .

Why should she, after all?

And Grace wonders, briefly, disloyally, whether she herself really wanted to visit the chilly rooms with their odour of sanctity. Somewhere in there was a photo of her brother Eddy, and she always went to see him, to press her fingers against the cold glass. It was all a charade, quite pointless. The photo didn't even look like him, he looked bluff and hearty, he was acting a soldier, and she was acting a sister in tears.

And most of my life I was acting a widow. If only I'd known that I'd been divorced.

'Well, goodbye,' she says, with a surge of good cheer, recalling that she's off to the Lighthouse, she doesn't need lunch, she's too old for that, her body survives and is not demanding, nor is there time, for it's already afternoon; and she's glad, in the end, to be going alone, it would have meant something different to go with Paula, something different to go with Ralph . . . She's ready for anything, even death. But it isn't so easy to slip out of the door, she has to push it open in the face of the wind, and the wind has the force of a giant hand which tries to hold her back from flying.

Arthur spends two hours with the police. They talk about drugs, and prostitution, neither of which, Arthur assures them, has ever cropped up at the Albion. They talk to Arthur man to man, they swell in their collars, they expand. Arthur is glad to put up with the boredom because it means that he can't ring Paula, if he's had to spend two hours with the police, doing his job, being a man.

As the policemen leave, Room 24 flows down the stairs in a tight leather skirt, shaking her yard of blonde hair forward, and both men turn to Arthur and smirk. 'Nice work if you can get it, sir.'

Sir feels better than he has all day.

'Arthur.' She's standing in Reception. Her voice shifts between husky and silky; today it's sad, but very near silk. 'If you're not awfully busy. The light bulb's gone in my room, and the ceiling's too high for me to reach.'

She was two weeks behind with her bill. He hated it when they got behind, hated having to chivvy them. 'You've got a bit behind,' he says amiably. 'I should have mentioned it on Monday.'

From silky to husky in a single move. 'No problem, Arthur. Sorry.'

'Normally Ian would do this, of course.'

But it's pleasant, walking upstairs behind her long bare legs, her long blonde hair, the swells and creases of her leather haunches. She smells nice too (and he remembers Paula; he didn't ring back; more clearly still he remembers her voice, last night's voice, neither silky nor husky, screaming at him that he stank of drink . . . Arthur is much too busy to ring her).

The room, inside, looks very dark, although it's only tea-time in June, and he looks at the window for a moment, looks at the rec-tangle of blue-black cloud, and just for a moment he hears the storm, a suppressed howl behind the double-glazing, and then he forgets about the storm, because she comes into the dark to join him.

Grace sees it bobbing round the curve of the cliffs like a tiny toy on a piece of elastic, the boat coming back from the day's first trip, and her eyes sting as she faces the blast; every second wave it disappears behind a shining wall of spray, then she sees the flash of a yellow oilskin and then they reappear again, pale, tipped faces, waving hands, they were being tossed about like dolls, and very, very faintly, fighting its way through the roar of air and the rush of water, the sound of a dozen voices squealing, and then what sounds like a surge of laughter; and she feels an irrational desire to be in that drenched, chaotic boat, shuddering up then screaming down with all those laughing, suffering people, and she only realises very late as a wild fling of foam from the incoming tide clears the rails of the promenade and spatters the side of her face with cold, that no boat will leave while the sea's like this, maybe nothing all afternoon . . . but it doesn't matter. There's still tomorrow. Nothing on earth will stop Grace now.

Afterwards there would be months of questions about why there was virtually no warning, why only two or three amateur forecasters noticed something was about to happen. With all the sophisticated monitoring devices, with every kind of advanced technology, with civil and military experts reporting and every kind of surveillance at work – how did it sneak in under the noses of all those dedicated, highly skilled men, the hurricane which came from the sea and collapsed Southern England like a pack of cards? Perhaps the technology let them down. But what went wrong with their eyes and ears, their ordinary human skills?

Was it because so many people were sitting not looking out of the window, watching electronic blips on screens, telephoning or with headphones on, double-protected from the world outside by tannoyed music and extra-thick glass and cavity walls and double-glazing?

The world outside was no longer of interest to most of the people in England that day, but later that evening it suddenly grew interesting, soon it became the one thing that mattered, that night as they lay there, intensely afraid, they knew that the skin was artificial, that no one was safe, there was no 'inside', nothing to keep the world 'outside', there was only one infinitely powerful world, one tremendous, unpredictable story in which all the characters were playing dwarfs, and had no words because nothing would help them.

Paula, actually, enjoyed herself until things were pretty far advanced. It didn't matter that Arthur didn't ring. Arthur had every right not to ring. She didn't feel lonely; she wasn't alone; she had her baby, her glorious secret, she'd hug it to herself till Arthur came home, for she knew absolutely Arthur would come, she had always trusted Arthur completely – well, *almost* completely, the faintest pang – and Arthur had never let her down.

She loved him. She approved of him. She was sure he would be as wonderful a father to *their* baby as he was to Sally. She couldn't wait to get her hands on him.

And as the happiness bubbled through her head and fizzed and whirled among the plants in the garden – the roses bobbing and nodding their heads, the clematis bower sighing, swooning, the hollyhocks straining at the leash as a fine fresh wind poured in through the window – while the world and Paula rejoiced in her baby, Paula was also clearing the decks, Paula was waltzing round the room and sorting out her files and notebooks.

By early afternoon she is hard at work, covering page after page with her strong, round, rather formless hand. Five or six months till the child is born. Since the play came off in April she has done frighteningly little work, but she'll work as hard as she can till then . . .

When she thinks about the murder of Hilda Murrell, she still feels an anger that's paralysing, blinding. That an old lady could be killed, perhaps by a seedy private detective, perhaps by a man who was sexually aroused and left those semen stains on her carpet. That the secret service might have been involved, however far away from the final violence. Or however close: '. . . those involved were men of the British Intelligence Service.' That *that* could be said in the House of Commons without the building falling apart, that nobody should be particularly shocked that this could happen in England. That somebody should be snooped on and harassed just because she objected to nuclear power, just because she proudly and openly said so in language that anyone could understand:

'Many of these very dangerous elements would never have existed at all but for man's meddling with the very building-blocks of the universe.' That the snooping should be contracted out to unbalanced, violent men. That someone who'd fought for good all her life should end it fighting off death on her knees . . .

But the story leaves Paula oddly mute, in a blind alley of indignation. She feels there is something very obvious that passionate anger makes her miss . . . Sighing, she turns to journalism. Maybe she's just a journalist.

There are simple things that she wants to say, things she is not too proud to say. That there *is* a future, that it matters, that we can't overlay it with a film of waste. That fission products like plutonium will still be lethal in two thousand generations. That the future is the child of us all, a child that's done nothing and shouldn't be punished and killed just because it stares at us.

She's completely absorbed in what she's writing but she suddenly stops to watch Sally's ball, a cheerful, red and yellow ball, rolling slowly then faster across the garden, propelled by no ordinary human hand, and she realises something rather grand is happening, a storm of splendid, epic proportions, for look at Arthur's favourite tree, the plum tree cartwheels its heavy green head, no longer a crown but a blowing fountain, no longer a fruit tree in an urban garden but something reverting, unravelling, and the light has changed, it's a low blue-green, a light that seems to have blown from the sea, a light of water and of night, but it's only tea-time, surely . . . and then it begins, a patter then stop, then start again, then a heavier drumming, drumbeats gathering, hundreds of them and it sweeps across in battering sheets as Paula watches the picture dissolve in a shining, curtaining blur of rain.

And that, she supposes, closing the window, enjoying a first deep breath of wet air, that will be more or less that for the day, for usually water damps down a storm. And she gets back to work with a sense of contentment, Arthur and Sally would soon be home, the new baby would come in November, at least a little of the future was known.

But nothing at all of the future was known. The storm got fiercer. They didn't come home. Arthur, the infinitely trustworthy Arthur, Arthur-the-father-who-could-always-be-relied-upon, hadn't shown up at Stephanie's.

'*Daddy!*' shouts Sally at the top of her voice. Perhaps the storm has killed her Daddy. She refuses to put her coat on ready. She refuses to sit down and read a book. She throws the offending book at the wall, and topples the minder's geranium, which falls to the ground and lies on the carpet in a mess of earth and broken pot. The minder manages not to get cross. Then Sally refuses to go to the toilet. '*Daddy!*' she screams, and clings on to the sofa, and suddenly it happens as Steffie foresaw, a little trickle, then a growing dark stain, and the other little boy that Steffie looks after, who's drinking his milk and watching TV, turns and points – 'Sally done a wee!' – and knocks the milk all over the table, and the howling wind roars through the minder and she hits Sally hard on the side of the head, something she's never done before though her father regularly did it to her, and everything inside the house goes quiet except the muttering of the TV: then Sally starts to howl in steady rhythm, Steffie says sorry, Arthur rings at the door.

By seven, Bruno is trying to hide. In the little terrace in Kensal Green the window next to the lighted, coloured window where Paula looks out on the night has dropped its neutral, slatted blind, but every so often the thin slats gape, every so often a pale, uncomprehending eye peers through. There is nothing alive in Bruno's yard but something clatters, endlessly, and he punches the wall with irritation every time it bangs again. But he doesn't go outside to see; he is double-bolted, double-locked, and all he can do as the dustbin lid laughs at him from the dizzy dark is bruise his knuckles on the inside wall, the wall that divides him from the next-door house, the wall that protects him from evil, chaos.

But Grace is happy on her final night. She will stay in Seabourne till tomorrow afternoon, and she sees herself rounding the shining rocks in the little boat, the sun will be out, Grace will be sitting high in the bow and it will rise before her, larger than life, more powerful than Grace's death, the Lighthouse, having survived the storm, and at last she'll see how wild and steep are the rocks on which they had to build, she'll understand how brave they were, those builders from the beginning of the age, dreaming foundations on those slippery stones, hacking and sweating the dreams into facts, scrambling across between the tides, clambering up at the very last minute above the hiss of the rising water; not giving up till they nearly drowned; she would bow to them and the Lighthouse keeper.

And the vision lasted, the work was good, for the Lighthouse had stood for eighty-three years, nearly the whole of Grace's lifetime, and how many storms had it survived? How many human lives had it saved?

As the noise grew worse, as the rattle from the window was all but drowned by the roar outside, as the crash and grind of the water on the pebbles turned into something that could shake the hotel, Grace thought of the light pouring over the water, the regular turning of the mighty beam. It could only reach out a certain space; it could only touch the edge of the void, but it would hold the human world together, it would bring the human ships safe home, and she drifts away down the shining pathway, drowsily thinking *all here, all one.*

But two hours later she wakes again in the darkest night she has ever known. Something is battering hard at her window, somebody's trying to get in, she remembers the sickening feeling yesterday that somebody was following her, she remembers the phonecalls, the breathing silence, and the void is here in the room all round her, and Grace turns into a pit of terror . . .

Even after she's awake enough to realise the banging is nothing human, a shutter or drainpipe that's broken free, the blackness doesn't drain away. Out of that emptiness her worst memory of Ralph rises to drag her down, Ralph's fist banging the table, banging and banging, that empty noise, the evening before he went away (and Grace no longer wants to think about this, but how could she ever evict the ghosts? They sat there still, they would never stop quarrelling.)

'No one could call thirty-seven young,' he'd shouted at her as she ate her apple and he finished the bottle of wine. 'You're not *too young* for a child, you know. Neither of us is. We're getting old . . .'

'I don't feel old,' said Grace. 'There's still so much I want to do' (and yet she had known it was slipping away, had perhaps already slipped too far, whatever things she'd once wanted to do. She had known it for years, since she'd gone to Spain and reappeared with the sketch-books that formed the basis of his Civil War triptych; 'Dunne's greatest work', they said in the thirties. Grace knew how good they were as soon as she saw them. And the passion of envy was a revelation, because they would never say it of her, 'Grace

Stirling's greatest work,' and it was her own choice not to go with him (*the girls at school depended on her, someone had to keep paying the rent*), her own choice to make sacrifices, long after Ralph stopped needing them, for she'd lost the knack of living for herself, she'd lost the habit of believing in her writing. A new kind of statement, duller than the old, had replaced 'I'm going to be a great writer': 'I used to want so much to write' . . . 'I once believed I'd be a writer.'

'I want a child,' he'd roared, slamming his glass of red wine on the table, wasting a little rain of blood. 'I'm wasting my time with you. You've never really loved me . . .' (she'd heard his voice as the voice of a drunk, faintly slurred, with a sob in it, and his nose had looked almost as red as his cheeks) '. . . not the way I love you.'

'I've had a long day at school.' She'd used her clipped, school-mistress's voice. 'I don't want a drunken argument.'

'I'm not drunk, you bitch, I'm *asking* you something. Begging you, if you like. You reduce me to this, drinking and begging,' and his fist came down on the table, banging at her again and again.

'You're full of self-pity, aren't you.' She couldn't bear him to say she reduced him; hadn't she tried to make him grow? Hadn't she given herself for him? And sudden anger made her spit it out: 'Baby boy wants a baby.'

'And you. You're bloodless. You're all dried up. You're turning into a stick insect,' and in the same second, the wine-glass flashed, something wet and dark shot over her front and the bloodstains lay solid and dark across her lap and down her narrow thighs and she never knew if he threw it at her or whether it jumped as he punched the table, she only knew she heard someone screaming, someone screamed in terrible pain and after a second she knew it was her but when he came and knelt at her feet she stopped abruptly; she was quite all right, she didn't want to talk about it, she found these quarrels such a strain . . .

I should have screamed when he left, next day, screamed and screamed and gone on screaming . . .

She hears Faith's screams outside on the landing and realises they are not her own.

At twelve, Faith was suddenly wide awake. She had looked at the dial of her watch in the dark and thought with a little quiver of dread I think it's starting, I think it is, and it couldn't be nearer the middle of the night, a funny little pain, a funny little cramp, she would have said it was a period backache but of course this couldn't be a period . . . then the cramp drifted off into the dark and she drifted with it on a wave of relief, just for a moment she had thought it was real and then her plans would have all fallen through; she meant the baby to be born in the morning; Faith would go down to Reception and ask one of the snooty receptionists (none of them spoke to her) to order her a taxi; she'd make the Housekeeper's mouth drop open – 'Mrs Emmett, I'm just off to have a baby' – she would strip off her sweaty nylon overall and cap, leave them in a pile with her broom in the foyer, and the taxi would carry her away from them all, 'Hospital, please, I'm about to have a baby . . .' Rehearsing it again, remembering their faces, she'd fallen asleep on a dwindling pain.

None of it worked when Faith woke next at a quarter to two and the pangs had grown sharper and closer together; she doesn't know much about having a baby but she knows for sure that this is it, and outside the window, all round the room, underneath the eaves and rocking the roof beams, the gusts of wind have grown sharper too, the wind is a high unholy scream, sharper and closer, not gusts any more, not pangs any more but almost continuous, all through her back and down her thighs, underneath her belly, rocking her rib-cage, and she realises she's forgetting to breathe, but why is everything going so fast, her mother had said it took years with the first . . .

She clutches for the light with a sweating hand. Tries it again. It doesn't work, and Faith has been cursed, for why should the bulb go now of all times? God must be punishing her for sin – and she drags herself across to her window to draw back the curtains and let in some light. But there *is* no light beyond the curtains; no lights along the promenade, nothing to show where the edge might be, no light to be seen on the length of the pier, in the howling dark she can see no pier, and Faith is howling, for it's all gone black, her baby comes at the end of the world, and she prays not to God but to her mother, who'd loved her until she began to grow up, *help me, help me to have the baby, I don't want to hurt it, show me how . . .* and for a long moment, the agony stops.

She manages a thought. Of course, it's a power-cut. A power-cut, not the end of the world. She grits her teeth and gropes for her clothes, her shoes, at any rate, a dressing-gown. If she can get downstairs to the floor below, the lift will carry her down to Reception and something is telling her hurry, hurry, she manages to feel her way through the door and as the next band of contractions starts she is pinned to the spot by a thunderous crack, then a shuddering, growing roll of sound that contorts around the knots of her body and she knows that the Empire is falling down as she claws up out of the well of pain and pushes herself to the narrow staircase, trying to get the baby out.

Grace is old, but she hears the voice in the dark, something that saves her from herself, not herself but another in pain, a real person, not a ghost, and she rises, slowly but without a second thought, pulls herself up and out of bed, she's eighty-five but alive and human and she isn't floored when the light doesn't work but walks through the night down the Lighthouse beam to the huddled form of Faith in the dark, not screaming, now, but panting hard, clutching the wall, trying to speak. Grace knows at once from the strange, hoarse whisper – 'Help me, please, I'm having a baby' – it's the cross little girl, the chambermaid, and Grace is as young as she ever was as she half lifts her, half holds her up and together they stumble into Grace's bedroom.

'Matches,' Faith says, 'In my pocket.' She strikes one and they see each other, her gleaming with sweat, Grace white as paper, and *why*, Faith thinks, *does it have to be her?* – but another wave comes, Faith drops the match and in the falling flash of pain she sees the eyes are wet and alive and then there's pain and nothing else, she grabs Grace's arm and squeezes so hard that Grace is proud it does not snap, it does not bend, her bones are old but they withstand and she takes the matches from Faith in the dark and lights another while she tries to remember, what does she know about having a baby, *newspaper*, one used newspaper, she wasn't quite sure what one used it for but she reaches across for the old *Observer*, nearly sets it alight as she flaps it open with her one free hand, spreads it chaotically across the carpet, and Faith gets down upon her knees, 'I must go and get help,' but Faith can't answer, the panting turns to rhythmic cries, no longer panicky, cries not screams, rising and falling like a cow lowing, and when they have diminished to pants again she says, 'Yes, get help,' and then, 'No, don't leave me, it's coming now, I can feel it coming, oh God, God help me, it'll never ... I *can't* ...' 'You can,' says

Grace, who knows nothing at all but something lifts her, she believes what she says, 'You're very brave, it will be all right,' *if the matches last out*, and she strikes another and sees the dark girl at her feet, kneeling there with her head tipped forward, almost touching Grace's knees then resting on them its heavy weight, and her knees are surely too sharp, too brittle, but they have grown strong and wide as stone; and she sees again, sweeping over the water, finding the two of them, wrapping them round, the steady, turning beam of light, touching them and sweeping on, the match goes out and the beam has gone but Faith says, 'I think I can hang on – if you go now – there's a Dr Glossop – floor below – I clean for him . . .'

'What number room?' Grace holds her head, queer to hold what she cannot see, strokes her hair, but no answer comes and she lifts Faith's face in the blind darkness, 'You'll have to remember which number room,' and she manages to pant out 'Sixty . . .' but the rest is inaudible, the pains are coming and this time her voice is not the same, more of a grunt than a cry this time, a rough barking, an animal sound, the sound of someone pushing and straining, 'I'll have to take the matches, I shan't be long,' and Grace is off, barefoot, in her nightgown, adrenalin driving her down the landing before she notices how strange it is, the feeling of carpet on her bare feet for at home she always wears her slippers, and even as the storm explodes around her, battering the bones of her head with sound, part of Grace thinks how nice it feels, her sole on the carpet, how real, how young, but then she comes to the top of the stairs; stairs are different, steep and frightening, she feels the Empire lean and tremble; slowly, clutching the banister, trying to remember when the staircase turns; step by step, she tells herself; *step by step, don't be afraid* though her head is spinning and she almost falls but she sees herself walking along the gangplank towards the boat, steadily forwards, step by step she's lived eighty-five years, step by step you manage to survive and that, in the end, was what counted; she had survived and Ralph had not, and the girl must survive, she must have her baby, and eighty-five years of being a lady don't stop Grace standing on the second-floor landing, a lighted match in one steady hand, roughly in the middle of the doors in the 60s, and shouting more fiercely than the storm, louder than she shouted at the girls in school, 'Dr Glossop! Dr Glossop! We need a doctor! Dr Glossop, wake up!' and as the match dies her voice grows louder and she adds, and for all she knows it's true, 'Dr Glossop! A woman's dying out here,' and because the words fill her with superstitious horror, she tries to say, 'Someone's having a baby,' but some strange connection fires in her brain, and the words break from her into the tempest, 'I'm having a baby, come quick!'

So what does he think, the small, fat man who opens the door with a torch in his hand, what does he think of the crazy old woman who stands and yells in the middle of the landing, a bag of bones with coal-black eyes that flash and burn in the narrow torchlight? – 'Dr Glossop, I'm having a baby.'

'We're having a baby. I can't believe it.'

The storm scoops out a place in its heart and weaves it round with layers of sound, a nest, and in it, safe and warm, Arthur and Paula lie with Sally who's crept in to join them, afraid of the noise, Arthur and Paula lie with their children, one of them still only hearing the storm as the dullest thunder a long way behind the immediate weather of rushing juices, thumping heartbeat, roaring breath, the weather of the body that keeps it alive.

'I can't believe you're having my baby.'

'Is it for me?' says Sally. 'My baby. Want it.'

'Course it's for you, as well,' Paula says. 'You can play with it. You can help with it.'

Sally, Arthur-in-the-middle, Paula. They are all back. They are all here. Arthur happier than ever in his life. He feels like a tree; they are under his branches (all over the country they're falling like skittles, but Arthur won't know that till morning).

'If I go to sleep, Daddy,' says Sally. She's dozing off in any case, sucking her nightie, hard to hear through the warm wet cotton, hard to hear through the crumbling heavens, clattering windows, crashing tiles, 'If I do. Will you make it stop?'

'You go to sleep, my love,' says Arthur. 'It'll stop of its own accord by morning. It's only a storm. We're safe in here.'

'Nurrican,' says Sally indistinctly, and sleeps.

'Did she say "never again"?' asks Paula. They are whispering now, the two of them, turned together, in each other's arms.

'Room 24 made a pass at me today.'

'You serious?'

'Yes.'

'I mean, I'm not surprised, you're very attractive. But what a cheek. Doesn't she know you're married?'

'I'm not married.'

'You *are* . . . in all but name we are.'

'In that case, my wife had gone off and left me.'

'Were you tempted?'

A fractional pause, then, 'No.' He loves her too much to want
to hurt her feelings, but he thinks, 'Yes, more than you can ever
imagine, and I stayed in her room for nearly an hour, it took me
that long to make up my mind; I wanted her to stroke me and
flatter me, I wanted to be wrapped in that long yellow hair, I
wanted to do what other men had done, all the men who've
traipsed up those stairs. I wanted to do whatever I liked, I knew
she would let me do what I liked. All the time I was there I had an
erection. I wanted to be a different person; I wanted to have some
fun. But the window shattered, without any warning. I was sitting
on her bed, we were drinking tea, and suddenly everywhere was
noise and glass, and we started to clear it up together but the room
was cold, I thought about death and it wasn't the storm, it might
have been her, she's so very pretty with those wide blue eyes but
she might have had it in her bloodstream. And so I pretended that
nothing had happened. I was bluff and hearty and I went away. I
didn't do it. Thank you, God.' He isn't religious, but thank you
God. Happy, happier, happiest.

'I shall tell Grace about the baby tomorrow,' Paula says, thinking
*Grace'll have to get to like him now. She's never given Arthur a
chance.* 'Let's move, Arthur. Before she's born. Or him, as the case
may be. I hate living near the railway line. I know it's only a tiny
risk. But if anything happened to the kids . . . How do they cope
with it, those parents. Near Windscale, and the kid gets leukaemia,
and they've stayed in the area because it was convenient . . . they
never thought it would happen to them . . .'

'Don't talk about it. Of course it won't.'

'That's what everybody says . . .'

Only Paula can't bear to think about it either, not in relation to
these two children . . . but she's doing her best, she *is* doing
something, writing about it, and today it went well . . . lying here,
pressed against his chest, his shaggy, Arthurian, barrel-like chest,
she can't hold out against happiness.

'Pity you've got to go away tomorrow,' he whispers, stroking
her heavy hair, then gently, tenderly over her nipples, it all seems
different, she seems brand new, for every part of her is pregnant –
'We could have celebrated all day.' Then he remembers. 'No we
couldn't. I've got to have a drink with James.'

And when he's recounted Pennington's plan for turning the Albion into a hostel, Paula and he agree; this is the chance he's been waiting for; Arthur will tell James where to stick it, he and Paula will start a new life, they'll sell the house and buy cheap in the north – 'What's the point of that? Let's get out of England, nothing's getting better, let's get out and go abroad' – 'So many people are saying that. Nothing'll get better if everybody quits' – but wherever they go, it will be all right, he has other talents, he'll make them work, and he's just beginning to make love to her, 'Are you sure it's all right? It won't hurt the baby?' when there is a series of shuddering crashes so fearfully loud and near at hand that Sally moans a little in her sleep and Paula at last begins to be frightened, and whispers, as Arthur noses inside her, gently, firmly, pushing inside, 'We're not going to die? After all this? We are going to survive the night?' and he replies, on a swell of tenderness, slipping inside the place he likes best, 'I wouldn't *let* you die. Nobody's going to die tonight.'

(He's wrong. That night there were many deaths. It wasn't what they expected, in England ... Disasters are never what people expect. The plutonium fire at Windscale was quite unexpected in '57. The little leaks in their endless series were somehow never expected either, and radiation-linked cancer deaths were always a horrible surprise; the poisoned airstream from the Ukraine astonished Swedish experts that spring, and the silent towns, the abandoned fields, the children shivering on railway platforms, no one anticipated Chernobyl, it wasn't what they expected, in Russia.)

'*Don't let the baby die*,' Grace prays, and she hasn't prayed since the Second World War when she'd prayed every day that Ralph wouldn't die. The doctor is here, and the doctor's wife, and her long thin room has become very small as the shadows press back into the beam of the torch and Faith hunkers down on the old *Observer*, pressing her baby down towards the earth. Grace has suddenly become very useful. She'd felt superfluous, standing on the threshold, till Dr Glossop wanted Faith on her back, and Faith refused, fighting his hand, 'Not on my back, it hurts on my back, my mother had Fion like this, I was with her,' but Glossop just went on pulling at her, and his wife, who was holding the torch for him, tried to help her husband turn her . . . Grace knew nothing but she knew about bullying, she also read Glossop as lower middle class, and she'd summoned her most commanding voice – every vowel was pure Compton Hall, Grace's voice when she was Head Girl – 'I think you'd better let her do as she wishes,' and she pushed past the doctor, she actually pushed, and began to stroke Faith's hair off her forehead, it was sopping wet, and Faith breathed, 'Thank . . . you', and then the grunts began again, but it sounded to Grace as though they were quieter.

'The contractions are weakening,' Glossop hisses. He has his hands between Faith's legs. 'She's getting exhausted. She ought to lie down,' and even his wife, who is clearly in awe, is aware this isn't a helpful statement and contradicts weakly, 'She's doing very well. She's doing her best, dear.'

'Aargh,' says Faith, and 'O-o-o-oh, I *can't*,' but it somehow means the opposite, she half rises from her knees, her head goes up, she starts to push down on a shuddering cry and Glossop is panicking 'Don't waste your breath, try not to shout, it just wastes effort,' but the roaring breath pushes on and on and Grace hears herself saying, 'Go on, *go on*,' and then Glossop squeaks like a little boy, 'It's the head! the head! I don't believe it,' and then something huge and coated with torchlight is hanging down between Faith's thighs, there's a long high howl of nasal outrage, a tiny animal's new to the room, and Glossop is helping the shoulders out and then there is suddenly a small bright wriggling pot-bellied thing which falls like Icarus but big hands catch it, and Grace, unthinking, touches its skin, and everyone and the storm is crying.

And minutes later the Porter arrives, with a hurricane lamp, blankets, a kettle, a medicine chest in which Glossop delves, and in this bright light Grace sees Faith transformed, no longer tiny-eyed and cross, rosy, smiling, shinging wet, two nakednesses pressed together, holding the boy to the mound of her stomach, (*so it doesn't go flat, I thought it went flat*), but the biggest surprise is the amount of blood, on the naked bodies, the Doctor, the carpet, and now Grace sees it has soaked the paper, 'Dunne's Dark Lady' is drenched in fresh blood.

'I think the wind's going down,' she says. Blood on her hands, blood on her feet, wonderful blood all down her nightdress. 'It doesn't want to frighten the baby.' She feels like a girl at a midnight feast which has turned out immeasurably better than expected.

'The sea came in,' says the Porter. 'Bloody washed in through the Empire door. I couldn't do anythink to keep it out. The roof's come down. And the sea came in.'

The storm goes down too late for Bruno.

He had tried above all things to stay on his feet, *if you can't fight be ready for flight*, but he couldn't hold out; the storm didn't stop; he felt the house collapsing round him, terrible noises of cracking and slipping, foundations shifting, roofs pulling off, the eyes close in round the creaking walls and he is to be exposed and naked, and then he will die, the watcher watched – and the lights went out, and Bruno lay down, flat on the floor in his mohair suit, flat on the floor so the wind couldn't catch him but he's still afraid that the roof will fall down and Bruno crawls underneath the table, telling himself that he's only being sensible, Bruno hides with his fingers in his ears, Bruno tries to think of concrete and steel and the perfect safety of banks and accountants, but when the crescendo of crashes comes he has to stifle the weeping child, since no one will come to comfort him, no one will hold him in her arms.

10

MEETING

Grace wakes in an unfamiliar room. They'd moved her after the baby was born, but it feels like waking to a different life. Sitting up, she aches all over, she supposes from lifting, holding, squeezing, but at any rate from being used; she had been used; she had been useful.

Outside the window, a different world. The sea has torn over the three-levelled promenade and converted it into a toddler's playground, seats sprawled up the bank at crazy angles, lampposts uprooted, the shelters roofless, the flowerbeds which helped to mark out the three tiers turned into crazy mud-slides. The pier is not a pier any more but a broken toy the sea has tired of, the pierhead no longer joined to the land, the legs splayed out at bird-like angles.

And the boats. Her boats. Her *Southern Queen*. Of the *Southern Queen* there is simply no sign. A heap of sticks where there was once a boathouse. So that was it: no trip to the Lighthouse. She'd never get to the Lighthouse, now, but this morning it couldn't have mattered less. The world is transformed, and so is Grace.

She stares down on the front in wonder. After eighty-five years when almost nothing had changed, the world had got bored with the pattern she knew, and everything had been erased, but she doesn't feel sad, she feels liberated; perhaps at last she is free to go.

But Bruno – what can Bruno do, waking up crumpled beneath the table, itchy and sweaty from sleeping in his clothes, bruised from hitting his head on the table-leg, Bruno, unable to accept his fear

– how can Bruno understand the morning, how can Bruno be expected to bear what he sees as he slowly raises the blind?

For there's too much light in Bruno's yard, and he sees something dreadful as he looks to the right, the wall between the houses simply isn't there, the long high wall that divided the gardens, and then he sees it, lying absolutely flat, almost in one piece, just the top bricks crumbled but it lies along the surface of his yard like a path, an ugly, useless, old-fashioned path.

Even as he watches there is something worse, a small white hand, an arm, a face, the face of a small fat child, spying, peering across from the slum next door, and then – he can't believe it – she *steps on the wall*, her stupid fat legs are standing on his property, and then she's walking along it, bow-legged, shrieking, 'Paula! Paula! Come'n see me! *Paula!*'

Too much has always been expected of Bruno. He's sweating, desperate, as she walks towards his house, shouting and grinning, he will have to kill her.

'SALLY!'

That's Paula, calling from the house, and Sally hears her and turns aside (how easy it was to save a life; how much depends on timing, how much on chance).

Bruno will be going down to Oakey today. He showers very carefully. He must be very clean. He feeds last night's suit into his boiler. Something unspeakable has happened in his underpants, something happened in the middle of the night for which there would have to be such suffering, such terrible punishment, such howls of terror, and he, Bruno, is the torturer, he, by daylight, now the storm has gone . . . He towels his face roughly, with tightly shut eyes, comes out of the shower and expects to see the wall, the wall will be back again, the world will be normal, but there isn't a wall, just the terrible light and the shivering form of Softly Softly, utterly bedraggled, pressed against the window, disgusting, pitiful, furred like a rat – and he flings his electric shaver at it, only to hear the window crack, and she jerks in terror through the shattered glass.

England awakes from the hurricane amazed, relieved, appalled, excited, grateful for once to be alive. For a few hours they live more intensely. In shops, on buses, on tube trains, people tell their stories, wave their hands; they exclaim, laugh, lament. Neighbours who haven't talked for months shout greetings across their flattened gardens. People are less alone, this morning (except for Bruno, who is more alone).

The damage will run to billions of pounds. Thousands of cars are pressed flat by trees, revealed in their wreck for what they really are, so many flimsy, silly tin boxes, imitation beetles chucked on their backs. Thousands of houses are punched in casually, minus a wall, the roof, the windows, as if they were built of paper, not brick; brick became paper in a wind like that.

Some of them realised that changed their world. Hills, for example, and valleys. Perhaps they haven't been there for ever, perhaps they will not always be there. Perhaps when the earth is in the mood it can crumple its surface like a piece of foil, perhaps it could throw us off its back. Perhaps overnight it could crush the barriers we build to last for thousands of years, trying to divide inside from outside, trying to divide bad from good, trying to protect ourselves from our poisons. Perhaps in the end the earth is one, and in billions of miles of empty space, the one place where life is . . .

Luckily a flask wasn't travelling that night, bringing nuclear waste through battered houses. They are very stable, very safe, but nothing is stable and safe enough. A train was toppled in a field of sidings where the wind reached a hundred miles per hour, a long blue caterpillar, feet in the air. And a railway bridge across a flooding river snapped like a match as a train was crossing, the last coach fell and was swallowed up and all the dreamers inside were lost.

On the whole, though, this morning, they feel refreshed, as if they had been given another chance.

Arthur has his showdown with Pennington, though it doesn't go according to plan (none of his life goes according to plan, which seemed to justify his shortage of plans). But this morning he drives to the Albion practising his speech. He has put a scarlet, unequivocal shirt on, one he has never worn for work, and Phyllis accords it a '*very* bohemian' as Arthur pushes through the swing doors, trying to make more noise than usual.

The whole thing is over in under ten minutes.

'Arthur,' says James, who's put on a little weight, and lost a little hair, and looks a little furtive. 'We've always been friends, which makes this more difficult.' (He doesn't say 'best friends', this time.)

'I've decided not to stay if you do it,' says Arthur, gabbling the lines he has prepared. 'It isn't right. These places are hell.'

'Precisely,' says James, not listening. 'It's had its day. It's simply out of date. Had a long natter with that boy of mine last night. Frightfully sharp. Thinks I'm an old duffer. I'm afraid he'll soon be off to New York . . . In any case, to cut a long story short, he thinks it's time to sell up. Going to be a crash, it seems. But the Japs are apparently sniffing round for property. They're coming here in swarms, you've probably noticed. They need somewhere to put their chaps.'

A long pause. Arthur is incredulous. 'You're selling up? You're selling the Albion?'

James is examining his well-polished shoes.

Arthur swallows, for here it is. Freedom at last from the fudging and the waste. An end at last to treading water. Arthur raises his glass to James. 'You'll be making a nice little packet out of this,' and is pleased to see how his old friend squirms. Looking at him he knows he never really liked him. He isn't just lazy and a bore; he's poisonous. The fat of his face is grey and inert. 'It makes me laugh, the way you're all selling up. I heard they were selling the Ashdown Forest. Most beautiful bit of land in the south. The family have owned it for generations . . . Everybody's selling their little bit of England.'

Flexing her arm with weary pride, Grace puts her suitcase on the Lewes train. She's starting to notice how little she's slept, she's starting to lose her concentration, but she has to concentrate, something's upsetting her, a little wire-worm of doubt. The train tries to rock her but Grace refuses. She mustn't fall asleep till she's got things right.

Something the Porter said. The Porter, at that extraordinary breakfast, which Grace enjoyed so completely that she didn't really hear the false note. The dining-room had been flooded, the power still wasn't back on, but bread and jam and orange juice were laid out for everyone in the bar, and they ate together by candle-light, the guests, the maids, the receptionists, and the room was alive with talk and excitement, and someone kept saying, 'It's just like the war, nothing like disasters for bringing folk together,' and part of Grace rejected it, for how big a disaster would it take, did we all have to die before we loved each other? – but part of her acknowledged the woman was right, it took mortal fear to remind us we were living.

A lot of people came up to her who had heard the saga of the baby. They were making her out to be a heroine, but Grace was clear that the brave one was Faith, or any other woman who had managed to give birth. *And they just go on living, as if mothers were ordinary* . . .

Remembering that night and the rhythms of Faith's pain through the rhythms of the train wheels, Grace starts to drop off. *But the Porter*, she tells herself. *Think about that.*

The Porter, who had always shown an interest in Grace, came and sat beside her, eager to talk. And talk he did, in a steady stream. She wasn't attending to all of it, there was a lot of noise, she was a little deaf, and she wanted to watch the young women, released from the rules of their role as receptionists, suddenly looking so much younger and more human, animated, without their caps – she didn't want to listen to a boring old man. His conversation was a long lament, running in the background like an underground stream that couldn't undermine her cheerfulness. 'The Butterfly House must be *pulverised*. Poor little devils, they wouldn't stand a chance. Makes me wonder if the place was unnatural. Mind you, a storm like last night's wasn't *natural*. And a ship ran aground on the rocks. Lifeboat put out and they got the crew off. Miracle anyone survived. Dunno, I wonder about that Lighthouse . . . does it do the same job now it's automatic? They took the last keeper off a year ago . . . do you reckon a machine is as good as a man?'

Then she realised his questions were no longer rhetorical. 'Did you have a pleasant time with your relative?'

'I don't know who you're talking about.'

'I told him you were at the Butterfly House. Don't say he missed you after all. Came to the hotel to find you, Thursday.'

'I haven't got any relatives. No men, that is. It must be a mistake. You're confusing me with another guest.'

'He was a red-haired fellow. It was you he wanted. Tall and red-haired.'

And she'd said without thinking, 'Oh, that was Ralph!' and the Porter smiled until she continued with a seamless transition to amazed dismay, 'But of course it wasn't him. Ralph has been dead for forty years.'

It was stupid, of course, it was all a mistake, the Porter was old and smelled slightly of drink, but he kept on insisting there had been a man, tall, red-haired, asked for Miss Stirling.

She supposed it couldn't be anything . . . sinister. The day is too glorious for anything sinister. She closes her eyes against the sun and the after-image is a tiny stain. The day she went to the Butterfly House. The day she thought so much about Ralph. Of course it couldn't be anything bad. The world had already survived its disaster, the air smells new, the sun is out.

She can't help remembering the phonecalls, though. That breathing which said *I'm here, I'm alive, you don't know me but I know you.*

Paula is getting Sally ready to catch the train for Oakey. The morning had been blissfully easy; overtired from the night before, Sally went back to bed and slept. Which gave Paula a chance to think. About Francesca, with astonished grief. About the baby, with quiet delight. About Grace, wonderful, ageless Grace. Well, I know she's old, but she seems so young. Sometimes I think I'm older than her. I'm less romantic, for a start . . . Maybe she seems young because she's . . . *unused*. A lot of Grace is still potential . . . And most of that's the fault of that bloody man. All right, he could paint, and I suppose he was handsome, if you like those corny old movie-star looks. Personally, Paula didn't like redheads. But he had the most shattering effect on women. She was reading Vera Boccione's memoir. Ralph had been her lover for weeks, not months, but those weeks were the centre of the woman's life. It was fascinating and repellent at once.

He was an extraordinary man. I have never forgotten him. A genius, without doubt. Myself and my daughter were so lucky. But I do have one regret; Ralph never said he loved me. Despite that, his pictures made me real. I tell myself that that's what love does. I tell my daughter, I think he loved me, in his way, if not as I loved him. It's all so very long ago, and how can I discover, now, what's true?

My daughter knows all her father's paintings. She loves his paintings of the Other One, so full of light, so full of life, so different from those paintings of me. 'Never mind, mother,' she says. 'The world has changed. You were too late.'

'Sally! Come on! Bring your teddy bear!' yells Paula, as she closes the last page, and she disapproves violently of all this rubbish, but the shine by her eye might be a small tear.

That woman at the exhibition. Must have been his daughter. Those deep blue eyes . . . *I'm glad that he loved Grace best . . .*

All the same. That kind of love could be fatal.

The train rocks onwards, a little delayed by trees which had to be cleared from the line. Now it lifts Grace through brilliant sun, the astonishing light that follows a storm, and she stares across the wide tracts of Sussex that open on either side of the line, long green glades and crowns of trees, half closing her eyes she could hardly see the damage, and they looked like offers of adventure and freedom, but she was too old, she was going home.

What opportunities I missed, living my life through my love for Ralph. It was all untrue, in any case, that they had been 'fated' or 'meant for each other' or 'could have loved no one else'. Because Ralph *did* manage to love someone else, he saw what he needed in life and took it, whereas I tried to see what my loved one needed and then took the scraps that were left for myself, and of course I starved and my writing stopped.

The new generation of women wouldn't do it. They wouldn't mortgage their lives for romance. Take Paula (Grace smiles through the carriage window at a green-shirted man hanging out some washing, both he and the flying clothes seem to dance in a dervish whirl of wind and sunshine), Paula isn't brainwashed into being unselfish. Paula's selfish; Grace knows it well. And careless, Paula is often careless. Her writing is careless. Mine *never* was. (She has sometimes re-read those old magazines, in the last ten years, after a lapse of decades. To her relief, the poems were good. *But I didn't go on; one has to go on.*)

One needed to be selfish; she saw that now. One even needed to be careless, about the tiny, hairsplitting details, the guilts that stopped one getting things done. Paula would railroad everything through. She would say what she meant, and be understood. She would direct her attention to what was important, not waste it making myths about men . . .

But Grace isn't going to back down about Arthur. Arthur is ugly, embarrassing, weak. Arthur is a mix-up of a man and a woman. But at least Paula couldn't fall in love with him, she's entirely safe from that fatal error . . . Grace smiles at herself in the window. She longs for Paula, and six o'clock.

Arthur is nearer than Grace knows. Arthur feels anything but weak. Arthur is driving down to Oakey by a roundabout route to avoid blocked roads. He can't remember when Paula was expected; Arthur has always been vague about time. But Arthur doesn't give a fuck about time. Arthur is lord of time and space. He's a father-to-be, he is eight foot tall, he is driving through the sunlight to meet his wife, for why shouldn't he ask her to marry him? Who better to act as a witness than Grace? (though she's sometimes curiously stiff with him). In the back are two bottles of champagne that he means to crack with the two of them.

The showdown with Pennington runs through his mind as he winds his way through the country lanes. It was true what he'd said; they were all selling up. But as he meanders through green-and-gold Sussex – and even the scars are a rich, earth-red, the up-turned tree-roots are knotty and real, not flaccid and watery and false, like Pennington – he thinks that the main thing is how much is left; for all that is lost, so much remains; if people would only take care of it . . . if people had a little bit of pride in England . . .

He looks at his watch. It's four o'clock, so he won't get there in time for tea. He has a choice of two routes to Oakey, one more scenic, one more direct, and he stops in the sun for a moment to think, watches the light on a battered dog-rose, creamy petals bruised semi-transparent but the buds survive and there in the distance, just as if nothing had happened, the bees, the sleepy, timeless sound of bees – and he realises how lucky he is, because just for today he can do as he pleases, Sally's with Paula, he isn't expected, in all the world not a living soul will be affected by what he decides, and the bees direct him to drive round the valley, the longer way, the more languorous journey, but does he want to be bossed by bees?

– A rainbow shoots from a wet red leaf, a drop of dull blood that breaks into diamonds.

Does she want to get to Oakey slow or fast? Grace has to decide; there are always decisions. She has mixed feelings about going back. Tonight will be lovely, with Paula and Sally, she hasn't seen Sally since Portugal, but they will be gone in the morning, and then she will be alone ... That silly business with the phonecalls. In the Empire it was an irritation, but she knew there were other human beings around her. At home it jabbed like a nerve in a tooth. She didn't want it to start again ...

Should she get a taxi from Lewes, or carry on by train to Oakey in the knowledge that then she'd have to walk all the way from the station, carrying her cases? Once there was a bus which ran right past her door, but the eighties had put paid to that. Suddenly Grace is tired. She wants to be back home, at once, turning the key in her own front door, stepping into the cool and dark of her own quiet life, her own secrets.

Home. She's going home. Never mind the cost, she'll go by taxi.

The single mini-cab driver waiting ignores a leather-jacketed yob who was strictly speaking in front of Grace, and Grace for once does not correct him. He puts her suitcases into the boot without being asked; he touches his cap; he even calls her Madam. Of course it is rather a silly salutation, but Grace enjoys his gallantry and the way he whistles under his breath.

'Here on holiday, Madam?' he asks. 'Hope we're going to have some better weather, then.'

'I've just been on holiday, as a matter of fact. I'm coming home.'

'Can't beat Sussex.'

'It's beautiful country.'

'Can't beat England. Though I wasn't saying that in the middle of last night.'

The sun is bright on the tweed of his cap, soft grey and soft green, rather hot for June. His three-quarters profile is pink and bare. His voice is somehow familiar.

'How's business this summer?' she asks.

'Terrible year for us, this year,' he says. 'Next year it might get back to normal. Americans didn't come, this year.'

'No Americans,' she says. 'That's a pity.'

'Can't stand Americans, matter of fact,' he told her, half glancing over his shoulder. The sun picks up a pale line of stubble. 'Country needs tourists, though. I'm not complaining.'

'Tourism's just about all we've got left,' she surprises herself by saying.

'Don't you believe it,' he tells her, sounding his horn at two bicycles riding abreast, young people – children – blonde, tanned laughing, the boy's bright arm on the girl's thin shoulder. They shriek and veer into a sheet of water and are left behind, laughing. 'Don't underestimate us.'

For a moment she feels an unreasoning cheer, a resurgence of the joy of this morning. *That's right. The English could rise again.* The hedges here had hardly been damaged; they were thick with flowers of white Morning Glory, big as saucers, pushing up at the sky, springing back from their beating and shining again, dripping with flashing, generous light.

Now the road has become entirely familiar. They drive along in the shelter of the hill, following the former bus route where the country bus ran three times a day. It's all been a dream, she tells herself. That drystone church with the winding path and the blaze of petunias. Two boys in short trousers (so they still wore short trousers) straggling along the road leaping the puddles then splashing straight in, each carrying a stick which makes him look small, and the smaller one has Ralph's fierce crest of red hair. A bank of blue cornflowers by a listing gate that had listed for years, but survived the night, and the cornflowers are rarer, they have said so for years, but they are still here, the blue of blue eyes (Ralph's eyes, at any rate, that rare deep blue), and a fine confetti of butterflies, also, on the edge of the field, and ahead on the road, a faint white haze of steam in the heat that says *now* and *June*, obscuring the future.

Everything was still all right. Everything would be all right. OAKEY, says the black-and-white sign by the road that has named her home for the past twenty years.

'So nice to be nearly home,' she says, half to herself, but the man has good ears.

'You haven't been away very long, have you?' he asks, and the day changes colour. A breath which feels cold as the sea sucks inside her lips and leaks out again. His neck is thick, and pink, underneath the cap which hides his hair. How does he know how long she'd been away? How does he know the turning to her home, which he is taking now without a hint of uncertainty?

Her hands clasp and unclasp, old hands with thin skin, no longer strong. So he'd waited for her at the station. That's why he ignored the leather-coated boy. Why didn't she think. Why didn't she see.

'How did you know?' she asks. Her voice, she observes, is flat, detached, without a hint of the fear she feels. And part of her isn't afraid. Part of her's simply curious. After all this time, at last he's come. Mrs Proctor's cottage flashes white to the right and she thinks two things in rapid succession, *if only I'd got to the Lighthouse*, and

I should have opened the door and jumped out, it was what they did in thrillers, she knew, but she is too old to be in a thriller.

'Sorry, Madam,' the kind voice asks. 'How do I know what?'

Grace doesn't want to play games. She hopes he will get it over with. 'How long I have been away,' she says, keeping her voice quite level. (There are the cedars, her own blue cedars. Trapped behind glass, she imagines she smells them.)

His voice remains kind and normal. 'Oh, guesswork. You said Seabourne, didn't you. Couldn't stand it for more than a week, myself,' and as he speaks, he drives past her gate, he doesn't know where she lives after all and the world flips back into normal gear with a heart-stopping shock; she is drenched in cold sweat.

The unfrozen blood rushes gratefully back to her cheeks, her palms, her living centre, for she is alive, they would let her live, the world is large and full of sunlight, there *is* a future, they are all still free. Stupid, stupid old fool, she thinks, but her voice is girlish, insouciant as she says 'Oh sorry – you've passed the turning. I should have directed you.'

The car slows down and the blur of green hedge sharpens up into individual buds and leaves, blackberry leaves, there would be blackberries later, and a single small rose hangs out into the road on its spiny tendril, exquisitely pink, though the others all round it have lost their petals. The car stops, and the pink rose waves just above her eye-level, six inches away, intensely present, small as a shell, transfused with light. It is all still here, and her home's still here. I'm mad, she thinks. I imagine things. Ralph always said so, and he was right.

Crunching round into her drive. The familiar gravel her feet know so well. The house is standing, at any rate. Indeed, it looks peacefully asleep. Two tiles have fallen near the flower-beds, and the dark delphiniums lie flat. But Gray has obviously been in to weed; the earth between the rose bushes is dark and clean. She hears a blackbird, liquidly inventive, and hopes it might be one from the second clutch of eggs. The car stops in the blue shade of the cedars . . .

Shades of the olives in Portugal. We lay in the light wind under the trees.

'That's perfect,' says Grace. 'How much will it be?' The amount he mentions is rather less than she'd paid in Seabourne for a journey only half as long. Country, she thinks, is better than town. England is here, in the country.

'Thank you, Madam. I'll give you a hand into the house.'

Before she can demur, he is out of the car, opens the door for her and takes the cases, walking before her across the bright gravel, revealed as a little man with short, bandy legs.

She searches in her jacket for the keys; finds them. Her own front door. With the old-fashioned, too-narrow letterbox and the cracked blue paint. I'm glad I've come home.

'Thank you,' she says. 'Goodbye. I hope you don't get too many Americans.'

She stands momentarily transfixed, fingering the jagged edge of the Yale as his engine revs, roars, and finally dies away in the distance, blending into the dim veil of warm sound (children somewhere, bees, a small plane) that means an English summer day.

But Grace is no longer in England. Grace is in Portugal, with Ralph. An aged woman in a patched dark skirt discoloured like a mussel shell had given Ralph the keys to the villa. They walked to it along the edge of the fields, pale feet, big daisies, tiny blue iris, feet which would later be coppery dark. When they saw the villa, white against the sea, Ralph handed her the keys. 'I want to pretend I'm giving it to you. This is our house. We'll live here always.' Those months turned out to be their always, the clearest happiness they lived together, and somewhere it must be beating still, the small hot heart that the white walls held, the knot of their bodies safe asleep.

Her fingers are stiff as they turn the key, or the lock is stiff with age; the hand that had been so long and fine, the hand he had painted, is like a map, where blood had retreated or stagnated, where cells had turned brown and never turned back, where veins had become small runnels of stone . . . While she stands dreaming, the door gives suddenly, and as the cool darkness calls her inside, half of her perceives that it *simply wasn't locked*, that was the reason the key wouldn't turn, and wonders if something odd's going on, maybe she should get back outside, but half of her senses have moved into reverse, hearing festive trumpets upon the silence, seeing on the black that surprises her eyes the dazzling brightness of a Portuguese morning as Ralph pulled the curtains back from the sea and sunlight broke on her naked body, *'They're out there practising. It's Mardi Gras.'* She sighs, and slips into the friendly shadows, dragging her cases like the weight of the past, in the end it's too strong, she cannot escape, and she misses him still as she missed him then . . .

But he's inside me. I still hear the trumpets.

193

And then she sees him, through the door that opens from the living-room into her study, kneeling on the floor with his back to her. The sun from the window sets his hair on fire. She'd forgotten how red, and his back, how muscled. The music played from behind his back. All round him there lay a lake of white paper, bright as swans' wings in the blaze of sun. Every hair on her body stands on end. She opens her mouth, but her throat shuts tight. She tries again. This is real. It's him.

'Ralph,' she cries, and her voice is old, cracked and old but loud with joy as she moves towards him in a staggering run, but in the same split second he turns, startled, and is pale and crewcut and utterly strange, not Ralph, a loose-mouthed stranger.

'What are you doing?' she pants, 'How dare you come in here?' (*How dare you make me think it was him?*)

'Get back,' he says. 'Stay where you are.' An ugly voice, nasal, metallic, frightened and therefore frightening.

'You're in my house. What the devil ae you doing?'

'Don't move, I told you.' He's on his feet now, his right hand flashes, he has a gun – this can't be real; bigger than Grace thought a gun would be; a man with a gun is threatening her, but she isn't afraid; she will not be afraid; the girls of Compton Hall were never afraid, she keeps her eyes steady and keeps on walking and the miracle happens, her spirit is stronger, the barrel wavers and turns aside and he flings it away with a deafening clatter, and then it is easy, there is so much anger, a lifetime's anger drives her on.

'I told you. Get back. Stay away from me.' He is very muscular, an animal. Three yards away she can smell his sweat. If she stops she is lost so she keeps on walking. A wave of something – fear? disgust? – rips across his stubby, shiny features and in the same instant Grace staggers back as something sharp and heavy jabs at her nostrils, his fingers, is it, but they feel like knives, steel nails claw and drag at her mouth and water, not tears, rushes to her eyes from the pain at the tender root of her nose; she is staggering, but must not fall; she steadies herself on the bookcase, panting.

'How dare you. Disgusting little coward.'

The blow, however, has given him courage. She sees a small smile possess his face. 'Stupid old bitch,' he mouths. 'That's what I do to disgusting old women.'

It was like the beginning of something very complicated, something that they were both nervous about, staring at each other, waiting to begin. But Bruno has hit her; she's lost her armour.

'I suppose you're a thief,' she says, the stronger for hearing he own calm voice. 'There's no money in this house.'

'Haven't you got any money?' he says, with a leering grin. 'Poor old biddy. Spent all your money.' His hands are very large. As she stares, he slowly opens and closes them, opening and closing like mechanical grabs. He's mad, she thinks. And it's going to break. I have to keep him talking.

'What have you done with my papers?'

He isn't a thief. It's the phonecall man.

'What am I going to do with you?' His hands move more and more slowly and deliberately, *a strangler's hands* but as the thought flashes she forces herself to ignore those hands, her life depends on seeing nothing but an ordinary burglar, an ugly boy.

She speaks again without conscious decision. 'I advise you to leave. I am calling the police,' and sets off walking across the long reach of blue carpet towards the telephone, her eyes still fixed on his pale face. The telephone is on the dresser by the mantelpiece. She knows he will not let her reach it. In the fraction of a second she has left she casts about desperately for a weapon – not the paper-knife; she could not stab him – not the poker; it took her too long to bend down – the tablelamp was too fragile – *why hadn't she ever anticipated this?* – but two feet from the telephone he comes for her, wrenching her left arm behind her back, his other hand, horribly, pulling at her hair, no one had touched her hair for decades, a hideous brutal intimacy and then there is only animal pain as he tears it down from the comb that held it and she hears herself scream, no longer human, but a voice inside her says *No, I shan't, I shall not let myself die like this*, and with her free right hand just before she falls she grabs at the silver cup on the mantelpiece, a heavy silver cup from seventy years ago, the Victrix Ludorum from Compton Hall in which she kept some dusty guineas, looking up at him, he clutches his eyebrow which is ragged with blood where the sharp-edged handle of the cup has cut him, and the blood drips all over her face as he wheels round wiping his eye and cursing her, 'Cunt . . . Fucking cunt . . . I'll murder you,' but he's hurt, she can see, he's staggering, and she tries to get up but her ankle buckles, *don't let me down* but it lets her down so she crawls for her life towards the stairs for the enemy stands between her and the door, her and freedom, she has to climb.

Intense effort; intense pain. Her knee has gone as well as her ankle. Upstairs there's another phone extension. Please, oh please, let him be concussed. She had heard the metal thud against bone, she has seen the long tear in the skin by his eyebrow, his socket streaming with brilliant blood. Is the blood on her knuckles hers or his? *Climb. Don't think. Climb, keep going.* Her breath is tearing like ancient cloth. Behind her now she can hear him coming; he's hurt, she's sure, the noise behind her is uneven, lumbering, and only the obscenities spit at her heels in a steady stream but as she rounds the bend at the first half-landing and looks behind her, *oh* – for then she sees how close he is and knows how little strength she has left, she is very old, she is eighty-five, she would have done better to have begged and pleaded, and a hand grabs at her ankle, *missed*, and then there is the terrifying sound of his laughing, inches behind her as she reaches the top.

With the last of her energy she turns on her back, half sitting, half lying, to face him – if she faces him he will at least be real, behind her back he is nameless horror – and sees a panting mask of blood; and enormous hands, in gloves of blood, and then the gloves come out towards her and *yes*, she thinks, *but I'm not afraid: whatever he does, I am not afraid* – and for a moment there is stillness; perhaps she has entered another life; she sees the white sunlight behind his head, and then there is a pounding, a thundering, and, 'Don't you dare,' a great roar of sound, and two big arms come round from behind and pinion the maniac's arms to his sides, two great arms are lifting him up, and his feet are kicking hopelessly.

'Are you all right? Grace, it's Arthur.' His enormous shape surrounds the other; he towers before her at the head of the stairs, holding Bruno with his feet off the ground, holding him helpless as a baby, using his weight to keep him still.

'Arthur,' she acknowledges, with a long sigh. 'Oh Arthur. I thought . . . Arthur.'

'You get to the phone. I'll take care of him,' and then, in an afterthought, because it comes out, 'We're having a baby, Paula and me.'

As she dials the police she looks back at them, frozen. Bruno is dangling, not kicking, now. There is only the sound of their heavy breathing, and another odd yet familiar sound; the murderous boy is a baby again, a beaten thing running blood and tears. And then Paula and Sally are behind them on the stairs, their faces burning with fear and surprise, love and terror and the child to come, and Grace sees this is the end of the age; they can not be split up, they are finally one, so the old could go, she would leave no shadow, and the child would live to see the world in the morning.